Fic
James

700044

OTHER BOOK BY BRETT JAMES

The DeadFall Project

THE DRIFT WARS

BRETT JAMES

FALLACY PUBLICATIONS OAKLAND

This is a work of fiction. Names, characters, places, and incidents either are the product of the author's imagination or are used fictitiously, and any resemblance to actual persons, living or dead, business establishments, events, or locales is entirely coincidental.

COPYRIGHT © 2013 BRETT JAMES
ALL RIGHTS RESERVED.

FALLACY PUBLICATIONS

http://thedriftwars.com

ISBN 978-0-9850864-3-5

First Hardback Edition

PRINTED IN THE UNITED STATES OF AMERICA

2 3 4 5 6 7 8 9 0 1

COVER ART BY ANDREW LEUNG
BOOK DESIGN BY MOBIHUE

Acknowledgments

My enduring thanks to my editors, Jeff Stark and Jenna Kamp. Thanks as well to Jeremy Roth, Nicholas Sher, Barri Evins, Jennifer Wilkin, Allen White, Ian Saunders, Pam Susemiehl, Megan Caper, Jason James, Donna Bell, Bill Loeb, Ed Overton, Skunk, Jeanne and Lance James, Mo Flaherty, Paul Ford, Paula Z Segal, Jason Engdahl, Kristin Campbell-Taylor, Fred Ohler, David Hagberg, Danielle Hlatky, Andrew Leung, Libby Stephens, Pablo Morales, and so many others that have offered support, both moral and tangible, through the years.

Thank you Rob, and damn you Rob, for encouraging this.

Science fiction plucks from within us our deepest fears and hopes then shows them to us in rough disguise: the monster and the rocket.
- W.H. Auden

Truth's a menace, science is a public danger.
- Aldous Huxley,
  Brave New World

[19.17.4.1::7743.4569.619.1D]

"No recon!"

"What?"

"No recon!" Saul's voice was barely audible over the metallic vibrations of the ship. After three hours of traveling through the eerie calm of space, the ship had slapped against the planetary atmosphere and was skipping violently. In a few moments, Peter would make his first combat jump. He hoped it would go better than in training. His helmet still smelled faintly of vomit.

The cabin was sweltering; the hull glowed from the friction of atmospheric entry. The ship's engine screamed, pushing them even faster.

The hull was 95 percent effective at these speeds— it would fail one time out of twenty, vaporizing the ship and its passengers. This would be unacceptable in civilian spacecraft. Only marine transports played such odds.

"You ever heard of a drop with no recon?" Saul yelled over a closed channel.

"No," Peter shouted into his helmet mic.

"Me neither. I bet no one lives to talk about it."

Peter knew better than to let Saul psych him out. "Command put the satellites on the other side of the planet," he yelled back.

"Misdirection."

"Smart."

"Smart is being tucked away in the commandship," Saul shouted. "I don't see any generals lined up for this drop."

"Dispersal altitude," the captain said over the intercom. He was calm and relaxed, piloting the ship from ten thousand miles away.

Men stirred throughout the cabin, prepping weapons and themselves. The ship held a full regiment: twenty-four hundred men in ash-gray combat suits packed in shoulder-tight rows along the curved floor. They were all recruits, privates on their first mission. Their suits shone like they had been made this morning—all but one, that of Colonel Chiang San, who watched his men from a raised seat up front. His suit was dulled and chipped from use, and even though they were inside, the protective silver coating was down over his visor, masking his face.

Anonymous in the crowd, Peter pressed his hand to his chest, where, beneath his suit's hard crust, hung a locket containing a curl of soft, silky hair.

Saul started to speak, but the ship's floor fell away and wind roared through the cabin. The men, clamped in by the backs of their suits, were rotated to face the green world below. It was drawn with the clarity of distance—the sharp-edged mountains and lakes, and an ocean of jungle as soft as cotton.

The clamp behind Peter snapped open, and a blast of compressed gas shot him straight down. The other men disappeared in a blur.

Six transports screamed through the white sky overhead, their massive impulsor engines burning the air in a trail of roiling orange and black. They spit out fifteen thousand marines in five seconds, staggered just enough to avoid collision, then arced back toward the safety of space. The sky was poked with little black dots—men plummeting to the surface.

The first time Peter tried out for football, the varsity players took the hopefuls out for a little bonding session. Several jugs of fiery moonshine were passed around, and then the young players, mostly freshmen, were taken to Culiver's Gorge. The gorge had a high dirt bank that overlooked murky, green-coated water. A narrow iron pipe crossed between the banks some fifteen feet over the water. The hopefuls were told that the unwritten requirement to make the team was to walk the pipe, blindfolded. They didn't want to, but the older boys insisted.

As his classmates hemmed and hawed, Peter stepped to the front. He figured that since he couldn't get out of it, he might as well try to look enthusiastic. He was blindfolded, balanced on the pipe with drunken steadiness, and then pushed forward. He managed two wobbly steps before he went over the edge. Though terrified, he kept his mouth shut as he fell through the air and flopped into the water.

Not one of them made it across, but Peter was the only one who didn't scream when he fell. Back then, that was brave. Back then, walking blindfolded across a water pipe was scary.

Now, plunging through the high atmosphere of an enemy-occupied planet, he knew that while the stakes were higher, the setup was the same: no matter how scared he felt, there was nothing to gain by showing it. Screaming wouldn't bring the ship back; it would only make him look bad.

Peter fell freely at first, but as he descended the atmosphere thickened, pushing his arms and legs backward, and pressing against his chest as he slowed to terminal velocity. Frost crystals formed around the edge of his visor, and the wind settled to a dull rush. He brought his legs together, drew his arms to his side, and angled into a dive.

The green world approached rapidly, its topography rising as his angle lowered. Red lines drew out over his visor, the computer in his suit marking the target landing area.

He felt a jolt as he punched into the lower atmosphere, and a red light flashed in the corner of his visor: incoming fire. Below him, the green jungle faded under a gray cloud of bullets that rose to meet the men.

Peter angled his hands like fins, corkscrewing. He wiggled his fingers, weaving his body randomly and crisscrossing through the other men, who were all doing the same.

Something crashed into his back, knocking him end over end. He flailed, slapping at the air, but that only made it worse. Then his training clicked in: he tucked his arms in tight and fanned his legs to drag at the air, angling him back into his dive.

Peter was breathing hard and trembling with adrenaline. Sideways collisions were expected during evasive maneuvers, he reminded himself. Even at this speed, they were nearly always harmless.

He looked up and saw Saul flying overhead, an enormous white grin beaming through his visor. Saul had hit him on purpose. Saul was like that. Playful—bored even—no matter that they were plummeting into hostile territory at three hundred miles an hour. Peter had grown used to this attitude back in Basic Training—five intensive months meant to hone men into deadly weapons. Frankly, they'd had much greater success with Saul than Peter.

Peter turned back to the incoming storm of bullets, forcing himself to relax. *Just like falling into the river*, he told himself. Of course, he didn't make the team that year. He might have impressed the older kids, but they didn't decide who made the cut.

Moments later the cloud of bullets collided with the swarm of men. Most of the bullets rattled harmlessly against the heavy armor on the marines' shoulders and helmets; they had spent most of their power on the long climb up. The bullets were mainly intimidation anyway, broadcasting the size of the force waiting below. But they also provided cover for the rockets that followed.

Thunder came from all sides and great orange fireballs filled the sky, shattering the unlucky and knocking around the rest. The explosions came one after another, their black smoke choking out the light. Someone—or some part of someone—struck Peter's shoulder and ricocheted away.

Sergeant Mickelson had advised them to have some sort of distraction on hand for the dive. Loud music, particularly metal, would drown out the noise of battle and pass the time. "Pornography is even better," he said, "but it's against policy, so don't let me catch you."

Neither idea appealed to Peter, so he hadn't brought anything. Instead, he tried to think about home, and about Amber. It had been seven months since he'd seen her, seven months since he'd felt her arms around him. His memory of her had been his strength, but he couldn't bring it up. Not while he was careening though the thick smoke and dull pounding of rockets, wondering if the next one was meant for him.

Having no other distraction, he started to hum.

The explosions stopped. Peter dropped below the smoke and saw only the plush treetops as he crashed into them. A charge on his back fired with a loud bang, flipping him upright. His rocket pack roared to life, its long flame licking his feet as it strained to slow his descent.

The leafy canopy closed overhead, sealing Peter into a murky world of long, spidery tree trunks. As Peter strained to pick a clear landing site, a leg-thick tree branch caught him square in the chest. He was knocked over and his rocket drove him straight at the ground. His suit's stabilizers tried to right him but, designed for the weightlessness of space, lacked the power.

His rocket sputtered out thirty feet from the ground; he slammed into it headfirst.

The jungle floor was thick with leaves, cushioning Peter's fall and sparing him serious injury or death—effectively the same thing this deep inside enemy territory. He scrambled out of the crater made from his own impact, ran for the cover of the nearest tree, and tucked himself into a protective ball. Shrapnel and debris drummed the ground. It tapered off after several minutes. He eased to his feet and looked around.

The trees were as straight as pencils, their white cabbagey trunks rising a hundred yards into the air, then sprouting into a green roof. Down at ground level, the trunks split and tangled together. Low scrub, like moss magnified a hundred-fold, circled the trees in wreaths, wisps of steam billowing off their crowns. In the dim light, the wet ground was the color of blood and dented by debris—parts of rockets, parts of men.

Alone in the jungle, Peter felt exposed; the enemy seemed to lurk in every shadow. He retreated further into the tree, ducking into the cave of its high roots, and waited.

It was fifty long seconds before the satellites moved into place. Peter's visor lit up with information, and he studied the translucent map that appeared in the corner. There were blue dots to indicate the other marines, but no red dots yet—the satellite's sensors couldn't detect the enemy through the thick foliage. It fell on the marines to dig them out here on the ground.

Peter's regiment was spread over several dozen miles, and he was a thousand yards from the nearest friendly. The rendezvous point was a mile and a half away, labeled by a green circle. He did a quick visual inspection of his suit, then tested his arms and legs. The artificial muscles in his suit whirred smoothly.

Everything seemed okay. He drew his sidearm and crept out from his cover.

The thick foliage cast dark shadows in the haze, providing the enemy ideal camouflage for an ambush. The jungle was dead quiet, with no sign of the indigenous otter-like creature that supposedly thrived there. Maybe they were hiding from the coming battle. Or maybe they had been slaughtered.

Fog condensed on Peter's visor, making beads of water that jiggled as he walked. His suit was climate controlled, insulating him from the jungle's heat and humidity, and its smell. The air from his tank was scentless and filtered, and gave no sense of the world around him. But his mind brought the jungle inside, the sense of danger, the presence of the Riel.

His eyes darted around, hunting for anything that seemed out of place. His suit had a battery of sensors, everything from emission scopes to wide-band motion detectors, but the dense jungle overpowered them. Even his thermal imagers were useless—the Riel were cold-blooded, so their body temperature matched that of the air around them. Despite his complex array of sensors, the best tools he had were his own eyes.

A tall, flat boulder loomed in the mist ahead. Perched on top was a short, muscular tree, its roots running down the stone like melted wax. It was exactly the sort of place where Peter would set an ambush, and he figured that a Riel sniper would think the same. He crouched low and gave the rock a wide berth, watching for a trap.

A yellow light pulsed on his visor—a warning from his Life Control System that he was breathing too quickly. The planet's atmosphere was poisonous, so running out of air here would be as deadly as it was in the vacuum of space. Peter stopped and took slow, measured breaths. Then he saw movement in the corner of his eye. He whipped around and fired.

The impulsor ray from his pistol was invisible, but it burned a line through the air, hissing and leaving a trail of curling smoke. The gun sliced through several plants and charred the trunk of a tree, but there was no one around. The movement had only been water running down his visor. Peter cursed, dropping low and peering back at the rock, seeing nothing.

He backed up, turning a slow circle and jerking his gun from target to target. His heart thrashed wildly and the oxygen warning light turned orange, then red. Unable to control his fear, Peter sprang up and raced through trees, slashing with his arms to clear the foliage, careless of the racket he was making.

His only thought was to reach the rendezvous point and the safety of his platoon.

Peter was watching his map, following his blue dot as it approached the green rendezvous point, when his legs tangled and he fell forward. He face-planted, scattering leaves and knocking into something solid. He jerked his gun out, but it was another marine, dead, half-buried from impact. Shards of red-stained metal jutted from his chest, and a stump of an arm rose as if saluting the sky.

Peter crept forward on his elbows, lay his pistol down, and pushed up to peer into the corpse's visor. The face inside was still and ashen. Peter didn't know him.

"I'll shoot you my damn self, Garvey," Mickelson snarled over the comm, "if you keep making all that goddamn noise."

The sergeant stood over him, glaring with anger, Peter's gun clenched in his hand. He leveled the gun at Peter's face, his finger tightening, but then changed his mind. He let the gun drop to the ground.

"Strip off your rocket and get over here," he said, walking away.

"Yes, sir," Peter said. He hopped up, holstered his gun, and pulled a catch on his shoulder; the spent rocket clattered to the ground. He considered grabbing the rocket off the corpse but shied away. He piled his own on a small stack over by Mickelson; if they won the battle today, the rockets would be collected, refurbished, and reused. Peter joined the men who were already there. Their names were stenciled on their backs, but Peter recognized none of them.

As if reading his thoughts, the battle computer broadcasted a full-channel update. The regiment had arrived 48 percent operational, which was the optimistic way of saying that 52 percent of them were killed before they even reached the ground. Of Peter's platoon, only Mickelson, Saul, Ramirez, and himself had survived the landing. Four of twelve. A thousand miles away, back on the commandship, that was just a figure on a spreadsheet. But down here they were men, like Peter, with families and friends who hoped and prayed to see them again. Now most of them would not, and the battle hadn't even started.

The attack would go ahead as planned, no matter the casualties. There was no choice. The transports couldn't land until the marines eliminated the Riel's anti-ship defenses. If they could eliminate them. Only Command knew the odds, and they wouldn't bother to tell anyone down here.

Twelve men gathered at the rendezvous point, an ad hoc platoon assembled by the battle computer from those who had survived the drop. Peter fidgeted with his pistol as men trickled in, relaxing only when Saul appeared, strolling out of the jungle as if he were arriving at a party. He moved through the men, exchanging hellos and learning names. His presence calmed the others, infecting them with his air of indestructibility.

"The good news," Saul said, settling next to Peter, "is that we landed in the middle of the regiment. That means we're completely safe. The bad news is that we've got a long walk before we get ourselves killed."

Sixteen minutes after touchdown, the newly formed North-58 platoon rolled out. Their target was three and a quarter miles away, and their orders were to be there in seven minutes, so they had to hump it.

Even though this section of the jungle had been declared clear, the men stayed in formation, guns at the ready, wary of ambush. In the field, *clear* was a relative term. More than once, men had stumbled onto Riel encampments right in the middle of their own.

"Let the suit do the work, Garvey," Mickelson growled. Peter's oxygen light was glowing yellow again.

Running should be easy—he just needed to guide the artificial muscles with his own. Peter had run literally thousands of miles during Basic, but while he could remember the motions, his body seemed to have forgotten. His legs struggled against the suit, tiring him out and wasting precious air.

Thankfully, they soon reached the no-man's land, and Mickelson motioned to slow down. "Stay low," he warned. "The Riel see you first, you'll never even know it."

The platoon took up an arrowhead formation with the seven general infantry marines forming a V on the perimeter and the three heavy-weaponry specialists—including Saul—just behind them. As the platoon's sniper, Peter walked to the center with Sergeant Mickelson.

The platoon crept forward, the GIs expanding and contracting to maintain their field of vision through the trees and underbrush. One of them glanced at Peter with bloodshot eyes, a side effect of Battle Heat.

Heat was a drug cocktail administered by the suit's Life Control System to maximize a marine's effectiveness in combat. Peter knew it only by reputation—it was never issued to snipers for fear of impairing their aim.

They arrived at their target three minutes late. There had been no resistance along the way, and when they saw what they were up against, they understood why. Who would skirmish in the jungle when they could hole up in a fortress?

The Riel stronghold was an oblong shard of reddish rock that towered over a wide clearing. Its rough-hewn walls tapered to an impossibly narrow base, like a massive spike balanced on its tip. A few green patches were scattered around the rock face—trees and plants that somehow found purchase. In several places sunlight glinted off crystal shields, Riel fortifications impenetrable to even the heaviest rifle in the marine arsenal.

Mickelson brought the platoon to a halt and moved to the front. His face distorted as the glass in his visor thickened and reformed, magnifying the distant rock. Peter tuned his visor to Mickelson's to see what his sergeant saw.

Each of the crystal shields—a half dozen in all—protected a gun nest, either armed with a heavy-caliber recoiling rifle or twin machine guns. Rocket batteries were spread over the stronghold, unmanned, either sentient or operated by remote.

All these Riel had to be guarding something important, and Peter guessed it was a Delta-class heavy-impulse blaster, which was exactly the sort of antiship weapon they'd have to destroy to get back off this planet.

Mickelson tracked along a recessed walkway cut into the rock face, spotting a patrolling Gyrine.

The Gyrine was the smaller of the two Riel species. It was several feet taller than a man, but from this distance its squat body made it look short. Its black skin was dry and scaly, like the skin on a bird's legs, and its face was pinched, with squinting eyes and the heavy jaw of a bulldog. Thick white fangs jutted up on either side of its flat nose, the effect more cartoonish than ferocious—not that Peter cared to put it to the test. This particular Gyrine had no cybernetic augmentation, which made it an officer.

"There's your first target, Garvey," Mickelson said; a yellow dot appeared on Peter's visor map.

Peter unlinked from Mickelson's video feed and crept off to find a good vantage point. Two GIs peeled off and followed him, his own personal guard.

More likely, Peter thought, *their orders are to recover my rifle when I get shot.*

After five minutes of scouting, Peter found a small boulder among some scrub ferns. He had been warned not to use rocks as cover, but he couldn't remember why. Meanwhile, Mickelson berated him impatiently. Absurdly, Peter was more worried about getting bawled out than getting shot.

Peter motioned to his escorts, who took up positions on either side, far enough that they couldn't all be killed by a single rocket. Peter clipped his pistol to his thigh, reached over his shoulder, and drew his rifle from its protective case. He unlocked the gun's barrel, extending it from the stock until it was taller than himself, and twist-locked it into place. He popped the rubber cap from the barrel and inspected the lens. He withdrew the battery clip, checked the contacts, and shoved it back in, seating it with a jiggle. This would be a synchronized attack; there was no room for mistakes.

Peter popped the cap off the optical scope, leaned against the rock, and raised the long gun toward the Riel stronghold.

Peter bent his arm and locked his combat suit's artificial muscles, making his hand a stable pivot for the gun's barrel. He pressed his visor to the rubber cone on the back of the scope, tunneling his vision down the gun's sights.

The Gyrine officer had moved, but Mickelson still had eyes on it. An arrow appeared on the left side of Peter's visor, and he shifted the gun up the walkway; he then centered on the Gyrine's chest. A second set of crosshairs appeared near the first—the battle computer's suggestion of where to aim. The computer took into account everything it knew, from the video feed of every marine's combat suit to the atmospheric information gathered by the satellites. Technically, the computer-generated crosshairs were the more accurate of the two, but a good sniper could outshoot the computer two to one. It was instinct, as all snipers have claimed since the invention of the rifle. But Peter wasn't feeling any instinct, so he just split the difference between the computer's crosshairs and his own.

The Gyrine was restless, pacing nervously, as if it could sense Peter's gaze. No doubt it expected an attack—this operation was far from covert—but it wouldn't know where or when. The UF satellites were flooding the planet with so much interference that a Riel couldn't detect a dog humping its leg, much less a small platoon three thousand yards out.

The Gyrine's black skin blended in the overhang's shadows, making it hard to track its movements. When Peter finally settled into his target's rhythm, he gave the trigger a light squeeze, signaling that he was ready to fire.

"About time," Mickelson snapped. "Fire at zero." A countdown appeared on Peter's visor. Ten seconds.

Nine.

Peter would fire the first round, followed by Heavy Weaponry; their countdown was just a quarter second behind his own. Getting the first shot meant catching the enemy unaware, practically guaranteeing a kill but also making his gun the first that the Riel would register. He would draw most of the return fire.

Getting the first shot right was critical; the marines had to kill enough Riel to offset the advantage of higher ground and protective shields. And officers, like Peter's target, were of particularly high value.

Something is wrong, Peter thought. The countdown had stopped; the number seven was frozen on his screen. He waited one second, two, but still it didn't change.

He tried to stay focused on his target, but his eyes were drawn to the seven on his visor. He was holding his breath to steady his shot, but his lungs began to ache. He took two quick tugs of air, and then the number dropped: *Six.*

Peter instantly felt relieved, then foolish, no longer sure that the pause hadn't just been his imagination. He looked back to his target, but it was gone.

Five.

Four.

The countdown raced now. Peter panned his rifle side to side, searching the empty walkway. *Where is it? Did it see me? Did it run?* The green, computer-generated crosshair remained where it was, aimed at nothing.

Three.

Salt stung his eyes. He blinked, trying to clear them.

Two.

His oxygen light pulsed red, the glow filling his visor.

One.

The Gyrine popped back into view—it had been bent over, hidden by the walkway's low wall. It stretched lazily, gazed into the distance, and scratched its chin, oblivious to both Peter's panic and the impending assault.

Peter swung the rifle toward the Gyrine but overcompensated—the slightest movement of the gun was yards at the fortress. He eased the gun back, his muscles tight, working against each other. The crosshairs found the Gyrine just as the countdown flashed zero. Peter squeezed the trigger.

Peter had never fired on a live target before. He closed his eyes, unable to watch the results. When he opened them a second later, the Gyrine was gone. *Did I kill it?*, he wondered.

"Christ-all-fucking-mighty, Garvey," Mickelson barked, and Peter knew he had missed.

Peter whipped his gun around, searching for the Gyrine, but it was gone. The rock face disappeared behind a cloud of dust, pounded by the giant impulsor cannons carried by heavy weaponry. He shrunk down behind the rock; all he could do was wait for further orders.

Distant machine guns cracked and rockets whistled in close, pounding into the ground and tossing up columns of dirt. Peter listened to the bullets rattle against the rock; then they stopped. The ferns around him vaporized and a nearby tree blackened like a match. The Riel were sweeping the area with lasers.

Lasers weren't a direct threat. Even if Peter weren't shielded by the boulder, his suit's ceramic coating would easily disperse the heat. But the beams would burn away his cover, and once they could see him, the Riel had plenty of other ways to kill him. Peter grew anxious just sitting there; he queried the battle computer.

"Negative targets," it replied.

We're in the middle of a battle, Peter thought. *How can there be nothing to shoot at?*

He stood up and aimed his gun at the towering rock, searching. On the very edge of the left face, he saw the top of a Gyrine's head sticking out over a crystal shield. It wasn't much—not enough for a kill—but it was something.

The Gyrine worked a thick-barreled, turret-mounted gun that recoiled heavily with each shot. It fired in the opposite direction, which Peter found reassuring, since it meant there was at least one other platoon involved in this assault. Peter centered his crosshairs just over the Gyrine's head, thinking perhaps to first draw its attention by shattering the rock.

His chest was warm. Not just warm, hot. Searing. He pulled back from the scope; the boulder he was leaning against was glowing red. Peter suddenly remembered why he wasn't supposed to use rocks as cover.

While his combat suit was immune to lasers, rocks were not. They would become superheated and explode. A melon-size rock had the destructive power of a fragmentary grenade. This boulder was a hundred times that.

Peter felt the rock tremble and crack, expanding from the heat. He might have even heard the explosion before everything went black.

[14.08.2.14::3948.1938.834.2D]

A white light clicked on—bright, painful. Peter blinked, his eyelids scratching over the crust that coated his eyeballs. His head was fuzzy, and the room's silence pressed against his ears. He heard footsteps—soft and light-footed—padding toward him. A pink blur slid into the light. Peter blinked again and saw a woman in a green surgical mask. She was leaning over him; he was lying down.

"There you are," she said. Peter couldn't place her accent. She wore a white smock with short sleeves that jutted off her shoulders like little wings, leaving her arms bare. The uniform was cut slim, but not as slim as she was. It dangled loosely over her body. Her dark brown hair was pulled tight, and a ponytail hung in a net behind her head. Gunmetal eyes inspected him from over the mask, faint wrinkles radiating from their corners.

The nurse settled onto a stool and raised a long finger, its nail trimmed short, with a dark stain under the tip that looked like dried blood. "Can you see this?" she asked. Peter nodded. "Follow it, please."

Peter followed the finger up and down, left and right. The woman ignored him, watching the video monitor that hung over his head.

"How many letters in the alphabet?" she asked.

"Twenty-six," Peter said.

"Recite them, please."

Peter did, feeling silly.

"What's the last thing you remember?" she asked.

"What?" Peter asked, confused.

"What's the last thing you remember?" the woman repeated impatiently.

Peter thought back. First he was crawling through the mud on his elbows. Then he was being thrown from a ship into the black nothing of space. And then he was free-falling through a white cloud, his stomach tight and sore. And finally, he stood at attention with the rest of his platoon. They wore full dress, and a general spoke on a distant stage.

"Basic Training," Peter said. "Graduation."

"Good," the woman said. She tapped around her monitor. "Anything else?"

There was something else, the memory of a memory. It felt important, but his efforts to remember it only pushed it farther away. His head ached from the effort, and he felt a sharp pain, like a hundred needles pricking his skull.

"No," he said. He tried to rub his head but found he was strapped to the bed.

"Easy, kid," the woman said, taking his wrist. "Don't rush." Her hand was searing hot; it burned his skin.

She flicked a finger at the crook of his arm, then dug her thumb in. A vein swelled with blood. The woman smiled warmly, raising a long syringe of oily liquid.

She slipped it in with practiced ease.

[19.17.3.17::1845.9671.402.7D]

The ship was so minimal that it didn't even rate a pilot, much less a name. It was designed to be cheap and disposable, and it served but one purpose: to transport marines to and from extra-planetary combat.

It had no hull, just an open frame made from thick bars that curved like a down-facing rib cage. Where there should have been a bridge, there was only a small metal box for the remote control. Marines were packed to the frame on all sides, crowded ass-to-knee. It was a full regiment: twenty-four hundred men, plus their colonel. Far in the back, at the tip of one rib, Peter craned his neck and watched the tapered flame of a relay module. It fired its rocket as it left the ship, then flipped around and fired again to fix its position. Next it fell still, disappearing against the black background.

Space was unnaturally dark inside the Drift, which had a scant few thousand stars.

The relays had been dropped at regular intervals, leaving a trail between them and the commandship far behind. They allowed the transport to be guided by tight beam, thereby protecting the location of both ships. The transport was fed its route one coordinate at a time to keep its destination from falling into Riel hands.

"Is that sixteen?" Saul asked over a closed channel. He was seated opposite Peter, his face hidden behind his mirrored visor. But you didn't need to see Saul's face to recognize him; his suit was twice as wide as—and a full head higher than—any other in the regiment.

One small benefit of Saul's size was that he was seated at the very tip of a rib, since he would otherwise fill two seats. And Peter, by virtue of being his best friend, got the next seat in.

"Nineteen," Peter said.

"I thought it was sixteen?" Saul asked disingenuously.

"Nineteen," Peter repeated.

"And they launch every four hours?" Saul mumbled, making like he was calculating. "So this is our fourth day. And you lost the bet."

Neither man had any real idea of how long they had been in transit. The computer in their suits had been disabled before they left the base, leaving them without a clock or access to movies, music, or anything that might give a sense of time. If they knew how long they had been traveling, they could guess how far they had come. And if they were captured, the Riel could use this information to locate their base. The United Forces had only one base, so losing it would be tantamount to losing the war. Protecting the base's location was a top priority, certainly more so than entertaining a few divisions of marines.

"I didn't say we were betting," Peter replied.

"You didn't say we weren't."

Peter shook his head, but the gesture was lost inside his helmet—their artificial muscles were locked to keep their movements from affecting the transport's course.

"You haven't won yet," Peter said, deciding to play along.

"I don't see any Riel creeping around," Saul replied. "So I figure we've still got a long way to go."

"So you hope," Peter said, but he did as well. The journey might be boring, but it was far better than the destination. This was his first combat mission, and even after five months of Basic Training, he still felt completely unprepared.

Two hours later a half dozen relays shot off all at once—a redundancy that anticipated enemy fire. More relays lit up the sky around them. It was jarring to suddenly be in the middle of so many ships; they had been alone since they left the base. Every ship in the fleet had taken a different route to reduce their energy signature and thereby avoid detection. That they had converged could mean only one thing.

Incoming rockets exploded on all sides. The transport banked hard, pulling at Peter's guts. A dozen rockets lanced through the ship, which twisted to let them pass harmlessly out the other side. One shot past Peter's head so close that he felt the heat of its exhaust.

His suit sparked to life and his visor flooded with information. There was a click as his suit separated from the ship's umbilicus, followed by the hiss of oxygen flowing from his own tank. Sergeant Mickelson shouted instructions over the open channel, but Peter didn't catch a word of it. Another rocket raced by, exploding right in the ship's belly. It was terrible and silent, and the orange flame reflected on the visors of a thousand marines. Then the shock wave slammed against Peter, knocking the air from his chest.

The ship bucked, then recovered, rolling one hundred and eighty degrees and whipping straight up. Peter had been through these maneuvers in simulation, but there was no comparison.

He jerked his head around, trying to see where the ship was going. Mickelson cursed sharply as more rockets shot past. And then it was over. With a blaze of engines, the ship wrenched to a stop and lay still.

They had ducked behind a wall of rock that floated in empty space. The rock flickered in the light of a nearby transport, which smoldered like the coals of a campfire. The ship was dead, rolling slowly as if capsizing. It twinkled as the air tanks of the attached marines exploded.

Another rocket plowed into the burning ship. Peter shielded his eyes with his hand as the explosion lit up giant rocks floating all around them.

The Teisserenc Asteroid Belt. They had arrived.

Muscle relaxant tingled through Peter's body, delivered automatically by his Life Control System to ease the stiffness of the long journey. The motors in his combat suit whirred as he flexed his arms and legs, stretching, working in fresh blood. There was a heavy clunk as the ship unclipped him, its rib sliding up and away. The ship drew out from the jumble of men and then shot off to safety.

Peter pressed a hand to his chest, where, beneath the combat suit's hard shell, hung a locket of soft, brown hair. *My dearest Amber*, he thought. *If you ever pray for me, pray for me tonight.*

Saul floated over and took Peter's arm. The platoon locked together, hands grabbing elbows, forming a ring. All were quiet. Each man soberly watched his visor and waited for the order to move out.

Somewhere deep inside the Teisserenc Asteroid Belt was a Riel base. Where exactly, or even how large, nobody knew, but the mission was to find and neutralize it. Even if everything went according to plan, Peter would never lay eyes on that base. His regiment, along with a half-dozen others, was running a diversion far from the core assault.

There would still be plenty of action. Several outposts had been scouted in this area, each protected on all approaches by missile turrets. Peter's platoon would either take out the turrets, allowing for a naval assault, or they would attack the outposts directly. They had trained for both, but would only now find out which. Either way, there were a lot more Riel in this area than they could hope to handle. Their orders were simply to fight until called off. Or, the unspoken alternative: until they were all dead.

Back on the base, Colonel Chiang San had called this battle "risky." "Don't think of yourself as men or marines," he had said, "but as the last line of defense for the Livable Territories. Any man who gives his life today does so to secure the freedom of his homeworld."

Peter wasn't impressed. He had no desire to die for his homeworld or for the entire Livable Territories. But if he had to, he'd do it for her. For Amber.

A fleet of missiles trailed far behind the marine invasion force. It had followed them here from the base and had taken up position just beyond the reach of the Riel sensors. Most were armed with warheads to strike as critical targets were identified, but a few—like the one approaching—carried a more specialized payload.

It wasn't visible until it passed overhead in a great gray shadow. And then it was gone, the blazing ring of its impulsor engine shrinking away. The engine flared out, replaced by twelve smaller ones as the missile broke into sections, each heading in a different direction. Those sections divided again, spreading like intricate fireworks, and the smallest ones exploded, scattering silvered marbles. These were sensor pods. They flooded the area with frequency-coded radar waves, indicating time and place of origin, which allowed the marine's combat suits to interpret their signals directly. While the suits had their own sensors, using them would be like wearing a neon target.

The battle computer merged the gathered information into a single picture, and a green-mesh diagram of the asteroids drew out on Peter's visor. This overlay, called his scope, blended with what little he could see and, when he focused on something, gave him information about its size, distance, and composition. Peter zoomed his scope all the way out to get a view of the battlefield.

The Teisserenc Belt stretched out for thousands of miles, like a massive stone wall with the mortar removed. It was so calm, so beautiful. Peter didn't want to spoil the view by thinking about how many Riel were hiding in there.

Orienting in the three dimensions of space was far more complex than doing so on the ground, and Peter was still fumbling into position when Mickelson gave the order to move out. Their first target was a missile turret a few thousand yards inside the belt, which was close enough, Mickelson decided, to burn gas. It was a calculated risk: their fuel was limited, like their oxygen and batteries, and once they ran out, they would be stuck.

Mickelson fired his rocket pack and flew ahead, diving below the asteroid that had been their cover. The platoon fell into a double-V formation, like the twin blades of a broadhead arrow. The other men readied their rifles, but Peter had to settle for his pistol.

They weaved through the asteroids, which were invisible beyond the green outlines on Peter's scope. The occasional flash of distant rocket fire echoed through the rocks, but it became less frequent as the platoon moved deeper into the belt, away from the battle and into the eerie stillness beyond.

Mickelson called for helmet lights, and a bloodred asteroid leaped from the dark. The marines banked, their formation flattening as they skimmed along the rock face, heading toward a small cave. The cave walls were smooth, machine-made. The men formed up around the rim, as if protecting it, and Mickelson motioned Peter inside.

"You're up, Garvey," Mickelson barked. Snipers were rarely useful in the close quarters of an asteroid belt, so

Peter had drawn double-duty as the explosives team. He eased himself to the edge and, pistol first, peered in.

His helmet light reflected off something large and flat ten yards down: a crystal shield that blocked the way. Something moved on the far side, but Peter couldn't tell what.

He took a deep breath, grabbed the rim, and flung himself down.

Peter aimed his pistol forward as he descended, his hand clenching the grip. The glare from his helmet light was blinding, so he switched to a smaller one mounted on his wrist, holding it wide to reduce the reflection.

The pistol clinked against the shield, and Peter brought his face to it. A cross-hatched electronic eye, mounted on a missile turret, stared back at him. It was flocked with a dozen missiles, each as large as his arm, all of which were aimed at him. Peter started, pushing himself back, his heart pounding.

"Hop to!" Mickelson shouted over the comm. Peter lurched at the sound, knocking against the crystal.

I'm wasting time, Peter thought. Back on the surface, his platoon was exposed to attack.

He slipped an explosive from his belt—putty packed into a shallow metal bowl, which focused the blast. He peeled the plastic film from the flat side, pressed it to the shield, then twisted it to set the adhesive. He placed another bomb in the opposite corner and, for luck, a third one in between. Sweat trickled through his eyebrows, but he had no way to wipe it.

Underneath the crystal, the turret tracked Peter's movements, keeping its missiles aimed at his head. But the shield remained closed; the turret felt that either the crystal would protect it or that reinforcements were on the way. Peter suspected the latter.

Peter armed the explosives and the countdown started on his visor: three minutes. Plenty of time, but no reason to waste it. He flipped around, banging against the tight cave walls, then shoved off the crystal's surface, leaping away. He rose through the cave, reaching the top just as the onslaught began.

Flaming tracers zipped by Peter's head. They would be mixed with more deadly rounds that were invisible in the dark. Something rattled against his helmet, but it was only rock fragments that had chipped from the asteroid behind him.

A half-dozen machine guns twinkled in the distance, the Riel behind them hidden by the bright muzzle flash. Peter's blood ran warm as his suit injected him with Battle Heat.

Heat was a volatile drug, its use limited to the most desperate of combat situations. Peter had never felt it before, but knew it by the warmth and by his swelling muscles. His mind sharpened and his thinking cleared. He could see now just how frail the enemy was, how outnumbered—their weapons were inconsequential. Killing them would be easy.

He charged forward with a quick burst of his rocket pack, diving straight at the machine guns. He raised his pistol and clicked the trigger. His gun had no flash or kickback. The only indication that it worked was a red light blinking on the back. The machine guns hammered Peter, bullets glancing harmlessly off the sharp angles of his suit's shoulders and helmet. Then his arm caught a solid hit, knocking it back.

Peter had no way to tell if the bullet had penetrated. If it had, his combat suit would instantly anesthetize the wound, and his artificial muscles would compensate for any damage to his flesh. In case of an air leak, the suit would seal his arm off from his body, leaving it to fend for itself against the freezing vacuum of space.

The Gyrine appeared behind a blazing machine gun. It was naked, its tough body as comfortable in rancorous space as on any planet—more so perhaps, since the creature drank oxygen instead of breathing it. From the chest down, its right half was completely robotic. Its arm ended with a multi-barreled minigun, which spit a continuous stream of bullets.

Peter's confidence wavered. The creature was enormous, its machinery powerful. But then the warmth in his blood grew to fire. He aimed at the creature's head, holding the trigger until the battery ran dry.

There was no impact from the shot; the Gyrine's skull simply dissolved, its head melting to a jiggling sack. Peter had never killed anything before. He stared, transfixed.

Bullets strafed his feet. Peter shoved a fresh battery clip into his pistol and spun, but the battle was over. Four marines stood nearby—the survivors—while eight others floated lifelessly in space, forming a trail that led back to the asteroid.

Saul flew up to Peter, thumbs up, waving at the dead Gyrines. Their bodies were drained, their robotics warped and twisted. Peter returned the gesture, trying to be enthusiastic, but the Heat had dissipated and with it his confidence.

Two men for every Gyrine, Peter thought, counting the corpses. Mickelson had told them they'd be lucky to see that ratio. So they had been lucky, but Mickelson had not. Their sergeant's body floated among the dead.

A red light blinked in Peter's visor, reminding him that the charges he had set would explode in less than a minute. It wasn't much time to clear the blast radius. He checked the gas level in his rocket pack; he'd be lucky to get a three-second burn. It wasn't enough. The only asteroid in that range was the one they needed to escape.

Peter searched his map for options and found none. The battle computer suggested a route off to the right, drawing a blue line on his map, but Peter knew it wouldn't work. While they might clear the initial explosion, shattering a crystal shield would require tremendous force; the resulting shockwave would reflect several times with deadly power, catching them squarely. So either the computer had made an error or was simply offering false hope in lieu of none at all.

The other men had already started along the computer's route when Peter squeaked, "Stop," his voice cracking.

Peter reddened as the other men turned to him, but he couldn't take it back now. Seconds were ticking away.

"This way," he said, pointing back to the missile turret. "The asteroid is too big to explode, so we can take cover on the other side."

The men looked at one another, unsure. They had all seen the flaw in the computer's plan, but in Mickelson's absence, the computer was the authority.

"You're sure?" Saul asked.

"No," Peter said, but he didn't back down.

Saul chewed on it. "Better idea than what Command had," he said, considering. Then he nodded, waving Peter ahead.

Peter took a deep breath and fired his rocket pack, leading the men straight at the explosives.

Peter used his stabilizers to flip around, approaching the asteroid feet-first. He banked, skimming over the surface, the rock passing inches from his face. He was heading toward the edge of the asteroid where, according to his scope, the rock tapered to a thin wall that would offer cover. His plan was to swing around behind it, somehow.

The explosive's timer fell to ten seconds as his feet passed the bottom of the asteroid. He dragged his hands along the surface, feeling for anything large enough to grab.

When the counter hit five, he was halfway below the edge. He clawed at the rock, his fingers slipping on its smooth surface. The bottom rose to his chin, then slipped away. Beyond was nothing but empty space.

He stretched his arm up, grasping for the very tip of the rock, but it was too thick. His hand wasn't wide enough to get a grip. The asteroid climbed out of reach, floating away. The counter dropped: *Three.*

Two.

One.

Something slapped into Peter's hand; his fingers closed automatically. By sheer luck, he caught a spur at the edge of the asteroid. He tightened his grip, kicked his legs, and swung behind the rock.

A flaming geyser shot from the cave. The asteroid trembled and the rock in Peter's hand broke free. He was adrift but safe. The shockwave passed, tickling his feet.

The other marines swung behind the asteroid right behind Peter, each with better form. Three made it, but the last, Alan DeGrazzio, wasn't fast enough. The shockwave—a haze of gas and microscopic particles—struck him full on. He was pressed flat as a door, and then his suit sprang back into shape, filled with the paste of what had just been a man.

The remaining four men watched him float away, his visor tinted red. One by one they turned away.

Peter's map was a complete blank; the explosion had knocked out all the sensor pods in their area. Blind beyond the range of his headlamp, he turned in a circle, guessing what to do next. Then a blue light blinked in his visor. He was being hailed.

"Sergeant Peter Garvey," Colonel Chiang San said, his projection appearing in space, as if standing beside him. "Promotion effective now. Sending you coordinates for a nearby Riel outpost. Battle is in progress. Get over there and take charge."

The projection dissipated, leaving Peter so dumbfounded that he didn't see the approaching asteroid until it hit him in the face.

Peter was knocked into a backward spin, scrambling his sense of direction. He tried to orient himself using the headlamps of the other marines, but Saul was shouting frantically, making it hard to concentrate. Peter had never heard the big man panic before. It was alarming.

A second asteroid pressed against his back, shoving him toward the first. The two rocks were on a collision course, and Peter was in the middle. The math part of his brain figured that the explosion had blown the asteroid backward, hurling it—and him—into the other. The rest of his brain didn't care; it just wanted out.

Somewhere in Saul's garbled shouting, Peter caught the word "legs." He curled his legs up just as the two asteroids connected with shearing force. The rear asteroid slammed his head into the other, scratching thick white lines down his visor.

The remaining gap between the two asteroids was a V-shaped canyon that narrowed as the two rocks rotated toward each other. The other men were already scurrying up the rock, heading for the opening at the top.

The asteroid was rich in iron, providing traction for the magnets in Peter's boots. He climbed along a crystalline vein, gripping its rough surface with the rubber pads on his fingertips.

He was halfway up when the asteroid jolted backward. He hugged the rock to keep from being thrown and looked up just as Donaldson crashed into his visor. Peter was knocked back. He lost his grip and went spinning into the chasm. Below him, Donaldson disappeared into a cloud of rock dust; the two asteroids were pulverizing each other and everything in between. Peter would be next.

He gouged at the rock but found no purchase. The walls tightened, the rust-colored dust engulfed him, and then, suddenly, he wrenched to stop.

"Gotcha," Ramirez said. He was dangling in the air, holding Peter by his oxygen tank. At first it looked like Ramirez was floating, but then Peter saw a green line on his visor. The micro-cord, a carbon weave only a few dozen molecules thick, was invisible to the naked eye but coded for his suit to detect. The line ran up to Saul, at the top of the canyon. The big man tugged, and Peter and Ramirez flew upward.

Halfway there, Ramirez's chest plate got caught in the shrinking gap and jerked him to a stop. Peter reached the top and Saul caught him, palming his helmet in one giant hand. He set Peter down and heaved on the microcord.

Twenty feet down, Ramirez was sandwiched between the tightening asteroids. Saul yanked him free, but the rocks closed, catching him a few feet later.

"Give me a hand," Saul said, panting.

Peter took the end of the cable and pulled, his artificial muscles whining. Ramirez finally came loose, shooting up. He was nearly out when his foot got stuck. Saul and Peter pulled on his arms, but his metal boot was wedged tight, bending under the press of the walls.

Peter dove headfirst into the narrow gap, pressed his pistol to Ramirez's boot, and fired. The boot glowed red, warping and melting, and then exploded into vapor, along with the foot inside. Ramirez popped loose, colliding with Saul and sending them both tumbling.

The resistance of Ramirez's boot gone, the asteroids lurched together, clamping onto Peter's helmet.

Peter tried to twist free, but he was stuck. The fibers in his helmet cracked and snapped, so loud that he thought his skull was splitting. His only hope was for a painless death, but even as his thoughts turned toward acceptance, he was overpowered by the urge to escape. He didn't want to die here; he wanted to get home, to see Amber.

He flailed wildly, bucking and screaming. The cracking grew louder and louder, and then came a terrible thud, twisting Peter's neck. A foot flew at his face, connecting with another thud. The foot swung back and came hard, bending Peter's head to his shoulder, but he broke loose. He was yanked up, dangling by his ankle, face-to-face with Saul.

Saul spun him like a baton, set him on his feet, and stood back. He smiled expectantly.

"Thank you..." Peter started, but he was shoved forward. He took several long steps to recover his balance, and then turned and drew his pistol. He was facing a rock wall; Saul had set in him in the path of the approaching asteroid.

"You better watch out for those things, sir," Saul said. "Get yourself killed and they'll try to make me the new sergeant."

Peter whirled on Saul, ready to be angry, but saw the smirk on his face.

"I wish they would," he said with a weak smile.

The ground shook as the two asteroids came together. Ramirez, standing on one leg, hopped to keep his balance and fell over. He laughed like he was drunk, and soon they were all laughing.

"Thanks, Sarge," Ramirez said as Peter helped him up. "Man, I need a new foot."

Ramirez's missing foot outlined on Peter's visor. It was annotated with a dozen details—his estimated top running speed and how much weight he could support, as well as a list of which painkillers and mood enhancers his suit was administering, the latter explaining his good mood. Peter turned to Saul and saw similar data.

Must come with my promotion, he thought. He looked at the bullet wound in his arm, but nothing appeared.

"So what's next?" Saul asked, clapping Peter on the back.

Peter shrugged. His map was blank—he had no connection to the battle computer and no idea where the Riel outpost was. He turned in a circle, taking in the nothingness. Even the stars had abandoned him, blocked out by unseen asteroids.

"When I'm Sergeant," Ramirez said, "I'm gonna have all my men carry a spare gas tank."

"You'll never be a sergeant," Saul said.

The men were still on the asteroid with no idea where to go and no way to get there. Peter paced the rock's perimeter; the asteroid was still moving, and he hoped to pick up a signal from Command. Ramirez sat in seeming thin air, having bent his leg and locked his artificial muscles. Saul was sprawled out on the ground, which in zero gravity was more of a statement than a comfort.

"Why not?" Ramirez asked.

"Who ever heard of a sergeant with a missing foot," Saul replied.

"They'll give me another one," Ramirez said. Then, to Saul's dubious look, he added, "A better one, like what the Gyrines get."

"With a gun?"

"Sure. Why not?"

"You ever seen anyone with gun feet?"

"We're recruits," Ramirez protested. "We just got here."

"What about you, Sarge?" Saul called to Peter.

Peter ignored him at first—this was the third time they were having this conversation, even though they'd been stuck here only a few minutes. But then he was struck by a thought. "Mickelson has a limp," he said, and then corrected himself. "That is, he *had* one."

"No, he didn't," Saul replied, firing a look at Ramirez.

"I never saw him limp," Ramirez said, thinking. "Not in Basic, anyway."

Peter thought about it, but then his visor flashed; it had found a connection to the battle computer.

"Hang on," Peter said. "I've got the location of the outpost."

Both men got to their feet.

"Where?" Saul asked as the asteroid slowly rolled down, revealing a battle in progress.

"There," Peter said, raising a finger.

Not a hundred yards away, a platoon of marines advanced over an asteroid the size of a small mountain. Peter had an overhead view of the men as they moved over the rough surface, trading shots with what he assumed was the Riel outpost—from this angle, all he could see was a steel base at the top of the rock.

Peter, newly crowned Sergeant Garvey, had orders to take charge of the battle, but had no idea how to do so. His map showed eight blue dots on the face of the asteroid, as well as four red ones—unidentified Riel clustered at the outpost. The battle computer scrolled through possible attacks, filling his screen with lines and arrows mixed in with confusing code names. It was beyond comprehension. Peter was about to pick one at random when three Riel fighterships shot into view.

The fighterships were perfect spheres, fifteen feet in diameter, gleaming of polished steel. An assortment of armaments dented their smooth surfaces, both guns and rocket launchers. They moved in a tight line arcing out from behind a far asteroid and heading straight for the other marines. Machine guns strobed as they approached, and through the green trapezoidal cockpit window, Peter saw a Gyrine sneering with pleasure.

The ships streaked past, curved away, and disappeared into the belt. The screech of their engines came to them in the gas from their exhaust, and then all was silent. Across the expanse the eight marines floated lifelessly.

"That your new command?" Saul asked.

"Yeah," Peter said, "my very first."

Peter had known from the start this was a suicide mission, but that abstract idea was now spelled out in three concrete, and equally hopeless, options. They could wait for reinforcements, which were unlikely. They could retreat to the edge of the belt and call for evac, but with no gas for their rocket packs, that would take days and they'd run out of oxygen long before they got there. Or they could attack the outpost by themselves—an idea well past the line where courage becomes stupidity.

"So what's the plan?" Saul asked.

"I'm open to suggestions," Peter replied.

"Right," Saul said, whipping his giant multi-pulse cannon up to his shoulder. "We know those fightership saw us, so I vote we start this attack before they circle back."

Saul was right. Peter nodded. He backed up to get a running start and leaped into the void.

Peter dove for the asteroid's bottom, staying below the enemy's line of fire. He doubted they would leave the safety of their outpost to come get them. *Bother to leave*, he thought, *might be a better way to put it.*

They sailed past the lifeless marines from the other platoon. Ramirez grabbed one to check its rocket pack.

"Empty," he reported.

"Just keep on cheering me up," Saul replied.

Peter's boot magnets locked to the asteroid, and he took off at a full sprint. He had a scavenged general infantry rifle in one hand and a grenade in the other. He kept an eye on his scope, matching his pace with Saul's, who was racing up the far side of the asteroid. They would attack the outpost from both sides while Ramirez, with his limited mobility, would draw their attention to the front.

The outpost appeared on the shallow horizon. It was three stories tall, covered with opaque crystal blocks, and held together by a steel framework. It was round and narrow, like the turret of a castle.

Ramirez opened fire, and machine guns replied from the high walls, their bullets tearing through his chest and drawing red strings of blood out from his back. His blue dot disappeared from Peter's map, leaving only Saul's and his own.

Peter leaped up, flying through the air and firing at a thin slit in the wall. A thick steel leg swung over the wall, taller than the entire outpost. It was triangular in cross-section and had several joints that tapered down to a spiked tip. The first leg was followed by a second, then a third. It was a Typhon.

The Typhon was the other species of Riel, a monster so large that, even with the legs right in front of him, the top half was still hidden over top of the outpost. Peter had seen diagrams, pictures, and even full-size holograms of the beast, but nothing had prepared him to meet one face on.

He dropped the rifle—it was useless—and cocked the grenade back. The Typhon's battery of machine guns blazed high above, knocking Peter down and flattening him to the ground. The grenade slipped from his hand, floating just over his head, its three-second fuse counting in Peter's visor.

Everything went black.

[14.08.2.13::3948.1938.834.2D]

White light pulsed like a failing fluorescent tube, jarring Peter from sleep. Something hot clamped to his wrist, searing the skin. His eyes popped open; a nurse leaned over him, her hand on his wrist. Her thumb dug into his artery, its short nail biting his skin. She counted silently, her face hidden behind a surgical mask.

The room was covered floor to ceiling with white tiles, and a hose was coiled up in the corner. Medical equipment was stacked along one wall, piled haphazardly, looking long out of use. Peter tried to lean over to get a better look but was strapped to the bed.

"There you are," the nurse said, noticing him stir. "You had me worried." She didn't sound worried; her tone was flat, efficient. She tucked his wrist gently against his side and used a pencil-size light to inspect his eyes.

She peered into one ear, then leaned on top of him to look in the other. Her body was scorching, even through the fabric of her shirt. *She must be burning up*, Peter thought. He reached to touch her bare arm. Linda recoiled, glaring, but not at him.

"Everything seems normal," she said finally. "What's the last thing you remember?"

Peter thought back: He was in full-dress uniform, standing with Saul and Ramirez in a hanger full of marines. A general spoke on a distant stage. *Was that only yesterday?* Peter wondered.

"Graduation," he said. "Basic Training." *But if that was yesterday, what about...?*

"Good," the woman said. "Anything else?"

There was something else.

Peter reached deep into his memory, searching. Then it leaped out at him.

"Typhon," he gasped, adrenaline chilling his blood.

The woman frowned, crossing her arms. "That's not right," she muttered, turning to the monitor over Peter's head.

"Typhon!" he shouted, jerking against his straps. "I've got to warn Saul."

"Careful now," the nurse hissed. She clamped a hand under his jaw, locking his head to the steel bed. "Hold still."

Peter wrenched back and forth, but she was too strong. His strength withered and he lay still, panting, his heart racing. A door opened behind him.

"Everything okay, Linda?" a man asked.

"Everything is fine," the nurse replied, irritated. She jabbed a finger at the video monitor and electricity crackled in Peter's ears. The room shrank away, retreating down a long tunnel.

Black.

The white light jarred Peter awake. A nurse inspected him, her face covered by a surgical mask.

"What's the last thing you remember?" she asked.

Peter thought back. "Graduation," he said. "Basic Training."

"Anything else?"

"No," he said, shaking his head. "Just Basic."

"Good," the woman said, her gunmetal eyes smiling.

[84.3.4.3::4843.4534.345.2L]

"The one thing you children need to keep in the forefront of your feeble little minds," Sergeant Mickelson said, shouting in a strained voice, "is that what is back there is back there, and back there doesn't matter anymore. All that matters now is what's out there."

Peter had just arrived at the Marine Training Orbital. It was a flat disk, several miles across, in low orbit over one of the Livable Territories' rim planets. A clear dome covered the top, rising to a half mile at the center, encasing buildings and roads that could have been in any town on any planet. Except there was no sun, just the permanent green twilight of the orbital's plasma shield.

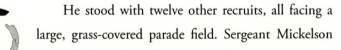

He stood with twelve other recruits, all facing a large, grass-covered parade field. Sergeant Mickelson paced the ramshackle line, scrutinizing them with increasing disdain.

Mickelson was a short, thin man with feline strength. His face was flat and weatherworn, and his eyes had a distant squint, as if you were standing in the way of what really interested him. Peter had only just met him as he left the shuttle. The sergeant had ordered him to stand at attention, though Peter wasn't exactly sure how.

The sergeant had been lecturing for twenty minutes, most of it insults and threats. Peter's attention wandered to the base around him, which would be his home for the next five months. Though it was supposedly a small orbital, its size overwhelmed him.

Beyond the wide field, buildings stretched down long roads. It dwarfed the town Peter had grown up in, and unlike the mismatched buildings and shambling farms of home, everything here was uniform and modern. Even the marines, marching around as if by interlocked gears, looked freshly minted.

Peter had never seen a real marine before, aside from the recruiters back on Genesia. "population control experts," as Saul called them.

He and Saul had grown up just three towns apart but had only met on the journey here. At least, Peter didn't remember him. And Saul wasn't someone you forgot.

Saul was big. Bigger than a linebacker. Bigger than two. Peter was tall himself, but his head barely reached Saul's shoulders—shoulders so wide that he had to step sideways through most doorways. He had large black eyes, skin like cream in coffee, and a pencil-thin beard traced around his wide jaw. His smile revealed a monolith of white teeth, and Saul was nearly always smiling.

This trip had been Peter's first in space—his family was too poor to vacation off-planet—and he was entranced. He spent almost the entire three-week journey in the observation lounge at the back of the transitship, watching the stars through a half dome of windows.

It had never been his plan to join the marines. He didn't want to leave Amber or his family, but he had bet everything on a football scholarship—ignoring his schoolwork and pretty much everything else—and it hadn't arrived. Then the war started.

Like the other men in town, he had wanted to defend his planet against the Riel. But that wasn't his main motivation. What he was really after was a way to start a life with Amber. For that, he needed money. Enlisting seemed the best of his limited options.

It hadn't been an easy decision, and it haunted him from the moment he signed the papers. But he found comfort looking out at the stars. There were so many; his own troubles seemed insignificant. His worries faded as the days passed.

For most of the trip, Peter had the back lounge to himself—the other recruits preferred the bar amidships. Then one day, as he sat watching a red-and-blue nebula float past, Saul wandered in.

Saul had a half-empty bottle of beer encased in one hand and a full one in the other. He walked a full circuit of the room and—even though it was both large and empty—dropped into the seat next to Peter's, his bulk forcing the shared armrest into Peter's ribs. Saul stared at the nebula for a few minutes, then said, "Now that's something."

Peter murmured, quietly hoping the intruder would lose interest and leave. But instead Saul offered him the full beer, popping the cap off with a flick of his thumb.

"No, thank you," Peter said.

Saul was incredulous. "You do know the drinks are free, right?"

Peter shook his head; he didn't.

"They're free the whole trip, but on the orbital they'll cost four times what they do back home. So allow me to suggest, with great humility, that you drink up."

"Okay," Peter said, taking the beer. "Thanks."

Saul tapped the neck of his bottle to Peter's and they drank. A few minutes passed in silence, both men watching the nebula. When it reached the back of the warp envelope, it stretched like putty and was sucked into the bright spot that floated in the ship's wake.

"Now that *is* something," Saul said. And Peter couldn't help but agree.

Mickelson gave the recruits a quick tour of the orbital, assigned them to barracks, and allowed them six hours to themselves before training. Most of the men, ragged from weeks of drinking, fell immediately to sleep. But Peter lay on his bunk, fondling the locket of hair that hung from his neck and thinking about the night the war started. It was a week after his seventeenth birthday, and just a couple hours after dark, when the Riel invaded the Livable Territories.

A blackout had been ordered for the entire planet; light made an easy target for the Riel bombers. Amber and Peter were in town and took shelter in the feed store basement, along with a few dozen other people. But after sitting on dusty grain sacks for a couple hours, Amber grew restless.

"Let's go outside," she whispered to Peter. "I want to see what it looks like."

Peter resisted, but Amber pushed, arguing that the cellar wasn't going to protect them from a high-powered bomb and that she couldn't think of a more dismal place to die. So they slipped out.

Downtown was small, a few short blocks of Craftsman-style buildings lost in a sea of wheat. They wandered out to the fields, stopping at the deserted general store to borrow a blanket and two bottles of wine.

It was fall, and the wheat was thick and tall, whispering in the wind as they followed a rutted tractor path. Amber's hair billowed like a soft brown cape. Her white skin glowed in the quarter moon, and Peter stole lustful glances at her neckline, where deep cleavage rolled with her every step. Amber was as pretty as any girl he'd ever seen, in real life or otherwise, and just looking at her made his heart race.

They reached a grassy rise in what had once been a cemetery. The bodies might still be down there, but the headstones were worn to nubs. They settled onto the blanket and realized they didn't have a corkscrew or glasses. Peter pushed in the cork, and they drank right from the bottle.

The invasion wasn't much to see. A few lights traversed the sky, but that was normal enough. Peter guessed they were navy ships, instead of the usual cargo freighters, but he had no way to be sure.

"Would you like to go up there someday?" Amber asked as they lay hand-in-hand, staring at the sky. "To see other planets?"

"I like it here fine," Peter replied.

"I think it would be amazing. Some of those luxury liners have clear bubbles where you can float out in the middle of space."

"Just float?" Peter asked, running a finger down her dress, from her stomach to her thigh.

"Peter Garvey!" Amber said, slapping his hand with mock affront.

"We might die tonight," Peter said.

"I bet you say that to all the girls," Amber said, but she knew better. She and Peter had been a couple for as long as either could remember. They grew up friends and didn't so much start dating as notice that they already were. They would get married too, as soon as they were out of high school.

"Come up here, instead," Amber continued, peeling her collar back slowly, tantalizingly. Peter stiffened, his eyes glued.

"You like that?" she asked.

"You know I do."

"You have a filthy mind," Amber said.

"You know I do." Peter sprang on top of her, nibbling her soft skin with his lips. He worked down her neck to her collarbone, then dropped to a breast, nosing back her dress and taking a bite. He pulled back before she could protest, then dug his fingers into her ribs and tickled. He had years of practice—once upon a time, his only interest in her body had been tickling. She giggled loudly, slapping his chest until he stopped. He settled on top of her, circling her face with his fingers and gazing into her eyes.

"Peter Garvey," she sighed, "I can't wait until we're married."

"I don't see why we have to."

"Because my dad owns a gun?"

"That's," Peter said with a laugh, "that's a pretty good reason."

"And because I say so. Girls like me don't come cheap."

Peter frowned, rolling off her. "I'm not sure I can afford it."

"You still bothering on that scholarship?" she asked, hugging his back. "It won't matter now. No one's gonna watch football with a war on."

"I suppose," Peter said.

"I don't want you to give it another thought. We'll find some rich old hag who won't mind you too much. I'll just take you on the weekends."

Peter lay back, and Amber slid on top of him. Suddenly the whole sky flashed white. Peter bolted up as an orange fireball ballooned in the distance. It was so low to the horizon he couldn't tell if it was on land or in space. He raised his arm to point, but Amber buried her face in his side, crying.

"This, gentlemen, is the Drift. You've all heard of it and you'll all be fighting in it. Most of you will die in it."

Colonel Chiang San lectured under the glow of a three-dimensional projection; a model of the Drift floated over his head. Chiang San was a stout man, Asian, with a thick chest and a wide wrestler's stance. He stood in a large auditorium that was packed with twenty thousand recruits. It was a lot of men but still only a tenth of the newly formed Digamma San Division, the youngest in the United Forces. Or they would be, as soon as they finished Basic.

Peter's platoon, lost somewhere near the back, were all sealed inside their combat suits. They had been stuck inside them for six straight days now and would remain so for the next two months.

"Starting now," Mickelson had told them, "you will train in your suit and you will sleep in it. You will eat through its feeder tube and you will use its map to find the bathroom. More important, you'll acquaint yourself with the delicate art of controlling your artificial muscles. Any of you morons can bend bars with them, but I want you to peel an egg. And you'll do that for me before I'll let you so much as flip your visor up."

It had been a difficult week. The artificial muscles were hard to control, and Peter had to relearn the most basic tasks. Things broke and mangled in his hands, and the first time he tried to walk, he launched himself into the ceiling. Worse, after a couple of days, the suit began to itch and chafe, especially at the joints. Peter wanted to claw his skin off.

"The Drift is a desolate place," Colonel Chiang San continued, circling the projection, which depicted a long, thin pocket of black with a burning orange skin. "It's large enough to pack several galaxies inside but has few stars and even fewer planets. Mostly it's just barren rocks and empty space.

"Passing through the Drift's boundary," Chiang San said, running a pointer along the Drift's orange exterior, "is such a violent experience that for centuries we were convinced it was impossible. At this scale, it looks peaceful, but in real life it's a terrible thing, an eternal storm of radiation and X-rays that will pulverize anything that gets near it.

"The boundary surrounds the entire Drift, but there are only two parts that concern us. Here, where we cross it, and way over here, where the Riel do. Right now, they're over here, by our side, ready to attack at any moment. Our job is to push them all the way back to their side and, just maybe, beyond it to where they live."

Chiang San paused, considering the model as if imagining a long and journeyed battle playing out. He nodded with satisfaction and turned back to the audience.

"There are scientists who argue that the Drift is the seam of the universe, the place where space wraps all the way around to meet itself like some vastly oversize doughnut. Others argue that it's a border, a no-man's-land between our universe and the next.

"Me? I don't give a shit what it is. I only care that it's full of Riel. And if we allow them back into our universe, then they will burn our cities and slaughter our families. The Riel have no mercy. Hell, they don't even have common sense. They exist only to kill, and they're damn good at it. To quote the Great General, 'This is a battle of evolution, from which only one species will survive.' Personally, I'd rather it be us."

The night the Riel attacked the Livable Territories, every power station on Genesia was either bombed out or shut down. As a result, the town received no news until the following morning, when a white pickup drove in from Genesia City. It was loaded with medical supplies and copies of a special edition of the *Genesia Tribune*, just two pages thick. The truck left some of the supplies and a half-dozen papers and continued down the road.

Peter and Amber were tucked into a booth at the diner, having breakfast. Amber had pancakes, but Peter ordered a cheeseburger, which was free on account of the thawing freezer. Downtown was nearly abandoned, so they got a copy of the paper to themselves.

The headline screamed, "SNEAK ATTACK!" The Riel had broken the sixty-year-old peace accord without warning, swarming out from the Drift and taking the United Forces by surprise. A counterattack hadn't been organized until the early morning.

The Great General declared the situation dire, but under control. The Riel had retreated, and the UF was on high alert. Civilians were urged to remain near shelters and to conserve water and food, particularly canned and dry goods.

The rest of the paper was just pictures of Genesia City, which had been pounded throughout the night. One photo showed a toppling high-rise; another was of a fire that ran for blocks and blocks. In the middle was a foldout of the skyline, taken at first light. It looked like a collection of shattered bottles. Peter had never been to Genesia City, but the image shocked him: the capital of his planet was on fire.

"What are we going to do?" Amber asked. Peter had no answer, so he wrapped his arm around her and pulled her close.

"It's war now," Chad McGuffin said, appearing over the far seat. He was a sturdy kid, muscular, but with a soft layer of fat that would win out in a few short years. His sole hobby was brawling, but in the presence of adults, he had to settle for just being an ass. "See if it's not," Chad continued, his S's whistling through a missing tooth. "I always knew those bastards would pull something like this. They only signed that accord so they could catch us jerking off."

Peter felt his blood rise—he didn't like McGuffin, and he didn't like him talking like that in front of Amber—but he let it go.

"I expect that you're right," he said dismissively, easing Amber from the seat. "Let's get you home," he said. She nodded, giving him her bravest smile.

As much as he had admired it through the window, Peter was petrified the first time he faced black space through an open door. His platoon had shuttled out to the middle of nowhere for its first space walk, and while the other men had filed out in an orderly manner, Peter couldn't even rise from his seat. His hand clamped so tight that the bench was molded to his glove.

Mickelson insulted him for a few minutes, then fell silent, standing by the open hatchway—the door to nothing. Peter worried what came next and kept his eyes on the floor in the hope that Mickelson would just give up on him. But the sergeant walked over. Even without air, and therefore no sound, Peter felt the weight of each approaching step.

"There's no going back," Mickelson said, his voice surprisingly soft. "You do realize that, don't you? You enlisted for two years. You will serve, and I will find some use for you. If you won't jump out of ships or shoot at Riels, I'll toss you out just to draw the fire away from those who will. A big guy like you will make a fine decoy."

Mickelson tapped his foot. Peter watched the floor.

"But you know what?" he continued. "I'd rather have a marine. I'd rather see you go leaping out of that hole shooting, killing as many of those sons of bitches as you can. Doesn't that sound better? To get out there and fight, instead of just floating around getting shot at?"

Peter remained frozen. In spite of Mickelson's reassuring tone, dread filled his stomach, thick and cold.

"Doesn't it?" Mickelson prodded.

"Yes, sir."

"Then I'll tell you what I'm gonna do for you. I'm gonna toss you out that hatch and we'll just see what happens."

Peter objected, but his suit moved on its own—Mickelson had taken control of it by remote. Peter's own muscles were no match for the artificial ones. The suit slowly stood up as he flailed inside. Mickelson hefted him onto his shoulder and walked to the hatch.

"You might hate me for this," he said, "but I hope not. You seem smart enough to see that this is for your own good." Mickelson might have said more, but Peter couldn't hear over his own screaming.

The sergeant cocked him like a spear and flung him into the dark.

The Riel didn't reappear after their initial attack. The United Forces sent scoutships into the Drift but found no trace of them. Down on Genesia, power was restored and the videos were flooded with news of the attack, which had occurred on all planets simultaneously. The Council of the Livable Territories voted unanimously to declare war on the Riel, which seemed a little redundant. Two days later the Marine Corps set up a recruiting table in front of the general store.

It was late morning when Peter walked into town. The sun was bright and the road dusty, and the line to enlist ran down the street. All of the upperclassmen from school were there, along with every other man who considered himself fit to serve.

It wasn't uncommon for the town and countryside to gather together on Election Day or for the Harvest Festival, but this was different. The war had aligned people as never before. Men moved freely along the line, talking and laughing with anyone whose name they knew. A new club had formed, and the only criterion was that you were human. Even Chad McGuffin got some laughs, making lame cracks about "Riel sandwiches." And Peter surprised himself by laughing as hard as anyone. It felt good just to be standing there, to be part of the excitement.

Two Marine Corps recruiters worked the table, interviewing one man at a time. As each man was accepted, the taller recruiter stood and called out his name, raising a cheer from the crowd. Men hung around after they had enlisted, not wanting to miss any of it.

As intoxicating as it was, Peter grew anxious. The word had spread and spectators were arriving. It wouldn't be long before the whole town was there—including Amber.

It had taken all night to convince her not only that his enlisting was a moral obligation but also that his salary could buy them a future. And then he still had to talk her out of coming along. He'd told her she would find it upsetting, but the truth was, he just didn't want her there. He didn't want the other guys to think he had to bring his girlfriend along.

Amber finally consented, and they made plans to meet for lunch afterward. But it was nearly lunchtime, and the line had barely moved. He knew Amber would grow impatient and come find him.

The crowd broke into laughter. Peter looked up as Charlie Davis's father—who was also named Charlie—

drove his truck right up to the line, got out, and dragged his son out of place by his ear. Young Charlie was only fifteen but had sneaked out of the house to come down anyway. The two argued, the younger stating that only the recruiters could decide about his age. "You don't even shave yet," the older Charlie snapped.

Peter self-consciously stroked at the soft fuzz on his own chin.

"We've been using tachyon technology to drive our spaceships for centuries," the armorer said, "but never once did we even consider using it as a weapon. In fact, we thought it was harmless."

Peter's platoon had been in Basic for a month now. The men were comfortable enough with their combat suits, Mickelson decided, to begin weapons training. And so they reported to the armorer, a short, thick man whose only visible hair was a white gull-wing moustache. He wore a suit but no helmet, and his bald head looked tiny atop the thick ceramic shell. Behind him a table was covered with a variety of impulsors, the tachyon-based weaponry that made up the Marine Corps arsenal.

The armorer drew his sidearm and dialed it up to its highest setting; then he pointed it at his bare hand and fired. It made a faint hum, but did nothing.

"Doesn't even tickle," he said. "But if I do this..."

The armorer lobbed a baseball-size rock over his audience and shot it in midair. The rock exploded, spraying through the room. Peter covered his face as fragments rattled off his suit.

"Quite a different effect," the armorer beamed, pleased by the men's reaction to his prank. "The pulse waves of the tachyon beam pass harmlessly through many elements—especially those with low boiling points, like what's in our bodies. I can only imagine the Riel's surprise when they discovered that we were impervious to their tachyon-based guns.

"Unfortunately, the opposite is also true. The Riel are evolved of harsh conditions and can live comfortably in freezing space, exposed to intense radiation and microscopic meteorites that travel fast enough to drill through steel. As a result, their hides are so tough that our bullets bounce off and our rockets are nothing but an irritation.

"Of course, it didn't take long for both sides to figure out the score. I find it one of this war's great ironies that the weapons used by both sides are the very ones each had developed to use against their own kind."

Peter was abandoned in space for almost twenty-four hours, his combat suit locked as tight as an iron maiden. Mickelson had led the rest of the platoon through their maneuvers, loaded them into the shuttle, and left without a word. Peter's fear had turned to anger, and as time wore on, to despair.

"How do you feel, recruit?" Mickelson said over a closed channel. Peter felt a flood of relief.

"Better," he replied.

"Better?" the sergeant barked.

"Better, sir."

"You get any shut-eye?"

"No, sir."

"Right," Mickelson said. Peter's suit relaxed as his artificial muscles returned to his control. He stretched, his own muscles bruised and stiff, and looked around. The sky was empty in all directions; he was completely alone. "Next time you'll have muscle relaxers," the sergeant continued. "I hadn't figured you'd be out here so long."

"Yes, sir."

"But as long as you *are* out here, you might as well learn how to use your rocket pack. I'm uploading some coordinates to your computer. Let's say...seventeen. You get yourself to each of them, and then I'll come pick you up. Sound good?"

"Yes, sir," Peter said, though nothing he could think of sounded worse.

"I don't expect you'll use more than half your fuel."

"Yes, sir," Peter repeated, and then added, "Sir?"

"Yes?" Mickelson snapped.

"I wanted to...to thank you, sir. For helping me."

"Carry on, recruit," Mickelson said gruffly.

Amber arrived at the town square just before one in the afternoon. The line to the recruiting table had grown sedate, the men's enthusiasm withered by the harsh sun.

She walked down the line swinging a small paper bag, pausing to chat with the boys she knew, who obliged her with smiles and jokes. Then she saw Peter and stopped. For a second, it seemed like she was going to cry, but her face grew hard. She tossed the bag at him and walked away.

Peter started after her, but she ignored him. He wanted to chase her, but anything he said now would only make it worse. He watched her go and returned to his place in line.

The crowd, which had fallen silent, burst into nervous chatter. Someone picked the paper bag off the ground, dusted it, and handed it to Peter. Inside were a sandwich and a note, "For my brave soldier."

"The general infantry rifle is, as the name implies, an all-purpose weapon." The armorer held a gun that, at a glance, could have been any rifle ever carried by a marine in the history of warfare. The basic design hadn't changed because neither had the men who used them. What had changed, however, was the technology inside. This gun fired tachyon rays instead of bullets; a two-inch glass lens capped its barrel.

"Model R-14," the armorer continued, "has an effective range of zero to seven hundred yards. This slider is the scatter control, used to focus or widen the beam. You want the beam to be six inches wide when it strikes the target. Pull the slider back to expand it for close combat, push it out for long range.

"A standard battery clip slides in here, providing thirty seconds of power. Click that off in standard quarter-second bursts or hold the trigger for continuous fire. You sight by eye, using these two marks on the barrel, or through the video link to your visor. Use the video when firing around corners, from behind barriers, or over your back as you flee from the enemy. You won't have much luck with that, though," the armorer chuckled. "The Riel can run a lot faster than you."

The armorer waited for a laugh, then grunted when none came. He swapped weapons, picking out the largest on the table. It looked like a boxy missile with a crystal ball jammed onto the tip.

"This sweet monster is for you heavy-weaponry types. It's a tachyon weapon, same as the R-14, but you might as well compare a bear to a muskrat.

"You hold it as such," he said. He balanced it on his shoulders, his artificial muscles whining from the effort. "This hinge locks to your shoulder here, stabilizing it. Aim and scatter is controlled via your suit's computer. You don't move the gun itself; its internal mirror will focus at whatever you target, up to forty degrees in any direction. Your main job is to just hold the thing steady. Believe you me, that's hard enough."

The armorer eased the large gun to the floor, then turned it around.

"On the back you have the recoil modulator, which vents as much energy behind you as the gun fires out the front. This keeps you from falling on your ass every time you fire, and that's just in normal gravity. Fire this thing in space without the modulator, and it'll be the last anyone sees of you."

He let that sink in, then continued. "As for power, you need far more than a standard clip's worth. There's a plug here for either a battery belt or a backpack, and the total firing time is limited only by how much weight you can carry. By the look of this guy," he said, nodding at Saul, "we're talking months."

This time, the armorer got his laugh.

"Last up is this sneaky thing," he said, picking out a rifle that was taller than him. "The MX-311d is the very latest in sniper technology. It has an effective range of up to twenty-two miles, though I hear tell of men getting twice that. Scatter control is here, but there isn't much. Even at its widest setting, the beam will pass harmlessly through anything closer than five hundred yards.

"It's aimed through this full-face optical scope. There's a video option, but at those distances you'd need a feed off someone closer to the target. This gun takes the same battery clips as the R-14, but you'll only get seven shots per.

"And, as a note to the rest of you, the MX-311d is the most expensive rifle that the United Forces has ever manufactured. So do us a favor, gentlemen, and protect your snipers."

The rocket pack had seemed straightforward enough when Mickelson explained it back on the orbital. The main thruster, gas-driven, moved the operator in whatever direction his head was pointed. To turn he used the stabilizers at each corner of the pack, which were small gravity generators that ran off the suit's batteries. So Peter understood the concept, but it was only now, stranded in open space, that he had to put it into practice.

Peter pulled up the list of coordinates Mickelson had assigned him, and the first one appeared as a green dot on his visor map. He tried to compare the map with what he saw outside, but there was nothing around him to use for reference. The marker was a random point inside a vast and empty void.

Peter rotated himself back and forth with his stabilizers, getting his aim just right, then fired his rocket. The green dot shot past his shoulder and disappeared behind him. He spun around and fired the rocket again, but his angle was wrong and, between that and his existing momentum, he curved off in a whole new direction. Peter panicked, flipped himself over, and tapped his thruster again. But he was only making it worse. The green dot had started thirty yards away and was now over a thousand yards back.

"In space," Mickelson had told them, "even the slightest bit of thrust will propel you indefinitely." The only cure was to use to point yourself in the exact opposite direction and then burn the exact right amount of fuel to counter your momentum. "You'll never figure it out yourself," the sergeant had said, "so don't even try."

Peter queried his suit's computer and was rewarded with two lines—a red one that indicated the direction he was moving and a white one that indicated which way he was facing. He rotated himself until the two lines were parallel and tapped his thruster. The red line shortened as he slowed. He tapped it two more times, coming to a standstill.

It took some fiddling, but Peter got the computer to draw a line between himself and the green dot. He rotated himself until his white line overlapped the other—both up and down, and left and right—then hit the thruster.

"Bull's-eye," he called as he shot through the marker, but the computer didn't agree. Apparently he had to not only reach his target but also hold the position for a full five seconds. Deflated, Peter stopped himself and again lined up with the dot. This time he flipped around as soon as he started to move, ready to fire a counter-thrust when he reached the marker.

He was too slow on that try and used too much thrust on the next. He pressed on, his frustration mounting, while the green dot slipped around as if greased. Finally, he lost his temper. He swung his fists in the air, cursing Mickelson, the marines, and the empty space around him. But his tantrum didn't get him any closer to his target, so he gathered his strength and started again. All said, it took five hours before he logged the first marker.

The next marker came no faster; his teeth ached from clenching his jaw. But Peter grew more adept, aiming with no more than a glance at his compass. By the end he whizzed from point to point, nailing each of the last three markers on his first try.

His elation was short-lived. His low-fuel indicator blinked; his tank was nearly empty. Mickelson expected him to use only half of his gas, and Peter worried that he might be forced to do it all over again. But he had nothing to fear.

The moment he radioed in, light blasted him in the face. A white line cut through the dark, expanded up to a full doorway, which was suspended in empty space. Mickelson stood a foot in front of him, amused.

"Gotcha, huh?" he asked. "Good old active camo." He grabbed Peter's air tank and hauled him aboard, where the rest of platoon was waiting. "You're head of the class now, Garvey," he continued. "These bums haven't done a thing this whole time but get drunk and watch you."

Saul stumbled forward with a beer can. "Stick this in your feeder tube," he said. To Saul there wasn't a problem in the universe that a few beers couldn't solve.

⤖ ⤖ ⤖

"I don't understand why it has to be now," Amber said. She was trying to be angry, but her voice was tinged with melancholy.

"There's a war on," Peter replied.

"I know that," she snapped.

They hadn't seen each other since yesterday, when Peter was enlisting. It was morning now, and they sat on her porch steps, he in the middle and she at the far end. Peter just found out he was leaving tomorrow.

Amber wouldn't come to the door last evening, and sleepless, Peter had looked in on her house several times through the night. Her bedroom light was always on, her curtains drawn. In the early hours, he chucked a stone at her window, like when they were kids. The curtains moved—he was certain that she peeked out—but they remained closed. Her light was still on at dawn, so Peter knocked on the front door and persuaded her father to send her down.

It was another half hour before she appeared. She was clean and fresh, wearing a dress that hung no lower than a T-shirt and that was thin to the point of translucency. No doubt she wore it to frustrate him.

I'm doing this for us, Peter thought. *So why am I the bad guy?*

They sat quietly on her porch for almost an hour. He couldn't think what to say and was terrified of saying the wrong thing. This was his last day on Genesia; he wouldn't get another chance.

"Come with me," he said, standing. "I want to show you something."

"What?" Amber asked, but Peter only motioned her to him. She stood reluctantly and followed him down the steps.

He turned down the sidewalk, and Amber fell in step beside him. They walked past the small, well-tended houses of the neighborhood, then turned in to the fields, which were deep with shadows from the low morning sun. Twenty minutes later they reached a thin row of trees that had been planted as a windbreak. Peter motioned to a trail that ran through them, offering up his arm. Amber frowned, but laced her arm through his.

The dirt path meandered, pushed this way and that by tree roots and small shrubs. A mile from the road, it ended at a muddy creek bed that was too wide to hop and too filthy to cross.

Peter walked back and forth, searching for a bridge that he remembered from some years back. He saw no sign of it.

"Is this what you wanted to show me?" Amber asked, forcing irritation into her voice.

Peter spun and grabbed her, kissing hard. She responded with anger, hitting his shoulders and chewing his lips, but then she wavered, grew still. He held her for as long as he dared and then released.

She looked struck.

"I wanted to show you that I love you," he said.

"What?" Amber asked, laughing with disbelief.

"I wanted to show you that I love you," he repeated firmly.

"Oh, Peter," she said. "That's so... stupid."

"I know," he said. "But I do love you, Amber. I want to marry you. And with the money from the marines, we can live..." Peter trailed off, losing momentum.

"Happily ever after?" Amber asked, dubious.

He nodded.

"I love you too," she said. "And I do want to marry you, but I... You're leaving, Peter. Going so far away that I can't even imagine it. Do you even know when you'll be back?"

"After Basic Training, we get leave every six months," Peter said.

"Six months?"

"It'll go fast. Everything is going to be fine."

"No, it's not. You're leaving tomorrow, and we've already wasted too much time. Come here." Amber grabbed his hand and tugged him toward a patch of fresh young grass.

"Why?" Peter asked.

"Because I want to show you something."

"If you attempt hand-to-hand combat with this creature," Mickelson said, "you will not live long enough to see yourself die."

He stood beside a projection of a Gyrine, the smaller of the two species of Riel—smaller being a relative term, since despite its hunched look, the creature was nearly twice as tall as the sergeant and several times wider.

It was a lumpy, lopsided beast, as if the work of some half-mad Frankenstein. Its left arm was shorter than the right, jointed in two places, and ended in something between a hand and an octopus's tentacle. The right arm was jointed in three places, and tapered to a bony spike. The rest was all chest and torso, which grew wide at the bottom and split into stumpy, jointless legs.

Its skin was coal black with tufts of gray hair spread about at random. Its face was pinched, its eyes squinty, and in spite of the carnivorous bulldog fangs, its mouth was webbed with a gelatinous membrane. It was commonly held that the Gyrine had evolved underwater, though, given their love of the cold, the water was more likely liquid helium.

"You can bend a knife on this thing's skin," Mickelson continued. "And you might as well punch a rock. I'm told its blood is some sort of liquid iron, whatever that means. The damn thing weighs more than a marble statue, but it's fast. Don't be fooled by those little legs—this thing can haul. And its reaction time is off the charts. He'll plant that spike of his in your face before you even know he's there."

The projection changed to another Gyrine. This one had three-quarters of its body replaced with robotics.

"God made the Gyrine a natural killing machine, but these bastards weren't satisfied. Most have some form of cybernetic enhancement. The most common mod is to replace the lower body, to make up for their small legs, but a close second is a split down the middle, head to toe. And they love to replace at least one hand with some sort of weapon."

Various Gyrine cyborgs flashed by, each more terrible than the last. The projection ended back at the original, unenhanced one.

"The rule seems to be that the fewer robotics, the higher the rank. That makes this one here your most valuable target." Mickelson studied the Gyrine. "Probably a colonel, or even a general. We don't know if they choose their officers at birth, sons of generals and whatnot, or if the restoration of limbs comes with each promotion.

"Hell," he said, "for all we know, they just grow new bodies by the vat. They're certainly eager to mutilate the ones they're born with."

The ship slapped against the planet's upper atmosphere and skipped along the surface. The cabin rattled and creaked as if being torn apart, and every bounce threw Peter's guts twice as far as the rest of him. He pressed his back to the seat, trying to ignore the tempest in his stomach.

"Cripes, Garvey," Mickelson said, strolling up. "You're white as your own ghost. You gonna make it, recruit?"

Peter tried to reply but couldn't unclench his jaw.

"Anyone in there?" Mickelson asked, tapping a finger on Peter's visor. Peter bent forward and threw up, flooding his helmet with khaki vomit.

"Son of a..." Mickelson said, hopping away instinctively. He yanked the emergency release—disconnecting the marines from their seats—and threw Peter to the floor. He raised Peter by his legs, upside down, so that the vomit pooled at the top of his helmet. It puddled over his eyes, but his mouth was clear. Peter gasped for breath, chunks of food flying down his throat.

"Someone get that goddamned helmet off," Mickelson barked. Saul hopped over and fumbled with the clasps at Peter's neck. The helmet dropped to the floor, leaving a gooey smear. Mickelson threw Peter aside and slammed his fist into the wall, muffled obscenities spewing from his helmet.

When he had calmed, Mickelson linked to Command. "High-altitude jump aborted," he said. "Bring us home."

In the basement of the barracks, there was a computer room filled with long rows of terminals for the men to send and receive mail from home; the Training Orbital was too far away for video.

Peter plodded in, exhausted, barely able to stand. His face was scrubbed red, but the smell of vomit lingered on his skin. His stomach was empty and sore, not only from throwing up but also because Mickelson, arguing that Peter had nothing left to lose, kept him on the shuttle for another three hours, doing one planetary entry after another. When they finally docked, Peter was so shaken that he had to crawl off the ship.

The silver lining, if only for one night, was that he was finally out of his suit while it was getting cleaned and checked for damage. After being sealed inside for six straight weeks, his skin tingled in the open air.

Peter searched the room for a free terminal. He was due for a letter from Amber.

After he enlisted, she wanted to help out with the war effort but quickly found there wasn't much for her to do. Most of the factories were automated, and she didn't have the education to oversee the machinery. She joined an effort to send care packages to the troops, but it turned out the distance between the Livable Territories and the Drift made shipping prohibitive. They couldn't even send handwritten letters, but had to scan them to send by computer.

She finally settled on organizing a local conservation awareness program. Raw materials—steel and petroliates—were limited by production, and the less they used domestically, the more was available for ships, suits, and weapons. The work kept Amber busy, and she always had plenty to report, which made Peter feel guilty about his meager replies.

Despite his hectic schedule, his life just wasn't that interesting. There were hours of marching and drills, followed by endless target practice—Peter had been selected for sniper training. By the end of the day, when he finally got to the computer room, he was too tired to think. But Amber didn't seem to notice that their conversations were one-sided. And that was good, because she was Peter's only link back to normal life.

It took Peter a moment to recognize Saul without his suit; Mickelson must have given the whole platoon the night off. Also, Saul only ever came to the computer room for a quick biweekly letter to his parents, which he considered an obligation. But there he was, face glued to a terminal, knee bouncing with excitement. Peter worked down a crowded aisle and looked over his shoulder.

A topographic map filled Saul's screen, the overhead view of mountainous terrain. Red symbols of various shapes and sizes were scattered over the highlands, while down on the plains blue dots were organized in grids. Saul flicked his hand over the screen frantically, sending the blue dots toward the red symbols, where they blinked and disappeared.

"Damn," Saul shouted, slapping the monitor. He turned to apologize to the men on either side and spotted Peter. "Look who's back," he said. "I was sure Mickelson would leave you out to dry again."

"I think I wore him out," Peter said.

"You keep everything down?"

"Wasn't much left."

"I'm sure. Good to be out of our suits, no matter what the reason. Nice just to pee in a toilet."

"Yeah," Peter said. He didn't want to talk about it. He pointed at the terminal. "What is that?"

"Battle simulator," Saul said.

"Really?" Peter leaned in for a better look.

"Yeah," Saul said. "Lets me play general in some of the hardest battles in the war." He tried to make room for Peter, but as was usually the case with Saul, there wasn't much room left.

The big man leaned back, scratching a toothbrush on the metal interface port installed just below his ear. The men all had neural webs stitched into their skulls on the very first day of Basic, and the port connected magnetically to the collar in their combat suits, giving them direct mental control. It was much faster than buttons or joysticks, but you were screwed if the connection went bad, so cleaning their contacts was basic hygiene.

"It's called the Sim Test," Saul said. "You ever wanna be a colonel, this is how. When a promotion opens up, it goes to whoever has the most wins. You'd pick up on these important facts if you weren't off getting private flying lessons."

Peter tried to imagine Saul as colonel, barking orders with a six-pack under his arm. "How does it work?" he asked.

"Just like on our visor maps. You're the blue guys, and the Riel are red. You can't see the Riel to start with, so you send out scouts and sensor pods. Each Riel has a different symbol. These are Gyrines and this is a missile turret, and that big *X* over there is a Typhon. You move your men by dragging a finger across the screen. Tap to assign a target and the battle computer handles the details."

Saul demonstrated, flicking his hand over five blue dots and sending them toward the Typhon, where they blinked and disappeared. Peter frowned.

"That's all there is to it?"

"It takes practice," Saul said defensively. "You've got to give it some strategy."

"Show me," Peter said, pulling up a chair.

Saul scanned the map. "This is a cluster of four Gyrines," he said. "So I'll start by firing a few missiles at them to soften them up. Then I'll send in these two platoons, plus this one from over there. Hit them from two directions." He moved his hands over the monitor, putting his words into action.

"It won't work," Peter said.

"You a sudden expert?"

"No, but look at that rocket battery. It'll pick off your missiles. And this platoon here, their heavy weaponry has laser sweeps. Those are useless against Gyrines."

"Doesn't matter," Saul assured him. "It's ten-to-one. I've got them completely outnumbered."

The two men watched the blue dots move across the screen. The missiles disappeared as they passed the rocket turret and the platoons. They reached the target at different times and blinked out as quickly as they arrived. Peter fought back a smile as Saul punched the terminal off.

"This thing is stupid," Saul said.

"If you two generals are done playing," Mickelson said, appearing behind them, "then I'll remind you that your first high-atmosphere jump is less than six hours away. Assuming this time everyone has a good hold on his breakfast."

"Yes, sir," Peter and Saul said in unison, rising and saluting. Mickelson walked off, muttering and shaking his head.

"There are scientists who postulate that the two species of the Riel are simply the two sexes of a single race," Mickelson said. "If that's so, then my money's on this one for the female."

The projection beside the sergeant was so large that, were it real, they'd have to cut a hole in the roof of the four-story lecture hall just so it could stand up.

The creature had two distinct parts. The bottom was like a mechanical spider, with each of its six legs broken into four joints, and each of these joints larger than a man. Capping the legs was a round metal plate, above which the colossus became flesh—a monstrous Lucifer, with red skin over rippled muscle. Two god-thick arms swung to the ground, with human-shaped hands, yard-long fingers, and shovel-head fingernails. High at the top loomed a bearded, triangular face, with horns jutting from the forehead. Its eyes were golden yellow, the edges curving up like a screaming mouth. It was the most horrible thing Peter had ever seen, in life or in nightmare. It was a Typhon.

"Whenever I look at this thing," Mickelson continued, "I can't help but wonder if one of them didn't happen upon the original homeworld, back when men were jotting down the great book. But Satan himself was never so evil—and probably a hell of lot easier to kill. I figure that if just one of these had shown up back in biblical times, there'd be nothing left of the human race but a well-chewed pile of bones.

"As terrifying as it looks, there's more to this thing than size. There are motorized turrets at the top of each leg, mounted with either a rocket launcher or a ninety-three-millimeter recoiler, which is strong enough to shoot clean through your average naval destroyer. And it'll have any number of armaments mounted on that plate up there, where the monster meets the machine. Sometimes, just to mix it up, it'll strap a few missiles on its back or carry a Delta-class heavy impulse blaster around like it was a rifle.

"In other words," Mickelson concluded, "the Typhon is a walking fortress. Nothing in your armory will even tickle it. If you happen upon one of these in the battlefield, the best you can hope for is that your last will and testament is in good order."

The sun dropped behind the distant hills, purpling the sky and raising a cool wind. Peter cupped Amber as they lay facing the sunset. She had been sleeping, but now stirred, rolling her head toward him.

"You have your knife?" she asked.

Peter reached for his pants and dug out a bone-handled pocketknife. She combed her fingers through her hair, separating out a pencil-thick clump. "Hold this," she said. He pulled it taut as she sliced off the last few inches. Then she grabbed her dress and pulled out a well-worn gold locket.

"I brought this just in case," she said sheepishly. "It belonged to Mimi." Amber curled the hair into the locket and snapped it shut. "For you," she said. "So I'll always be there with you."

They sat up and faced each other. Amber slid her arms around his neck and fixed the clasp behind him. Peter pulled her close, her bare skin warm and soft. She hugged back, hard, and then pushed loose.

"We have to go," she said, standing up and motioning for him to do the same. His lust slaked, Peter admired her coolly. The gentle curves of her white body and the soft definition of her legs and stomach. A wisp of hair trickled up her belly, and full breasts pillowed to her ribs, tapering to light pink. She was perfect. They dressed in silence and began the long walk home.

The next morning was overcast. Amber borrowed her father's pickup and drove Peter to Bentings Naval

Base, which was no more than a half-dozen small buildings with a fenced-in landing pad. A rocketship was parked on the pad, a dull-gray bullet with stubby wings. It was visible for miles over the empty farmland and, as they approached, seemed to scrape the sky.

"Is that your ship?" Amber asked, wide-eyed.

"That's just a shuttle," Peter replied, trying not to be impressed. "The transitship's up in orbit."

Cars were backed up for a half mile. When they finally reached the base, Amber pulled up to the curb and threw the truck in park. She turned to Peter and took his hands in hers.

"Promise me..." she started.

"I'll be careful."

Amber seemed to want to say more, but instead she just threw her arms around him, kissing him all over his head and ending at his mouth. They were interrupted by a knock on the roof. A man in fatigues walked by, swinging a riding crop. "Kiss and go," he called to no one in particular. "Kiss and go."

Peter pulled away, their lips separating like warm glue. He slid backward from the truck, keeping his eyes locked with Amber's, then turned away. A man at the gate checked his name and waved him to the shuttle. He climbed the metal steps to the hatch, then stopped to look back.

Amber was still at the curb, watching through the dog-wire fence. She made herself smile, and Peter, feeling his throat tighten, turned and rushed inside.

Military graduation ceremonies are for the generals. After five months of the hell that is Basic, the last thing any marine wants is to stand at attention in full dress for an hour while an old man rambles on about honor and valor.

When the general—whose name Peter had forgotten—ran out of things to say, all two hundred thousand marines of the freshly christened Digamma San Division hefted their duffels in unison and marched through massive hangar doors to the launch pad.

The men were shuttled up to the transitship a few hundred at a time. Peter's platoon was late on the list, so the men spent the afternoon lounging on the grassy parade field. It was the first free time since arriving at the orbital, and no one knew what to do with it. They didn't even have a deck of cards.

The shuttle ride took an hour, after which they joined a long line of marines in the transitship's cavernous landing bay, waiting to be loaded into cryo chambers. It was a long journey—the UF base was deep inside the Drift—so they would be frozen to conserve resources. Passing through the Drift boundary was hard on the human body, killing one in ten men and injuring the rest. Being frozen somehow protected them. Peter didn't understand the explanation, but he was used to that by now.

When he reached the front of the line, Peter stripped naked and stuffed his clothes into his duffle, which he tossed onto a nearby cart. Then he lay in his assigned chamber, flinching as his skin touched the cold vinyl. Unsure what came next, he crossed his arms as if in a casket.

A silver-haired med tech appeared. She smiled down at him, then apologized that he couldn't keep his locket inside. Peter unclasped it and handed it out. She slipped it into her pocket and assured him that she would put it in his duffle. Then she jammed an IV needle into his wrist and attached a bag of greenish fluid. She checked that it was flowing, hung it inside, and closed the lid. The chamber was dark but for a blue indicator light by his head.

The chamber moved, rolling into the ship's cargo hold. Peter wondered whether he would be filed alphabetically or by his platoon's ident-code, but he forgot the question before he could decide. He took a deep breath and released it as the blue light faded away.

[14.08.2.21::3948.1938.834.2D]

Peter blinked, squinting as the white light clicked on. He lay on a bed, a nurse in a green surgical mask working on the monitor over his head. But there was something else, something that had happened in between. He searched his memory, but it only made his head ache. He tried to rub it, but his arm was strapped down.

"Don't rush," the nurse said sternly. "You're still quite cold."

She unstrapped his arm and raised it, injecting him with oily liquid. The warm fluid trickled in, spreading through his body. The nurse turned back to the monitor, nodded, then walked to the top of the bed. She tugged at his head as if pulling his hair out a strand at a time. Each tug was followed by a metallic ping. She hummed, but Peter didn't know the tune.

"What's your name?" he asked, his voice hoarse.

"Linda," she said, tapping the tag on her jacket. It read Linda 75.

"Seventy-five?"

"The room number." She motioned to the door, which had a large 75 painted on it.

"They worry you'll get lost?"

Linda laughed, surprisingly warm. "More worried that they'll lose me. This is a big place, you know."

"Not yet," Peter said.

"Of course not," Linda said, frowning. "You only just got here." She moved back beside him, wiping her hands and inspecting the monitor.

"Only just," he tried. "But I'm in for the long haul."

"Squeeze this, kid," Linda said curtly, offering him a foam ball. "It'll speed up the resuscitation process."

Peter reached for the ball but stopped, feeling the heat radiating off her hand. He touched her skin warily, curious. Linda took his hand and pressed the ball into it.

"Pump," she ordered. She let go, grabbed a steel tray at the head of the bed, and walked to a sink on the far side of the room. She dumped the tray; Peter saw a flash of red as its contents clanked into the basin.

"Boys," she muttered, spraying water around the sink.

Peter pumped the foam ball and watched Linda work. She looked to be about ten years older than him, which put her in her late twenties. But her movements were slow and deliberate, like those of someone much older.

Linda finished cleaning and sat at a desk across the room, her back to Peter. She stared at the wall for a few moments, then pulled a stack of worn papers from the side drawer. She flipped through them, selected one, and began to scribble.

The scratching of Linda's pen and the wheezing of Peter's foam ball filled the next two hours; then a chime sounded overhead. Linda put the papers away and walked back to Peter.

"Hear that?" she asked, unstrapping him. "You've only just arrived and already they put you to work."

Linda pressed a button and electric motors whirled, folding the bed into a seat. Peter saw that he'd been laying on a steel table, with runnels like a cutting board, leading to drain holes in each corner. Water trickled down his back as the bed angled up.

Linda felt Peter's forehead, then pulled back his eyelids and peered in.

"Looks good," she said. She offered her hands; they were so small that they disappeared inside his own. They were no longer hot, only warm. "Gently," she said, leaning back and pulling him to his feet. He towered over her.

"Lift your left foot and rotate it," she ordered. "Good. Now the other." She watched him, nodding. "You're good to go."

Peter stared down at Linda, trying to see the face behind the mask. She had wide cheekbones and a long nose that raised her mask like a tentpole. She cleared her throat and shook her hands—she had let go, but he was still holding on.

"Sorry," he said, blushing, letting them drop. "Which way to...?"

"Through the door," Linda said. "Just follow the arrows. And don't forget that." She pointed to his duffel, which lay beside the bed. Peter suddenly realized that he was completely naked. He lurched for the bag and held it over his crotch.

"Thanks," he said, backing out the door.

"Just doing my job, kid," she said, amused. She reached for her mask, but the door closed before it came off.

The hallway was long and wide, with freestanding steel walls that opened to the base's vaulted ceiling. Men shuffled like zombies, knocking mindlessly into Peter. He stepped to the side, pulled on his clothing, and joined the flow.

The roof arced upward as he moved toward the center, fading into the heights. The base looked large enough to swallow the Training Orbital a dozen times over.

Corridors appeared on either side of the hall, and men split off, thinning the crowd. Peter found one labeled with his division, Digamma San. It was lined with doors. Halfway down, he found his platoon's ident-code, DS-52.

The door opened to a small dormitory with twelve tightly packed bunks. Peter was the last to arrive; the rest of the platoon was dressed and unpacking. Saul and Ramirez played cards at a small table in the middle.

"Don't be shy," Mickelson said from behind Peter, urging him inside with a hand to the shoulder. Seeing their sergeant, the men hopped to attention.

"Form up," Mickelson barked, and they snapped into a line. After five months of Basic, you could have trimmed the entire platoon's nose hairs with one shot of a laser.

Mickelson walked down the line, inspecting the men as if they were used cars. He had a slight limp that Peter had never before noticed. The sergeant gave each man a once-over and then put them all at ease.

"I have some good news, gentlemen," he said. "Command wanted to give you a warm welcome, so they've given us a priority mission. We move out at fourteen hundred, which is one hour from now. So skip the makeup and get your asses in your suits."

"You heard about the third race?" Saul yelled. Peter could barely hear him over the rattling ship, which bucked and swerved as it sliced through the planet's atmosphere.

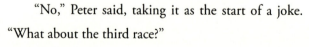

"No," Peter said, taking it as the start of a joke. "What about the third race?"

"I heard a rumor that there is one. Some new Riel that we haven't seen before. Command intercepted an enemy transmission, but the video was too garbled to get a good look."

"Great," Peter said. "We haven't even seen the other two yet."

The ship banked hard, weaving, throwing the men around inside their suits. Peter had expected his first combat jump to be harder than any in Basic, but this was too much. In addition to the normal turmoil, they had been dodging enemy fire for the last ten minutes. He clutched his chest where Amber's locket hung inside his suit. He was glad that she couldn't see him now, as scared as he was.

"Oh, crap," Mickelson snarled over the open comm. He leaped to his feet and cupped his hands to his helmet as if covering his ears. "Incoming!" he yelled as the ship's hull cracked open. Peter gazed up. The stars floated peacefully in a black pool; then a wall of fire ripped through the ship.

[14.08.2.22::3948.1938.834.2D]

The white light clicked on and Linda sat beside him, face hidden by a surgical mask. "Follow my finger," she said, moving it around, her own eyes on the monitor. "I said follow it." Peter did this time, not sure how she knew otherwise.

"Good, now recite the alphabet."

Peter did as he was told; Linda ignored him, typing on the monitor.

"What's the last thing you remember?" she asked.

"Graduation," Peter replied. "Basic Training."

"Good," she said. "Anything else?"

"Yes," Peter said. "You."

"Me?" she turned to him, confused.

"You," he repeated.

"Be serious," Linda said.

"I am," Peter said. "Linda."

She looked at the monitor. "No," she said, shaking her head. Then she figured it out. "Ingenious," she said sarcastically, tapping her nametag.

"Linda 75," Peter insisted. "Because of the room number."

"The room...?" she asked. Peter had meant to impress her, but she only looked concerned. She scrolled around the monitor, reading. "That's impossible," she mumbled. "How could he know—"

A door swung open behind Peter, and Linda started.

"Is everything okay, Linda?" a man asked.

"Everything is fine," she replied evenly. She raised a hand to her temple, pressing against the hair, and turned to face the intruder.

"That's good," he said. His voice was unnaturally calm, like a psychiatrist's. "Would you mind joining me in my office?"

"Yes. Of course, sir."

"Now?" the man asked with a tinge of impatience.

"But he's just—"

"It's not going anywhere, Linda."

"Fine," she said. "I'll start the epinephrine and be right there." She gazed at the unseen man, staring him down. The door shut.

Linda yanked off her mask and tossed it on Peter's chest. Her thin nose curved out over thick, dark lips.

She was the one thing Peter had never expected; she was beautiful.

"Nice work, kid," she growled. "You'll get us both in trouble." She spun Peter's bed around and pointed at a camera on the ceiling. "He watches everything."

She turned him back, unstrapped his arm, and jabbed in the needle.

"Just lie there quietly," Linda ordered. "I won't be a minute."

Peter pumped his fist, curled his toes, and worked his jaw, doing everything he could to raise his temperature. Fifteen minutes later, he was ready. He stretched his free arm over his chest, reaching for the strap. He got the very tip of his middle finger under the clasp, angling it back and letting it loose.

Chest free, he twisted further, releasing his other arm. He probed under the bed and found the switch to raise it to a chair; then he leaned over, unstrapped his legs, and pushed to his feet.

Peter's head went light. His knees buckled, and he teetered. He clutched the bed rails, crouched and panting, then slowly straightened up. He let go carefully, keeping his hands over the rails as he balanced on his feet. *So far, so good.*

At the back of the room was a wide roll-up door. He put his ear to it and listened, hearing nothing.

He eased the door open and peered out. A long hallway ran in both directions. It was wider than the one that Peter left by and completely empty. Roll-up doors lined both walls, each painted with a number. Peter went left; the doors counted up.

The hallway ended at door 96. Tucked in the corner, a frosted plastic door was labeled Supervisor. Peter padded softly up, his bare feet numb from the cold metal floor. He heard a familiar voice—the man who had called Linda away.

"If there's something wrong with the memory unit," he said, "then we kill the line. It's as simple as that."

"It's not a line," Linda retorted. "He's a human being."

"You're a nurse, so you're trained to feel that way. But this is different. Special circumstances."

"I can't see how."

There was a pause, followed by a sigh. "Try to think in terms of assets," the man said. "Take a broader view of our work. We can't let ourselves be distracted by the problems of a single unit, because it will lower our—"

A rattle echoed down the hallway; a garage door rolled up not twenty yards away. Peter dashed across the hall and flattened into the recess of a doorway.

An empty bed slid into the hallway, guided from behind by a nurse. She had the same brown hair as Linda, but hers was shorter and twisted into a bun. She pushed the bed into the distance, and Peter crept back to the supervisor's door.

"But there is nothing wrong with his memory," Linda insisted. "I checked the imprint three times. This has to be part of the design."

"You mean a flaw?" the man replied, incredulous. "A flaw in the design?"

"No, something else. Like an upgrade."

"An upgrade?" the man snapped. "And they didn't tell us?"

Peter winced—the man's tone was violent. But then he was calm again: "No, they wouldn't, would they?" he mused. "They like to keep us in the dark."

Silence followed. Sweat tickled inside Peter's ear.

"Well," the man said finally, "we can't call upstairs about every little thing, can we? We'll keep on for the moment. Who knows? Maybe this flaw will simply disappear in the next the version."

"I don't—" Linda started.

"We'll hope so," the man cut in. "You should get back to your patient."

"Yes, sir" was the last thing Peter heard as he sprinted up the hall. He slipped through door 75 and hopped onto the bed. He just had the straps back in place when Linda returned.

She ignored him at first, heading straight for the sink and violently scrubbing whatever was inside. Then she checked the clock on the wall and went to her desk. She sat down and stared at the wall, motionless.

She stood up ten minutes later, straightened her uniform, and pulled on a fresh mask. She walked to Peter, smiling as if nothing had happened.

"And how are you doing?" she asked. She grabbed his wrist, then dropped it, startled. "You're sweating."

"Squeezing," Peter said, motioning with his hands. "Like you said."

Linda inspected him suspiciously but found no other explanation. She checked the clock and then her monitor. "I guess you're done early today," she said with a shrug.

Peter kept his body limp as she helped him to his feet, then grabbed his duffel and lumbered out the door. He merged with the other naked men and headed for combat.

[14.08.2.23::3948.1938.834.2D]

After five successful missions in five successive days, Peter got his first R&R. He had been warned that things would move fast out here in the Drift, but he was still exhausted.

It wasn't the physical exertion or the lack of sleep—he had had plenty of both back in Basic—but the sheer number of casualties he had witnessed. He had seen men shot out of the air and transports burn in dark space, and he had fought across a field littered with the bodies of an entire division. Of the twelve men in his original platoon, only Saul, Ramirez, and himself remained. The most shocking loss was Mickelson; their sergeant had always been so casual in combat, as if he didn't even believe in death. He was shot by a Riel sniper who was too far away to see.

Peter knew that he should be upset by everything he had witnessed, but it just hadn't sunk in. There just hadn't been time.

Immediately after each battle, the survivors were re-org'd into new platoons, which meant new names, new drills, and new training. Then they were rushed through dinner, issued sleeping pills to ward off the nightmares common to active combatants, and marched to bed. Come morning they'd be hustled off to the docks again.

Now, when Peter finally had a break, all that was left was a jumble of images.

All missions had been suspended—word was they were waiting for reinforcements, but as privates, they didn't even rate that level of information. What they knew was they had a few days off. Peter persuaded Saul to go exploring with him.

Peter wanted to meet someone from the navy, so they walked to the docks. In addition to the ninety-six divisions—twenty million marines—the base was home to tens of thousands of naval craft. Most were unmanned transports, but even those would require repair and maintenance. Peter figured there was a sizable navy somewhere on base.

There hadn't been any navy recruiters back on Genesia, and Peter felt like he'd missed an opportunity. Flying a ship was far more exciting than just riding in one. Or at least that's how he figured it. He wanted to ask what it took to be a pilot, but so far he'd only seen them over the communicators.

Saul's interest was more practical. The navy had something that the marines didn't: women.

"What do you think of the new sergeant?" Peter asked as they navigated the halls.

"Anyone's better than Mickelson," Saul said.

"He's dead."

"Yeah," Saul said. "I was there too. Sarge wasn't the sort to get teary about casualties, so I'll return the favor."

Peter wanted to be shocked but found himself nodding in agreement.

"I'm just glad they kept us together," Saul continued. "You, me, and Ramirez. From what I hear, Command usually splits a platoon apart after the sergeant is killed."

"Why didn't they?"

"I don't know," Saul shrugged. "Maybe no one else wants us."

"Or we're too good to break up."

"Ha," Saul said. "I hate to think what that means for the other guys."

The docks ringed the base in concentric circles. Their hallways were large and hexagonal, with a grated steel column running up the center. The column was squared off, a box tube with gravity generators inside that allowed marines to walk on all four sides to rapidly load into the transportships. The walls were transparent—triangular windows in metal framework—and would have provided a spectacular view if the docks weren't encased by dormant transports. The little bit of space that Peter could see was tainted green by the base's plasma shield.

They hadn't gone far before Peter began to drag. He marveled at how quickly he'd become dependent on his combat suit.

Saul walked effortlessly, sighing as Peter steered him down yet another glass hallway. This one ended in a glass wall. Outside, a massive ship was parked in a wide gap in the docks. The ship was long and blocky, like a toppled building, and had an arched bottom, as if to sail on water. It was linked to the base by a dozen bridge cranes, and a continuous stream of containers poured out.

"Cargoship," Saul said impatiently. "Comes every week."

The UF base was deep in empty space, far from any habitable planet. Security by obscurity, but it also meant everything they needed—food, water, and weapons—had to be shipped in from a great distance.

"Could those be the new men?" Peter asked.

"Why not?" Saul replied.

"Not a very pleasant way to travel."

"What do they care? They're frozen solid. It's what you wake up to that counts."

"Your nurse?"

"Exactly. Beckie." Saul whistled appreciatively. "A little old, but..."

"The same one every time?" Peter asked.

"What 'every time'? I haven't seen her since they thawed us out."

"I..." Peter trailed off, not sure what he meant.

"Not that I would mind," Saul said. "This base isn't exactly full of excitement."

"Better than out there."

"Just go ahead and state the obvious," Saul said, drumming his fingers impatiently on the glass.

The containers trailed off and the cranes folded up. Three ball-tipped spires rose off the base and punctured the shield, forming a dark triangle. The cargoship backed out of the gap, turned in a wide arc, then passed overhead as it headed for home.

"Now can we go get a drink?" Saul asked.

"Yeah," Peter said, starting down the hall. He was disappointed not to have met anyone in the navy. Actually, they hadn't seen anyone at all. Peter wondered if he was the only person on the entire base who was interested in anything beyond the canteen.

"Cumberland is the best," Peter said to Saul, making his selection and sliding his mug into the autotap.

Golden beer rose inside, filled from a valve at the bottom. A ring slid up the outside, frosting the glass.

"Cumberland?" Saul said with disgust. "You would like him. Smallest quarterback in the history of the draft." Saul filled two mugs, making use of Ramirez's, who hadn't yet arrived.

"He's smart," Peter said. "He has a good sense of the field."

"He's a pushover," Saul said, downing one beer while the other filled. "If he can't make a pass, he's screwed. He has to hand off just to make a one-yard push."

Saul was right, but Peter still liked Cumberland. His off-the-cuff playing style had inspired Peter's own tactics.

"You think they're still playing?" he asked. "With the war and all?"

"Especially because of the war," Saul replied. "People need distractions during tough times."

The two men returned to their table just as Ramirez arrived. He spotted them and rushed over, waving a roll of paper. "That mine?" he asked as he took a full mug from Saul.

"What's that," Saul asked, pointing to the paper.

"My tat," Ramirez replied. "You know how once you make sergeant you get to put a design on your suit?"

"I thought it was colonel," Peter said.

"Some sergeants too. If they're senior enough."

"You get a sudden promotion?" Saul asked.

"Planning ahead," Ramirez replied. "Check this out."

The men raised their glasses as Ramirez unrolled the paper on the table. It was covered in blotches of orange, yellow, and black. Saul squinted at it, cocking his head.

"What do you think?" Ramirez asked.

"You're going to paint vomit on your combat suit?" Saul asked.

"It's a tiger," Ramirez snapped. "Like my nickname."

"You have a nickname?"

"When I'm a sergeant, my men will call me *the Tiger*."

The other men stared at him, waiting for the punch line.

"They'll see it in my eyes," Ramirez said.

"They sure won't see it in the drawing," Saul countered.

Peter drained his glass and stood up.

"Where you rushing off to?" Ramirez asked.

"Gonna check my mail."

"For a change," Saul added. "I'm surprised you waited this long."

Amber was pressed beneath Peter, her eyes closed, her back arched. Her lips parted, exposing the tips of her front teeth, and her naked breasts rolled up with every thrust. He wanted to touch them, to run his fingers over the supple pink skin around her nipples, but his hands were planted in the grass, keeping his hips raised and allowing them to move freely.

They breathed in unison, faster and faster, louder and louder.

Peter released with a shout and collapsed onto her. Amber trembled and let out a low squeal. She wrapped her arms around him and squeezed—inside and out—her skin like warm silk.

Peter leaned in to kiss her, but her mouth retreated. She slipped backward, falling out of focus and dissolving to colored squares.

Peter's eyes popped open. Hot water poured on his head and ran down his face. He sucked in water with each labored breath, dropping against the wall. He raised his hand to the showerhead, splashing water around the gray tiles, rinsing away the soap and scum.

Peter walked gingerly into the computer room, his head light and sore. After three days of drinking, the idea of combat was almost appealing.

The large room was empty, so Peter took the nearest terminal and pulled up his mail. There would be nothing new—for security reasons, radio transmission was restricted to official use, so electronic mail came aboard the weekly cargoship.

Peter scrolled back through his messages, all of which were from Amber, looking for something to read. None of them appealed to him. Just bland details of her life back home. It wasn't that he didn't appreciate her letters; he did. But what he really needed was her, here, in his arms.

He drew her locket from his shirt and fingered the hair inside. It was coarse and dry, and the smell had faded. He closed his eyes, calling her up. They were back at Benting's base. She leaned over, watching him through the truck windows as he boarded the shuttle. It wasn't his favorite memory, but it was the clearest.

"Thinking about home?"

Peter started, dropping the locket. Manzenze, his new sergeant, was at the door. He was a short, slight man with charcoal skin that rumpled as if made for someone larger. They had only just met at the last re-org.

"Yes, sir," Peter said. He started to rise but Manzenze motioned him back down.

"In the still of the night," Manzenze said, dropping into a seat opposite him, "home feels quite far away indeed."

"You been out here long, sir?" Peter asked.

"Drop the formalities, private. I have no use for them." The sergeant scratched his thin nose between two fingers. "And yes," he said. "I have been here a long time. You'd be surprised."

"Six months?" Peter asked. "That is the limit, isn't it? Before they rotate you home."

"Speaking of surprises," Manzenze said, "I was reviewing the playback of your last mission. That idea of yours, splitting your platoon like you did, it was ingenious. Caught those Gyrines unaware."

"Nothing to it, sir. Sergeant Mickelson used the same trick in the Peirescius Belt."

Manzenze squinted at Peter, as if questioning his honesty. "I've seen your record, private. You didn't fight in the Peirescius Belt."

"No?" Peter was sure that he had but knew better than to argue. "Must've been in the simulation, sir."

Manzenze held his squint, scratched his nose again, then smiled. "I told you to stop calling me sir."

"I'm sorry, sir. I mean..." Peter flushed, feeling like an idiot.

Manzenze laughed warmly. "It was good soldiering," he said. "No matter where you got the idea. But speaking of the Sims, I noticed that you were doing a fair job with them back in Basic, but you haven't touched them since coming on base."

"There hasn't really been time," Peter said, biting off the "sir." Formality was a habit easier learned than broken.

"That changes now. I'm spacing out your combat cycle, and I'll expect you in here every other day. I sense talent in there somewhere. Let's see if we can't find it."

"Yes, sir."

Manzenze motioned to the terminal. "You might as well show me your stuff," he said. "Unless you have something more pressing."

Peter practiced the Sim Test for the next six hours, with Manzenze looking over his shoulder. The sergeant had some good advice, but Peter still didn't manage a single win.

Peter shambled to the barracks, stopping by the bathroom to brush his teeth and his interface port.

Six months, he thought, staring at the mirror. *If every day is this long, it'll be like living forever.* He bent over the sink, cupped water into his hand, and swallowed his sleeping pill.

The medicine had kicked in by the time he reached the barracks, and he was so tired that he could barely climb to his bunk. Below him, the snoring hulk of Saul vibrated the bedsprings. Peter found it comforting, a constant reminder that his best friend was near at hand.

He closed his eyes and joined him in sleep.

[14.08.2.16::3948.1938.834.2D]

A white flash popped in Peter's head, jolting him awake. "Saul!" he screamed, wrenching against his straps, trying to tear loose.

The memory was so clear: floating behind a large rock in the Cylides Asteroid Belt, explosions strobing on the other side. Saul was in his giant combat suit, repeating some old story to the new recruits, grinning like the whole war was some big joke. His back was to the battle, so he couldn't see the rocket that swung around the rock. Peter shouted into the comm, but the rocket was too fast—the explosion engulfed Saul.

"Stop, stop, stop!" Linda yelled, racing across the room. She leaped up, landing on Peter's chest and slamming him to the bed. She clamped his wrists under her knees. Her mask was off and her face was wild with anger.

"What the hell are you doing?" she yelled, throwing a strap over his forehead and ratcheting it to the bed. Peter struggled, but she had him pinned.

Linda checked his other straps, jerking them tight, then collapsed on top of Peter.

Her breathing slowed and she sat up. She sat cross-legged on his chest and untangled her hair.

"I'm too old for this," she said with a dry laugh. She freed her ponytail and shook it out. Peter had never noticed how gray her hair was.

"You're early," she said, sliding to the floor and straightening her uniform. She walked to the top of his head and tugged. Peter felt something slide from his skull. Linda dropped it in the tray with a metallic ping.

"What happened to Saul?" Peter demanded.

"How would I—"

"Tell me," he said, angry.

The phone on Linda's desk buzzed. She raised a finger, warning him to be quiet, and went to answer it. "Yes?" she asked, then listened.

"Yes," she repeated. "I'll tell him." A pause, then, "I do understand. Yes, sir."

Linda set the phone back in its cradle and leaned on it, staring at the wall. It was several minutes before she returned to the bed. She moved with determination, opening a drawer and filling a needle from a small bottle. It was a clear liquid, different from what she'd used in the past. This needle was thin; he didn't even feel it.

"I'm sorry," she said, tossing the needle away. She wiped her hands vigorously and threw the towel in the trash.

"During your last mission," she said, "your entire platoon was killed by a rocket attack, including Private Saul Graff. Your leg was severed, so your Life Control System put you into hibernation. Your body was recovered and your leg reattached."

Saul is dead, Peter thought. The injection worked through his blood like steel splinters. His muscles trembled and then grew numb. He clenched his jaw as hot tears spilled down his face. Then came anger—at the Riel, at the generals, at everyone in this goddamn war. His mind raced furiously. He opened his mouth to scream but had only the strength to moan.

Linda bit her lip and turned away, walking out the back door.

Peter remembered it vividly. Saul was shredded by the explosion. Then another rocket took out Ramirez and Manzenze. Explosions were everywhere; all of space was burning. The men dodged and ducked, but there was no escape. They died in twos and threes, and then a rocket came for Peter. There was a flash, then nothing.

As Peter played it back, the memory grew thinner, less real. It was as if he'd seen it on video or heard it in a story. Finally, he lost interest altogether. His mind turned to a bigger problem.

According to Command, Peter had been on base for only two weeks and fought in just eight battles. Yet he could remember dozens of missions—six weeks' worth of near-constant fighting. But if he mentioned these other battles, he got only blank stares. Saul hadn't remembered them, and Manzenze had insisted they never happened. Either they were lying or Peter was going mad. And now there was no one left to ask. Everyone he knew was dead.

Everyone except her.

It was several hours before Linda returned. Her mask was off, her face grim. "I'm very sorry about your friend," she said, laying a warm hand on Peter's arm.

"Thank you."

"We can wait longer, if you…"

"No. I'm okay."

Linda almost said more but changed her mind. She freed his head and loosened the other straps, then dug her thumb into his arm and injected the oily liquid.

"What's the last thing you remember?" she asked.

"Fighting in the Cylides Asteroid Belt," Peter replied. "There was an explosion and then... I must have blacked out."

"Good," Linda said, nodding. "What else do you remember?"

Peter felt his resolve slipping. He looked her in the eye and took the plunge.

"I remember the other times that Saul died," he said. "That both of us died."

Linda stepped back.

"Every time I survive a battle," Peter continued, "I wake up on my bunk. But every time I die, I wake up here with you. You tell me the story of my narrow escape from death. My shuttle has failed eleven times, but—miraculously—everyone on board was only knocked unconscious."

Linda's eyes were wide. Peter continued.

"If I die in combat, I find my whole platoon waiting in the barracks. But if I live, like I did this time, then everyone that I saw die stays dead. Like Saul."

Linda retreated but Peter whipped his arm out, grabbing her elbow. As thin as it was, his hand wrapped all the way around. *Too rough*, he thought, but he held tight, twisting to keep her back to the camera.

"I know I'm not supposed to remember any of this. What I don't know is what happens if they find out I do. So I'll keep my mouth shut, but first I need you to tell me something."

There was long silence.

"What?" Linda asked.

"Can I trust you?"

Linda shook her head, looking away. Peter squeezed, Linda winced.

"Look at me," Peter said, but she didn't. "I know you're lying, but do you? Are you making up these stories, or are you just taking orders?"

Linda straightened up and turned. She locked eyes with Peter. "I only know what they tell me," she said. "I had nothing to do with your friend's death. I don't even know who he is."

Peter was dubious, but Linda stood firm, defiant. He had no way to know if she was telling the truth.

"Okay?" she asked.

"Okay," Peter said, releasing her arm. "Ask me again."

"Ask you what?"

"Ask me what I remember."

Confused, Linda asked, "What's the last thing you remember?"

"The battle in the Cylides Belt," Peter said loudly, angling his head at the camera.

"Anything else?"

"Nothing else."

"Nothing?"

"Absolutely nothing."

They both fell silent, neither sure of the other. Linda turned sharply as the door opened, and Peter stepped back. Colonel Chiang San strode in.

"Sergeant Garvey," he said. "I understand you know something about fighting in asteroids?"

[16.97.4.84::8233.2759.501.6D]

Peter watched as Private Tagomi drilled a pencil-size hole in the ship's hull. He pushed through and then unlocked the bit, leaving it sticking out from the hull.

At the top of the bit was a small plunger, a mechanical gauge that measured the pressure inside. Cramped beside Tagomi, Private Sabot opened the valve on a tank of compressed air. It hissed loudly; the dome-shaped plastic tent around Peter's platoon stretched tight, straining the three-inch-wide tape that sealed it to the hull. The plunger began to sink.

Peter linked to the camera that had been drilled through first, making sure that the hallway below them was still empty.

He knew he was being compulsive, but he was nervous. It was his first mission as a sergeant, and he didn't want to make any mistakes. He was responsible for more than just his own life now.

It had been a busy month since Chiang San had promoted him; Peter had trained both for his new job and this mission.

It was a massive assault, with forty divisions of marines storming the largest Riel base in the Drift. But that was just a distraction. The real job was here, twenty-five miles away, infiltrating the Riel flagship beneath Peter's feet.

Sabot closed the air tank as the plunger flattened to the hull. The pressure inside the tent was now the same as the inside of the ship, which should circumvent the ship's breech sensors. That was the theory, anyway. This was the first time anyone had put it to the test.

Peter did a final check through the camera and motioned for Tagomi to start cutting.

It had been pure luck that Peter's platoon was leading the mission. The plan, concocted by the Great General personally, depended on the Riel's bringing in a flagship to oversee the defense of their base. They knew the flagship would hide at the periphery of the battle—the ship was too valuable to expose to open combat—but the question was where.

Several days earlier, the UF scouted the area, then placed ambush teams of six platoons at each of the most likely locations. Each colonel had been asked to provide a platoon of his best men, and Peter was as astonished as anyone that Chiang San had picked him. By chance, the flagship stationed itself beside Peter's platoon, inside a hazy mass of gas and rocks that had either once been a planet or was on its way to becoming one. The ship moored so close that the men just leaped over.

Cutting their entry was taking too long; the assault on the Riel base was going to last no more than an hour, and they'd already used half of that. The saw was meant to be stealthy, with microscopic teeth and sensors that reduced power at the slightest vibration. But its designers had erred far on the side of caution, and the thing barely worked.

Peter swore quietly, fighting the urge to take it out on Tagomi. *It's beyond his control*, he told himself. *The best thing is to act confident, to set an example for my men.*

The saw finally completed its circular cut, and two marines lifted the middle out with suction handles. Peter dipped his head into the ship and looked both ways. All clear. He slung a polymer strap—two inches wide and as thin as dental floss—down the hole and secured it to the hull with a square foot of tape. He rappelled in.

It was a long drop. The hallway was cavernous, large enough to drive a commercial EMV through. Peter hopped to the floor and stepped clear of the others behind him. He motioned his men into two rows, back-to-back, to cover the hall in both directions. More holes appeared in the ceiling, and the other platoons streamed in. Peter motioned them into formation; their radios were disabled to avoid detection.

Seventy-two men was a sizable force, but they barely spanned the hallway.

Peter was already familiar with the ship's layout—they had practiced the mission on a holographic model that had been pieced together from fragments collected during previous battles. So he knew exactly where he was going and what sort of resistance he could expect when he got there. The team's objective was to disable the ship, allowing it to be recovered intact. That meant both crippling its engines and cutting all communication to keep it from calling for help.

Sergeant Garcia, the section leader, took four platoons forward to the bridge to take out communications. The other two, including Peter's, were to head aft under Sergeant Windham to cripple the engines.

Windham had a tall, sagging body and an undersized head, making him look like a giant from a children's book. His soft face was made softer by a thin beard. Non-coms weren't allowed to wear facial hair, but Windham had assured Peter that, because he held the top score on the Sim Test, he was all but promoted.

Windham motioned Peter's men down the left wall, then followed his own down the right.

The hallway was lined with structural arches, which the men used as cover, advancing in stages. It was a playbook move, but as far as Peter was concerned, the wrong one. Their principal concern should be speed—if they were spotted, the mission was blown, no matter what their cover.

Peter had said as much back in practice, but that had only irritated Sergeant Windham. Now, on the ship, the minutes felt like hours, and Peter had to throttle his own platoon to not outpace Windham's. Peter was the junior sergeant, so he had no choice but to defer to the other's judgment.

They had only fifteen minutes left by the time they reached the portside engine room. Garcia would have assaulted the bridge five minutes earlier, so the Riel onboard would already know about the invasion. Windham motioned Peter to the door, giving him the lead. Peter's men formed into a half-circle, standing just beyond the range of the door's motion detector.

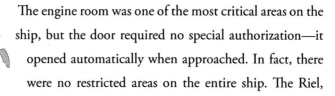

The engine room was one of the most critical areas on the ship, but the door required no special authorization—it opened automatically when approached. In fact, there were no restricted areas on the entire ship. The Riel, unlike the United Forces, seemed to trust all their soldiers equally.

Windham's plan called for Peter to run through each man's orders again to be sure they were fresh, but they had practiced this assault a dozen times in simulations so real that they might as well have been. His men knew exactly where the Riel were stationed and which was his target. It would be embarrassing to go over it again, not to mention a waste of time.

He bounced his arm, counting down with his fingers: *three, two, one...*

The fight was over in an instant. Within seconds of the door's opening, all five Gyrines were dead in their seats. Sabot confirmed that no alarm had been triggered, and by the time Windham led his men into the room, the bodies were piled in the corner. Peter posted two men at the inner door, which led to the engine itself, and was arranging the others when Windham approached.

"I'm impressed, Garvey," the senior sergeant said though the speaker in his helmet. Peter nodded absently, signing instructions to his men. He inspected each of them using the information provided by his suit, checking their status. They were fine.

"I'm tempted to give you a stab at the other side," Windham continued, louder, trying to get Peter's attention. "See how your beginner's luck holds out."

He wants me to volunteer to assault the other engine room, Peter thought. Their orders assumed that whichever platoon had taken the first assault would suffer casualties; therefore, the other platoon would handle the starboard. Peter's platoon was intact, so technically it didn't matter who went. But radio silence also meant no connection to the battle computer, without which Windham lacked the authority to override the mission parameters. Unless Peter offered.

"You'd better hurry, sir," Peter said as the timer dropped below ten minutes. "We'll get this room wired up."

Windham nodded, giving Peter a you'll-regret-this look, and lined his men up at the inner door to cut through the main engine compartment. As they moved out, two of Peter's men closed the door behind them, then stepped back and leveled their guns at it.

Peter's men set the explosives—the plan was to blow both rooms at the same time. As a precaution, Peter was wired to a dead-man's switch; if he died, his suit would trigger the charges automatically.

After that, they could only wait. Peter barked orders nervously, grouping his men at the exterior door, which seemed the most vulnerable. But as the minutes ticked by, he shifted more of them to the engine-room door, worried that Windham had failed. Then a piercing shrill filled the air.

Someone had triggered the alarm.

The alarm was bad news, especially if Garcia hadn't knocked out the ship's communications. If the flagship got a distress signal out to the nearby base, the mission was doomed.

Peter knew that it was Windham's fault; he had either been too slow or failed outright. Unfortunately, Peter's orders for either scenario contradicted each other: fortify this room or assault the other. He debated both sides, wishing—for the first time in his life—he had the battle computer's dispassionate guidance.

He decided to attack the other engine room. In a worst-case scenario, he would find Windham waiting for him. He ordered two men to stay behind and lined the rest up at the interior door.

Peter took up position at the back; the explosion triggered by his death would be fatal to everyone, so it was best if he led from behind.

He gave the signal and they moved out.

Peter was struck by the beauty of the engine. Clear glass tubes as wide as hallways filled the room in complex pipework. Arcs of pure energy crackled inside, feeding two massive helical chambers that pulsed with unshielded fission. He looked away; he had work to do.

The door to the starboard engine room was on the other side of the vaulted room, but there was no apparent way across. Peter motioned his men down to a tube thirty feet below that ran in the general direction. They leaped in, racing forward in single file.

The gravity here was weak and Peter landed softly. Energy attacked his feet, snapping against the walls of the glass tube. His radiation warning light flashed, but it was too late for that. He would just have to push through. Fortunately, he was the only one privy to that information; his men had enough to worry about.

The tube took a hard right and ran beneath a sun-bright fission chamber. The men banked through the curve, then suddenly stopped. Peter was furious, until he saw why.

A stack of bodies lay across the tube, Windham's entire platoon, set out as neat as firewood. Peter turned sideways and eased past the other men.

There was movement on the other side of the bodies. It looked like a marine, but something was wrong. His combat suit was pale white and deformed, flattened on both sides. Peter waved, but the man fled when he saw him, leaping from the tube and falling into the darkness below.

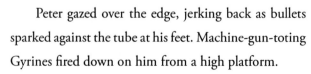

Peter gazed over the edge, jerking back as bullets sparked against the tube at his feet. Machine-gun-toting Gyrines fired down on him from a high platform.

Shoving through the pile of bodies, Peter raced toward the shelter of an overhead tube. He signaled his men to follow, but they were too busy to notice, firing back at the Gyrines. He opened the comm—no reason for stealth now—but before he could speak, the tube shuttered from a heavy impact, nearly throwing Peter from his feet. A shadow fell over him.

As he turned to look, he was knocked forward. Thick red fingers wrapped around his torso, hoisting him into the air.

The fingers squeezed, cracking his suit and then his ribs. The pain was far more than his suit could numb. He tried to scream, but his lungs popped, collapsing. He was lifted high and then stopped, weightless, as the giant hand reversed course. It swung him forward, his head aimed straight at a thick I-beam.

Peter heard a loud clunk and everything went black.

[14.08.3.17::3948.1938.834.2D]

Half-drunk and half-mad, Peter burst into the computer room wearing nothing but pants. The room was empty; everyone else had gone to sleep. There was a big battle tomorrow, but Peter had lost interest in such trivia. He had skipped the briefing and holed up in his room with a bottle of Saul's whiskey, thinking about Amber. Or trying to.

His memories of her had been fading quickly; when he tried to imagine her face, he saw only a blur. He came to the computer room to read her old letters, hoping they would bring her back to him. He missed her. He missed the good feeling that came from thinking of her. He needed that more than ever, stuck out here, all his friends dead.

Peter paged back to her earliest letters, those she had sent him in Basic. He was drunker than he'd figured, jerking and mistyping, but he finally managed to open one. It was blank. And so was the next.

"Stupid computer," Peter grunted, hitting the side of the monitor. He paged through her letters, pounding the keys, finding blank after blank.

The first actual letter was only two months old. "My dearest darlingest Peter," it read. "Today we held a picnic in the town square, offering to feed anyone who brought along steel to be recycled. Charlotte, as you would expect, brought only an old watering can, but Ms. Johnson drove up in her husband's front-loader and said we could have it if we wanted..."

Peter shoved to his feet and threw a kick at the terminal. It flew off, knocking through four rows of monitors and shattering against the wall. He felt a bone in his foot snap.

A picnic? Peter thought, disgusted. *That's what I get?*

He ripped the locket from his neck, breaking the chain, and fumbled it open. The hair spilled out. He rolled a clump between his thumb and finger. The color was wrong—light brown with sun-bleached highlights. He threw the locket at the terminal and limped away.

Back in his room, he took another slug of whiskey, then pulled on his suit, letting it numb the pain. He'd have to find someone to look at his foot, but who? Linda? He'd never had to deal with an injury before.

Of course, I have all-new recruits tomorrow, Peter thought. *They'll probably get me killed instead.*

"I refuse to answer that," Colonel Chiang San said, leaning his fork on the edge of his plate with much greater care than the task called for. The colonel was a precise man, but his current assiduousness was simply because he was drunk.

"I will say that I've been here longer than any of you," he continued. "I've been here so long that I can't even remember the Livable Territories. I doubt that any of you lot even have three months."

The colonel looked up from his fork and gazed, with bloodshot eyes, at the dozen officers seated in his private dining room. He picked out the hook-nosed, brown-skinned man opposite him. "How about you, Vadiraj?"

"Three months exactly, sir," came the sheepish reply.

"A real veteran," boomed Chiang San, knocking his fist on the table and upsetting his fork. He took a moment to replace it; then, satisfied, he picked it up to use as a pointer. He asked each man at the table the same question. Most had been on base for under a month. None of them ranked above sergeant.

The ranks of both lieutenant and major had been replaced by the battle computer. The computer made instantaneous decisions, taking into account every piece on the battlefield, with results far superior to those of human officers. It was only at the higher levels—colonel and up—where men still excelled. And at the lower.

Sergeants would be human for as long as marines were because no man would follow a robot into combat. They had to be inspired—or needled—by someone with as much at stake as them.

In the modern chain of command, sergeants reported directly to colonels, who then reported to the generals. Sitting at the top of the heap was the Great General, the four-starred commander in chief of the entire United Forces, marines and navy alike.

So when Chiang San wanted to loosen up, he did so in the company of his most senior sergeants. His Sunday dinners were one such occasion, during which he pointedly drank as much alcohol as the rest of the attendees combined. At least that's how it looked to Peter, but this was only his second time at the table.

"And you?" the colonel asked, offering his fork to Peter.

"Twenty-five days, sir."

"Twenty-five days?" The colonel said, making a show of not believing it. "So little?"

"Twenty-five days and sixteen missions, sir," Peter said, although his private count was well over a hundred. "It feels like a long time."

"I'm sure it does, son." The colonel set the fork down but missed the table. He bent over to retrieve it. "Nothing warms an old warrior's heart like hearing kids talk about hard times."

Chiang San reached for the fork, but it got away from him. "Let's see what you think when you have four hundred under your belt," he said, dropping to all fours and crawling under the table.

"You've fought four hundred battles?" asked one of the sergeants, awestruck.

"Four hundred and twelve victories," the colonel said from somewhere to Peter's left. "But to be fair, the odds of survival go way up when you stay at the back."

Sergeant Vadiraj stood up, puffed out his chest, and raised his glass. "To four hundred and twelve victories," he called out. The colonel popped up next to him, fork raised proudly.

"No," the colonel said, slapping the glass from the sergeant's hand. "What a terrible thing to drink to."

The room waited as the colonel pulled to his feet and tottered back to his chair. Vadiraj didn't even wipe the wine from his face. The colonel settled and replaced the fork, then lifted his own glass with sudden enthusiasm. "To four hundred and thirteen!"

The men toasted, pounding the table, then attacked the steaks in front of them. Peter didn't know how Chiang San managed to get real meat, but he fought the urge to rip it apart with his teeth.

"So tell us, my young sergeant," Chiang San said to Peter, "just how many victories in the Sim Test you've had."

Peter forced a hunk of steak down his throat, then gave the answer the colonel already knew: "One."

"One victory, says the officer who, in spite of his four short weeks of active service, and his..." the Colonel leaned back and peered at Peter, "his tall stature, already has four tactics registered with the battle computer. Four, gentlemen! I don't believe anyone in the room can match that."

Peter reddened as Chiang San drew confirmations from around the room. Peter knew he should be proud; few new tactics were registered these days.

The battle computer, as far as artificial intelligence went, was more of a librarian than an officer. It didn't invent tactics but sifted through its catalog and calculated the best fit for the situation at hand. Early on, when its memory banks were nearly empty, just about anything became a registered tactic. As the database filled, not only was it harder to think up something original, but there were fewer opportunities to do so. Peter's success was anachronistic and as puzzling to himself as it was to others.

"I myself have only two," the colonel said. "Whereas I had thirty wins in the Sim Test before I even made sergeant. Perhaps you could explain this... inconsistency."

"There's nothing at stake in the Sim Test," Peter said. "It's only a game."

"The most important game, if you ever want one of these." Chiang San tapped the eagle pinned to his collar. "Or maybe you like getting shot at."

"It's not so bad," Peter said. A look of shock passed over the colonel's face. He glanced at Peter, then into the glass in his hand. "That's strong balls," he said confidentially to the wine. "I'm surprised he's lasted twenty-five days."

"I—"

"I don't want your luck running out," Chiang San continued, looking at Peter. "I can't take you off the roster, but I can...and I do...order you to work on the Sim every chance you get. It can't be that hard. Just look at Vadiraj."

"Sir?" the sergeant asked, perking up at the sound of his name.

Chiang San looked surprised, as if he had forgotten Vadiraj was in the room. "Tell me again how many wins you have," he said.

"One thirty-seven, sir," the sergeant replied proudly.

"One thirty-two," Chiang San corrected. Then, behind his hand, he said to Peter, "Doesn't count if you win the same battle twice."

"If I might ask, sir," Peter said, hoping to sidetrack the conversation, "how many losses have you had? In the field, I mean."

The colonel glared at Peter, hard and sober.

"Only generals lose battles, son," he said. "The rest of us just fight them. And if they lose, we don't sit at this table. We lay out there!" The colonel pointed his fork at the window, out to the desolate black Drift. The fork trembled; he cast it to the table and pushed to his feet. He raised his glass, wine slopping. "To fallen brothers," he boomed. The men all stood, glasses high.

"To fallen brothers," the young men roared, then grew still, their thoughts turning to those they had lost.

The last of Peter's blue dots blinked out as a wave of red washed over them. He had lost the Sim twenty minutes ago—his eighth of the night—and was too tired to do anything but watch it play out.

"You'll have to try harder than that," Chiang San said, walking into the computer room. His combat suit was decorated with a stream of orange koi-fish, but scored black, and it smelled of burned carbon.

"I can't crack this one," Peter said.

The colonel squinted at the terminal. "That the Battle of Oenopides-7? I fought there, you know."

"You did?" Peter checked the date on the screen. "But that was thirty-five years ago."

"The dates around here are screwy," the colonel said off-handedly. He set his helmet down and took a seat. The cold of space radiated from his suit. "Government secrets and what all. Show me the playback."

The battle replayed at ten times speed—this time taking only three minutes for the computer to annihilate him. Chiang San gave a thoughtful grunt.

"You played football, didn't you?" he asked.

Peter nodded.

"Well, you need to stop." The colonel ran the playback again. "Look at that," he said. "You rush in the moment the ball snaps. Nothing covert there. Remember, the enemy doesn't know anything about you at the start of the battle. When they see you coming, they'll assume the worst, that this is a major attack and you're a hundred divisions strong. They'll hole up in the best spots and wait. But if you convince them you're weak, they'll find their confidence. Lure them out of their cover and they'll make a much better target.

"What's this?" The colonel said incredulously, jabbing a thick-gloved finger at the screen. "Did you just order a whole regiment forward without knowing what's to their north? These aren't just dots on a screen, Garvey. These are men like you and me. Men who are counting on you to bring them home alive.

"Try this battle again and forget everything you know about it. Use your sensor pods and your scouts to flush the Riel out, and double-check everything before you move. The Riel are fast, so don't trust their reported position. If the dot isn't solid red, then you haven't got eyes on them.

"Things move fast in a battle, but you still have to take your time. Only advance from a position of strength and keep your path of retreat open. A full regiment is a strong force, but if the Riel cut them off, they'll be swallowed up from all sides.

"As you see here," he added, as Peter's regiment blinked out for the third time.

Peter frowned. "I think it's beyond me, sir."

"You do, do you?" the colonel said, laughing with surprise. "Now that's irony if I ever heard it."

"Sir?"

"Never mind. The point is, we won this battle in real life, so I know it can be done. You only have to figure out how."

"But I haven't even studied military history—"

"The Sim Test is not about what you already know, it's about what you can figure out. And I have every reason to believe that you'll get the hang of this."

"Yes, sir," Peter said, trying to sound encouraged.

Chiang San studied Peter, then reached into his pocket and pulled out a golden locket. "I believe you dropped this," he said.

Peter stared at it.

"It looked important," the colonel said, setting it on the table between them.

Peter popped it open. The hair inside was dark brown, just as it was supposed to be.

"That hair belong to anyone I know?" Chiang San asked.

Peter shook his head, self-conscious, and clamped it shut.

"Someone back home then," the colonel concluded. "That's hard stuff. Hard enough when I did it, and back then the war was a lot closer to home."

"You have a girl, sir?"

"Had. A good one too. But this job changes how you see things. No one back home can understand what we do out here. What we've seen." Chiang San watched his own fingers drum the table.

"Enough of that," he said, looking up. "So how many of these Sims have you actually won now?"

"Three, sir."

"Not bad. That's two wins in as many weeks."

"Vadiraj's up to one fifty-three," Peter said.

"Don't compete," the colonel said sternly. "Not with him, not with anybody. It's us against the Riel, not against each other. Sergeant Vadiraj is good—he keeps his head and he's methodical. He wins battles and he brings his men home alive. Seems to me that you could learn something there. You don't get to be as old as I am without taking advice every once in a while. Or asking for it."

Peter nodded, unsure.

"You'll make it, kid," Chiang San said, clasping a cold glove on Peter's shoulder. "And that's the only promise you'll ever get out of me."

[14.08.2.64::3948.1938.834.2D]

"They bring you back."

"How?" Peter asked.

Linda worked on the monitor overhead, her mask off, relaxed. Peter's straps were undone, dangling over the edge of the bed.

"I don't know," she said. "Other people do that work. They heal your body and then bring you to me. I heal your mind."

"But I don't always die," Peter said. "At least, I don't always remember dying."

"You're never supposed to remember dying," Linda said. "Your memories are completely overwritten with a scan taken before the battle."

"And that's why we take sleeping pills?"

"Yes, exactly."

"Wait," Peter said, sitting up. "Did you do that when I first got here?"

"Down," Linda snapped, angling her head at the camera on the ceiling. "Or I won't say any more."

Peter lay back. Linda busied herself with the monitor.

"You're dead when you arrive at the base," she said. "Everybody is. Crossing the Drift boundary can damage living tissue, so they kill you before the ship even leaves port. Your body is frozen for the journey, and you're resuscitated out here. Your memory comes from a scan made aboard the transitship. We call that your version one point zero."

"And then what?"

"Then you wake up and go fight. If you die and we recover your body, then they patch you up and send you back to me."

"And Saul?"

"If he took a direct hit from a rocket, there wouldn't be anything left. Not that I know much about the medical side. I'm not even authorized for the Purple Area. But my point is that you're stuck in a loop until you survive a battle. I can only take a new scan if you come back alive. Some men will get stuck in the same version for months, fighting dozens of battles but always waking to the same memories, always saying the exact same things."

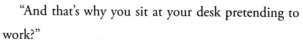

"And that's why you sit at your desk pretending to work?"

"Something like that," Linda said.

"Are you drawing?"

"Doodling," Linda said with a shrug.

"Doodles of what?"

"Things from back home, mostly. What I can remember."

"I'd like to see."

"Maybe," Linda said, but it sounded more like never.

Peter changed the subject. "So what version am I?"

"Two point thirteen," Linda said, checking her screen. "The two means you're a sergeant. Three for colonel, and so on. The point thirteen is because you've advanced thirteen times at your current rank. I have a chart where I can see what battles you participated in and how long ago it was—both real and in your perception. It helps me check the integrity of your memory."

"So how many real battles have I fought?" Peter asked. "How long have I been here?"

Linda looked away. "I can't tell you."

"What does it matter? It has to be over a year, right? I lost count of how many missions I've been on. Somewhere in the hundreds, and a few of those lasted several weeks—"

"You don't always remember," Linda cut in, anxious.

Peter shut his mouth and waited. Linda tapped her fingertips together, chewing her lip.

"How long?" Peter asked.

"I'll show you," she said.

She searched the drawer in the bed, pulling out a mirror and holding it to Peter's face.

"Look at that," she said.

It took Peter a moment to see the change, that his face was leaner, his skin duller.

"Oh," he said, taking the mirror and inspecting the thick stubble on his cheeks. "That long, huh?"

"Longer than any other patient of mine," Linda said.

"How many patients do you have?"

"Just you since you became a sergeant. You're only the second patient of mine who has."

"Out of how many?" Peter asked. "You don't look that old."

"That's some compliment," Linda said, hands on her hips.

"I didn't mean..." Peter said, struggling up to his elbows.

"I know," Linda said, smiling more to herself than to Peter. "It's more flattering than you realize."

She raised the bed and took his hands, pulling him to his feet. He landed very close to her. Linda smiled up at him, embarrassed. But she didn't back away.

"I like that you remember," she said.

"You do?"

"I do."

"I like it too," Peter said. "Except for the part about dying."

"Right," Linda said, laughing, covering her mouth. "I'm sorry."

"Don't be. I'm getting used to it. And there are benefits." He squeezed her hands.

"That's the other reason I don't talk to my patients. This far from home," she said, pulling her hands free and stepping back. "You marines are a little too eager."

"I'm different," Peter said.

"I've never heard that one."

The chime sounded, calling Peter to his post. He opened his mouth to speak, but Linda held up a finger.

"Later," she whispered. "Now get out there and do your job."

Peter all but danced down the hall, electrified. But he stopped short at the door to his room. Inside lying on the blanket was Amber's locket.

[18.23.7.32::3475.8563.331.1D]

Fist-size chunks of blue ice floated in the air as in a photo of a hailstorm. They rattled against Peter's suit as he pushed through, dragged by the dead bodies of two marines whose rocket packs he drove by remote. He moved slowly, the ice limiting the range of his sensors. He had no idea where he was going; he wanted only to be far away when the fightships returned.

The mission had been a complete bust, beginning with a serious miscalculation of the enemy outpost's location. Their target was inside the planetary ring of Catrols, a gas giant deep within Riel territory. Six platoons under Peter's command had been dropped several klicks away; they then advanced through the ring itself, using the ice as cover. But the cover worked both ways: Peter and his men couldn't see any better than the Riel, and when the outpost turned up closer than expected, they didn't even notice it until the Riel opened fire. It was a short, brutal battle. Peter won, but at the cost of half of his men. And then, just as they quieted the outpost, a squadron of Riel fighterships swooped in.

All the sergeants had been killed in the fight with the outpost. The remaining men were scattered and disorganized—most froze at the sight of the fighterships, and of the few who reacted, none did anything useful. Some fired on the incoming ship's thick hulls, others tried to flee. All were slaughtered.

Only Peter had taken cover, slipping behind a blue glacier as the fighterships made their strafing run. He doubted they had even seen him, but there was nothing to gain in taking that chance.

The dead men's rockets sputtered out, and Peter flung them backward, taking their last bit of momentum. He turned, watching them disappear into the quiet storm and marking their location in his computer. The men were basically intact—Peter had certainly been through worse—so he was sure that if they could be collected, they would be resuscitated. Not that he would ever find out. Even as a master sergeant, he still wasn't officially privileged to the UF's practice of bringing men back from the dead. And his knowing about it was a secret between Linda and himself.

It must be a lot to keep track of, Peter thought, *making sure no one ever meets anyone he saw get killed.*

Peter moved deeper into the ring, and the ice grew thicker and larger. Massive glaciers rolled by his scope in colorless dimension, shifting so rapidly that Peter had to use his computer just to dodge past.

Safely distant from his own mission, Peter scanned his map for nearby platoons that he could link up with. He was looking for a chance to redeem himself, but he was out of luck: the nearest action was a hundred miles away, too far to reach by rocket pack. For him, this battle was over. Irritated, he signaled for pickup. *Seventy men lost for only four Riel,* he thought. *Chiang San will give me an earful over that.*

To his surprise, the battle computer denied his request. "Fightership activity in proximity," it reported. "Retrieval prohibited until area secured."

Damn, Peter thought. He dialed up the Riel fighterships on his map and watched the four red dots spiraling through the ring. It was a search pattern; they were looking for him.

Based on their flight pattern, the fighterships would fly right past him. They wouldn't be hard to avoid—there were plenty of places to hide—but Peter wanted to give a little back. These were the same ships that killed his men.

Marines normally avoided Riel fighterships, and for good reason. They were fast and well armed, with metal hulls impenetrable to the heaviest weapon in the marine arsenal. But the ice complicated everything, perhaps in Peter's favor.

The ice in the ring shifted constantly, and sensors could penetrate only a few hundred feet, making it difficult to navigate. The Riel had solved this problem by sinking transponders into every glacier, which sent them up-to-the-second information on their position and rotation. As a result, their fighterships could plot hyper-accurate courses, weaving through the glacial ice at high speed with only inches to spare. But it was a blind trust, one that might be exploited. The fear, of course, was tangling with an enemy whose weapons far outclassed his own.

But so what? Peter thought. *If they kill me, I'll just wake up back on base.*

Though Peter had long taken comfort in this way of thinking when things got particularly grim, it was another thing altogether to willingly put himself in the path of death.

As long as I don't get blown up.

Peter drained his last battery clip and cast his rifle off into the blue ice. He looked down at the glacier beneath his feet, to the watery pit he had just melted. It was already crusted with ice.

He pulled all four explosive charges from his belt, dropped flat to the surface, and plunged his arm deep into the water. He released them, spreading his fingers wide to catch them if they floated back up.

Water clung to his arm as he drew it out, instantly turning to ice. He slapped it off and rocketed away from the glacier. The explosion was silent; light twinkled in the blue haze. Peter watched the glacier split in half, its two parts rolling away from each other.

The glacier was now directly in the path of the fightships. Assuming he hadn't destroyed the transponder, they would mistake one part of the glacier for the whole. By shifting course to avoid it, they would aim right at the other.

Peter flattened himself to the surface of a nearby glacier and killed all noncritical functions in his suit; it wouldn't make him invisible, but it would take the Riel an extra second to notice him.

And by then it wouldn't matter.

Moments later the four fightships appeared on his scope. They plowed through the icy belt in a tight line, leaving a hollow cone in their wake.

Peter glimpsed steel as they shot past, pelting him with ice. He wiped his visor clear just as the fightships rammed the broken glacier, exploding in such quick succession that they were just flickers of the same fire. But only the first three; the last one swung up, clipping and ricocheting off the glacier. It spiraled out of control, then came to a sudden stop. After hanging still for a moment, it flung back like a yo-yo rolling up its string.

Peter clicked on his suit and fired his rocket, racing to the other side of the glacier that he'd been lying against. He didn't have a plan; he was simply hoping that the fightership would overshoot, giving him a head start. But his luck had run out. The fightership whipped over the glacier and curved down, stopping right in front of him.

The fightership spun in place, the trapezoidal window rolling up from below, casting a green light that moved up Peter's body like a searchlight. It stopped at eye level, and the squashed face of a Gyrine stared out at him. The creature was upside-down, but then the whole ship rotated, orienting itself with Peter. It eased forward until its window practically touched his visor.

The Gyrine was expressionless—not that Peter knew anything about Gyrine expressions. He saw that it was only a face; the skin was stretched tight at the edges and then melded with the machinery. The entire fightership was a full-body cybernetic.

The creature inspected Peter with pale green eyes, then eased to his left, taking in his profile. The ship continued around back, disappearing from sight.

Peter remained stock-still, fearing that any movement would trigger instant death. He felt the

Gyrine's eyes on him, crawling over his back like sweat. An endless minute later, the ship came around the other side, finishing where it started, face-to-face.

"What happens now?" Peter wondered aloud. As if to answer his question, his rocket pack fired of its own accord.

Peter raced away as the fightership erupted in twin explosions—not, as he first thought, the ship firing on him. Two rockets shot out of nowhere and slammed into the fightership. Its thick hull shattered and the explosion engulfed Peter in roiling orange, searing his skin.

Peter's rocket fired again, lifting him from the fire, then aiming him forward. He raced at full burn, ice hammering his helmet. A massive glacier appeared on his scope, directly in his path. He tried to steer around it, but his rocket wouldn't respond. He tried the override, but it ignored him. He reached up to unbuckle the whole pack, but just then a doorway slid open in front of him. It was just a doorway floating in midair.

Peter hurtled inside and gravity pulled him to the floor. He tumbled down a short hallway and slammed into the door at the end. He was inside an airlock.

The outer door shut, and air hissed into the room. Peter's legs burst into flames—his suit, red-hot from the explosion, ignited in the oxygen-rich air.

An inner door slid open and two men rushed in, wearing black uniforms that Peter didn't recognize. They raised extinguishers and bathed him in a fog of halon gas.

"Nice decoy work," one told Peter as they hauled him inside.

"Yeah," the other said as they dumped him on the floor. "Good man. Now stay out of the way, right?" They left without waiting for an answer.

Peter sat up and looked around. The ship was no more than a single room, with the door to the flight deck set at the top of a high ladder. Figures moved through the dim red light, quickly but quietly. They wore black uniforms, with exaggerated shoulders and pants tucked into high felt boots. It was a menacing look, but they ignored Peter, their attention on the large table in the center of the room and the four men who stood around it.

Peter got to his feet, wondering how much of his legs were left inside his suit. He walked to the table, over which hovered a projection of Catrols' icy ring. There were blue and red marks, as in the Sim Test, but they were far more complex.

Each blue dot was captioned with a scrolling list of statistics—how many men, what sort of heavy weaponry, and how experienced. The red markers were shaped like what they represented, Gyrines or fightships in this case—and some had live video of fighting in progress. Large green pins rose at various points around the belt, each capped with the head of a colonel or naval captain.

The men around the table were generals. And this wasn't a Sim; this was the actual battle they were controlling.

Peter watched the generals move their hands over the table, their motions becoming orders, the troops at their beck and call. One of the green pins blinked and switched to a live feed—a colonel's face, bloated by his in-helmet camera.

"All clear here, sir," the colonel said. "Moving to two hundred and forty-four point twenty-one, but it's blind up there."

"Sending you eyes," the general replied, his face hidden in the dim light. Peter knew the voice but couldn't place it.

The general tapped the corner of the table, and a blue dot shot forward. It flew past the colonel and exploded, filling in details on a blank section of the projection. *Sensor pods.* The general leaned in to inspect the new information, his shoulder twinkling in the light—four stars. This was the Great General himself.

"I know it's fascinating," the General said to Peter, "but please don't stand so close to the table."

"Yes, sir," Peter said, seeing that his arm was inside the projection. "Sorry, sir."

The General's head snapped up at the sound of Peter's voice. He glared at Peter, his face twisted between recognition and rage.

"This is a mistake," he barked. "Kill this man immediately. And in the future, keep him out of my sector."

Several men rushed at Peter. Someone pressed a pistol to his helmet.

"No!" Peter screamed. He tried to knock the gun away, but his suit was disabled.

"Oh, get over it," the man said. "You marines are such sissies."

The man squeezed the trigger, twice, and everything went black.

[14.08.2.65::3948.1938.834.2D]

"Peter?"

Linda sounded close, her breathing quick, anxious.

He kept his eyes shut; the image stuck in his head—the Great General's face.

"Peter," Linda snapped. His eyes opened involuntarily. Linda leaned back, sighing with relief. "What is it?" she asked.

"I saw something," Peter said. "Back on Catrols."

"Catrols?" Linda went to the monitor. "You were never on Catrols."

"I was *just* on Catrols," he said. "In the ring."

"No," Linda said, scrolling around. "Not in the ring. Not even in the system. Not ever." She turned back to him and laid a searing hand on his forehead. Peter brushed it away.

"I was just there," he insisted.

"I..." Linda looked from him to the monitor. "The computer's never been wrong."

"Then they're hiding something," Peter said, sitting up. "Because of what I saw."

"Down," Linda said, shoving his chest. "You'll hurt yourself." She held him until he nodded. "Tell me what you saw."

Peter opened his mouth but stopped. *She'll never believe me*, he thought. *She already doesn't.* "I saw the General."

"You what?" Linda said, her voice cracking.

"I saw the General. The Great General. He—"

"Stop!" Linda said. She looked nervously to her monitor, then to the camera on the ceiling. Her face was drained.

"I need..." she sputtered. "I need to talk to the supervisor."

"No," Peter said, grabbing for her. But she was too fast.

"I have to," she insisted. "Just wait here."

"Linda," he called, but she was out the door.

Peter was unstrapped. He felt around for the button that raised the bed and then opened the drawer on the side. He found the long needle, already filled with oily liquid.

He dug around his arm until a vein swelled, then jabbed the needle in. It stung more than he expected. He pressed the plunger, withdrew it, and tossed it to the floor.

Peter pumped his hands and swung his legs, feeling the warm animation spread though his body. It was taking too long. Linda would have already reached her supervisor's office.

They killed me because I saw him, he thought. *The General himself gave the command. The General...*

Peter worked feverishly, flexing his muscles until they ached and pounding his fists on his legs. Then he eased himself to his feet.

There was a tray over his bed, splashed with bright red, filled with hundreds of long needles. He ran his fingers through them, rubbing the blood between his fingers. Then he touched his scalp; the skin was tender.

He let go of the bed, balancing himself, and started for the door. His legs buckled, and he threw himself into the chair at Linda's desk. He put his head between his knees, trying to still the room. After a few deep breaths, he sat back up. Linda's drawings were stacked on the desk.

The top drawing was of a church, done in black ballpoint, precise and detailed. It was an imposing cathedral of cut stone, its windows dark and foreboding.

The next one was of an alleyway between two tall buildings, the ink so thick it warped the paper. A shaded figure waited deep inside, a man.

The drawings were all similar—gloomy scenes rendered through intense pen work—except for the very last. It showed a man lying peacefully in bed, a faint smile on his face. It was Peter.

He pushed to his feet. He felt better, steady. He went to his duffel and pulled on pants and a T-shirt, to be less obvious, and walked through the back door. He started for the supervisor's office but saw Linda in the other direction, walking away, her ponytail swinging.

He sprinted after her, moving quietly on the pads of his feet. His muscles throbbed from the effort and were leaden before he was halfway to her. He considered calling out but was worried about what she'd do when she saw him back here. He hobbled on, reaching her just as she opened the door numbered 63.

"Linda," he whispered, slipping through the door behind her.

She started at his voice, then jumped at the sight of him. She opened her mouth—to speak or scream—but Peter pressed a finger across her lips.

"I'm glad I caught you," he said, panting. "This could all just be some crazy mistake, a bad dream. So before you go to the supervisor, let me just ask, have you ever seen the Great General?"

Linda retreated, wide-eyed. Peter followed her, staying close.

"No?" he asked. "The thing is, in my dream he... This is going to sound ridiculous, but..."

Linda tripped against a chair, falling into it. Peter knelt down in front of her.

"Let me put it this way," he said. "Is there anyone on this base who looks like me?"

Saying it aloud made it sound insane, but Linda gasped. She looked to the bed in the middle of the room. A man lay there, chunks of ice sliding from his body. He appeared to be asleep, but his eyes moved rapidly beneath the lids. A mass of needles grew from his skull, each wired to the monitor over the bed. The screen flashed wildly, symbols scrolling by in some foreign language. But it wasn't the monitor that caught Peter's attention, it was the man. It was him. Peter. An exact copy of himself.

"It's true," he said dumbly. He stared at himself on the bed, thinking back to the commandship, to the look of recognition on the General's face. Peter had felt the same recognition; they were the same person.

Peter turned back to Linda, looking first at her face, then down to her name tag. It read Linda 63.

Peter shoved past the Linda, toppling her from the chair. He dashed from the room and down the hall, the numbered doors passing in a blur.

Am I behind each of these? he wondered. He ran faster, pushing his stiff legs.

The alarm began to shriek as he passed number 8, biting his eardrums. Oversize doors loomed ahead, labeled Purple Area, Authorized Personnel Only. They swung open as he approached. He passed through into a different world.

Both walls were lined with glass that looked in on large rooms filled with frantic machinery, like an automated assembly line. The machine nearest Peter was a massive archway operated by small men in white arctic jackets. Under the arch was a steel bed, the same as the one that Peter had just woke up on. That he always woke up on. A robotic arm raced back and forth, extruding water, creating a long block of ice one razor-thin slice at a time. But it wasn't just water, it was flesh and muscle, blood and bone. The machine was a giant printer, printing a man encased in ice.

A hand fell on Peter's shoulder. He reacted instinctively, throwing his elbow back and finding something soft, probably a throat. Then he ducked low, stepped forward, and turned. A man in a black uniform charged him, another lay on the floor, grasping his head.

Peter drove his foot in the charging man's stomach, then walked over him as he fell. More black uniforms rushed into the room. *Guards of some sort*, Peter decided. They looked tough enough, but Peter was a marine.

They rushed him from all directions. One pulled a gun, but it fell as Peter broke his hand. Another grappled Peter's chest but crumpled as Peter's fist drove into his neck. Two more down.

Peter feinted to his right, then dropped to the floor, sweeping his legs under another guard, who fell backward and cracked his head on the floor. Another down, but more were coming. *Too many.*

Peter scooped up the gun and fired at the window. To his surprise, it spit out a bullet. This was a weapon to use against men, not Riel. The glass shattered and freezing-cold air blasted into the hall.

More alarms now, clanging ones. The men at the machine fled at the sight of Peter, escaping through a small door in the back of the room. It was the only exit, so Peter chased after them. He tried not to look at the half-printed man on the table, but his eyes were drawn to him. The surface of the ice was uneven, garbling the face. *Is it me?* he wondered.

Peter slammed against a wall and bounced back. But it wasn't a wall, it was a man. Enormous hands clamped on to his shoulders and hauled him into the air.

"Easy, buddy," the man said, his voice deep and rich, familiar.

"Saul," Peter sputtered, unable to believe his eyes.

It was him. His beard was gone and his hair was longer, but under that black uniform was the same old Saul.

"Do I know you?" Saul asked.

"Don't be an idiot," came a voice from behind. Peter knew this voice too—Linda's supervisor. "Just hold him still," the supervisor continued. "And turn him around."

Saul spun him easily, facing Peter to a man no taller than his waist. The man was bald, his sagging clown's face distorted by a snarl. He wore a white lab coat over a dust-colored suit and held a syringe of green-black liquid in his fat, carrot-shaped fingers. He aimed the needle at Peter's neck, but couldn't reach.

"Down here," he said impatiently, and Saul forced Peter to his knees.

Linda appeared at the broken window. She gasped, raising a hand to her mouth. *My Linda?* Peter couldn't tell. The needle went in and cold liquid coursed through his blood.

"I knew you were going to be trouble," the supervisor said as everything faded to black.

[14.08.2.69::3948.1938.834.2D]

"Just answer the question," Colonel Chiang San barked. "Have you downgraded his memory to before he met the General?"

"No," came the impatient reply. "That's what I'm trying to tell you. We don't even have a version that *includes* him meeting the General. That memory is coming from somewhere else."

Peter opened his eyes, blinking against the white light. He was back in his room, strapped to the bed, still wearing his clothes. The colonel stood over him, talking to Linda's supervisor. And someone else was there too, projected on the overhead monitor: a gray-haired man in a tweed suit. He wore wire-frame glasses and had buckteeth that could have been yellow plastic. Linda stood in the corner, kneading one hand inside the other.

"How is that possible?" the colonel asked the man on-screen. "It's not even the same body."

Ten slow seconds passed before the man heard the question; the delay meant he was far away.

"That's exactly what we're asking ourselves," he said. "I've conferred with the others, and we're leaning toward Randolph's Theory of Neural Transmission."

"Care to translate that?" the colonel said.

"You've heard of Dr. Jennifer Randolph, no? She proposed that each time the neurons in our brain fire, we broadcast a tiny bit of energy. A nano-size radio tower, if you will. It's a controversial theory, mind you—never been proven. Randolph claimed that the evidence lay in telepathy and precognition, which, between you and me, is a pretty shaky foundation."

The colonel shifted his hands to his hips. The last thing he wanted was a science lesson, but he knew that with the communication delay, interrupting would only drag it out.

"Randolph believed that while everyone transmits, only a scarce few can receive. And even then it helps if both parties have genes in common—siblings, a parent and child, whatnot. They're tuned to the right channel, you see. Also, certain thoughts and feelings will broadcast louder than others—traumatic ones, especially. There's a documented case of a mother knowing the instant her daughter was killed in an accident half a planet away.

"More important, Randolph felt these transmissions were residual, that the neural waves could leave a stain. Sometimes it's just a single emotion, a feeling—bad or good—about a place. But they can also be quite specific, like your dead uncle's ghost making a sandwich in the kitchen night after night. Or a murder victim quote-unquote haunting her place of death. This aspect of the theory is irrelevant, but interesting, no?"

The colonel sighed. He hauled his mouth up to a smile and motioned for the man to continue.

"Precognition—seeing the future—is nothing more than neural waves leaking backward through time." The man was quite excited now. "A traumatic event happens to you tomorrow, and you receive your own broadcast today, causing you to sense that something bad is going to happen—because, in fact, it already has. You see? It's even possible to see your own death before it happens.

"Granted, no hard documentation on that particular scenario. By the time you prove that it wasn't just paranoia, it's a little hard to record your findings, right?"

"I don't see how any of this—" the colonel started, but before his words reached the man, he was talking again.

"What we've got here is the exact opposite: a man broadcasting his entire life and his future self receiving it *after* his death. Who could have imagined? This is something completely new. Exciting, really."

The man appeared to have finally run dry. Chiang San waited to be sure, then said, "We've never seen this happen before. Not in this or any other model."

"Oh, I shouldn't think so. Transmission-reception is rare enough in the Livable Territories, and we've got a much larger gene pool than you do."

"But we have multiple copies of this very model here," the colonel insisted, his irritation showing. "Why don't all of the Garveys have this ability?"

"Near-exact copies," the man said. "We tweak each one a little differently. Apply a bit of chaos theory, if you will. Give Darwin a kick in the ass.

"You might remember that we first tried fighting with robots. Very effective, briefly. See, robots will always react the same way to the same situation, which makes them completely predictable. Once the Riel saw the pattern, they annihilated our defenses. Can't have our biologicals falling into the same trap, so we mix the formula up a bit.

"What's that?" the man asked, turning to someone offscreen. He listened for a moment, nodded, then turned back to the colonel.

"All of that is classified, by the way. Best to forget I even said it. Besides, we're only talking about a minor tweak here and there. You could spend a week with your original and never notice the difference."

"Well, this one is very different," the colonel said, red-faced. "Would you care to explain that?"

"Not really." The man frowned. "It's fairly complicated. Better if you just trust me."

The colonel seemed ready to burst with rage, but he swallowed it down.

"Hell," he said finally, "if I understood even half of what you just said, they'd have to give me one of those fancy white coats. Just tell me what you need."

"This is a discovery of epic proportions," the man said. "Scientifically, it's a chance to prove the Theory of Neural Transmission. But there are also immediate applications, both practical and military. Here's a man who can capture his own memories: details, sensory input, and even feelings. If we could harness this power, put it in other reproductions, it would be huge.

"I need you to send us everything you can—records, bio samples, memory scans. Get it all on the very next cargoship out. Freeze up that one on the bed, too, and send it along."

"Will do."

"Thank you very much, colonel," the man said. "I can't tell you how much we appreciate your cooperation."

The colonel closed the connection. He nodded at the supervisor, who turned to Linda.

"Roll this one back to the technicians," the supervisor said, motioning to Peter. "Get it frozen—they'll have a cryo chamber back there somewhere—and have them pull samples from its tanks. I'll be by later with the rest."

"Yes, sir," Linda said. Her voice was weak, weary. The supervisor laid an unwanted hand on her shoulder, giving her a mannequin smile.

"Once you've done that," he said, "wipe your machinery and prepare for a new patient. I think it's best that we pull you off the Garvey line entirely. It's caused you far too much stress."

"Yes, sir," Linda repeated.

The colonel had been leaning over Peter, inspecting him, but now wheeled around. "What's that?" he demanded.

"I was just telling her to prep for a new model," the supervisor replied. "Seeing as how we're terminating this one."

"We're doing nothing of sort," the colonel barked. He marched over to the supervisor and glared down at him. "What gave you that idea?"

"Well, the minister said—"

"The science minister said that he wants a sample. So send him this one and then make me another."

"But it's an unstable design," protested the supervisor. "And I have thousands of others waiting to go."

"I don't need more idiot grunts straight out of Basic. This is an experienced man, a master sergeant with fifty successful missions under his belt. I won't have you throw him away."

"But—"

"Don't misinterpret this as a conversation, supervisor, because the other thing I don't need is technicians who don't know how to take orders."

"Yes, sir," the man said, backing away. The colonel watched him retreat through the back door and then, with a nod to Linda, left by the front.

Linda went to Peter's bed and quietly prepped a needle. Her eyes were glassy, but she forced a smile.

"See you soon," she said, driving the needle in.

Peter watched her fade to black, warmed to think that she would be there when he woke up.

[unknown]

Peter's oxygen supply was low, ten minutes at the most. It was time to move. He could only hope that the Riel had left.

He released the cabinet, his cover for the past sixteen hours, and let it float away. To his relief, the room was empty.

The gravity was out, as was the power, so he crept forward using the magnets in his boots. The room was dark, and he didn't dare to use his sensors; after living on this ship for three months, he could navigate by memory.

The door to the main cabin was jammed, its electronic locks as dead as the rest of the ship. Peter gave it a kick, breaking its hinges, and continued forward. He headed for the reserve oxygen tanks; his life depended on their being intact.

Stars shone through a gap in the roof. The hull had been blown outward, leaving a hole like a jagged crown. Outside, space was littered with hunks of metal and glass fused into strange sculptures. A man twirled slowly past, still clutching his stomach against the pain of whatever had killed him. Despite the death and destruction, the view was peaceful.

There was no sign of the Riel spacecraft. Either Peter had escaped their sensors or they simply hadn't bothered to kill him. And why would they? He was but one man on a ruined ship, too far from home for any hope of rescue. As far as he knew, he was the only living human in this entire universe.

"This is an extraordinary assignment," Colonel Chiang San said to the ninety-six marines packed into the briefing room and to the four naval officers tuned in by video from their ship's bridge. "We're not just pushing the battle further into the Drift," he continued, "but shooting out the other side."

The colonel traced a pointer over a projected map behind him. "Over the past several months, we've beaten the Riel back to the very edge of the Drift, allowing us to send probes though the far boundary and to catch our first glimpse of their universe. Unsurprisingly, the first thing we found was this." Three orange dots appeared just past the Drift boundary: Riel bases. "The welcoming committee," Chiang San said with a smile.

"These bases are massive—twenty times larger than anything we've run into before. A direct attack would be useless. But what, we asked ourselves, are they protecting? It has to be something pretty important, so we started poking around. And yesterday we found ourselves a pretty good clue."

A grapefruit-size sphere appeared behind the bases.

"A probe at this location logged a flood of radio signals, spanning the entire bandwidth. In our experience, the Riel military—like our own—is frugal with its communications. No easier way to make yourself a target than with a bunch of radio transmissions. But civilians are different. The one place in our own universe where you'll find this level of radio usage is in the Livable Territories. And that, my friends," the colonel said, pointing at the sphere, "makes it a sure bet that there's a Riel homeworld around here somewhere."

A murmur spread among the men, a chain reaction starting from the back. The Colonel cleared his throat, silencing the room.

"It's just a hunch, so don't get your hopes up," he continued. "We don't know anything past what I just told you. There is no way to communicate through the Drift boundary, so the probe came back the moment it made this discovery—better to return with a little intel than to risk not returning at all. However, based on what we *do* know, the source is somewhere in this area."

The projection zoomed in on a sphere, revealing thousands of stars inside.

"It's a much bigger area than it looks," Chiang San continued. "And it looks pretty big. It's a lot of ground to cover, gentlemen—too much for probes alone. Which is why we're sending you.

"You'll be the first men in history to cross into the Riel universe. And, once you're there, you'll be completely cut off. You'll be self-contained, which means specialized training and a lot of it. You'll learn to triangulate radio signals, to perform spectral analysis on light, and a bunch of other crap that I can barely pronounce.

"You men are the cream of the crop, with a combined experience of a thousand battles. But you are not a combat force, not this time. You are a survey team. Your mission is to locate the homeworld, to catalog its defenses, and—by far the most important—to bring this information back.

"This will be tedious, low-brow work for fighting men like yourselves. It will take weeks or months, during which you'll be trapped on your ship with little to do. Nevertheless, you must remain vigilant at all times—if you are caught, you'll die. That far into space, we'll never even find your bodies."

The ship's oxygen generators had been breached, and the bacteria inside were dead from exposure, but the reserve tanks were full. With only Peter left to breathe it, the air would last months. And he had plenty of food, though it would be feeder-tube only—there wasn't an intact compartment in the ship, no room that could hold air or heat, and that meant he was stuck inside his combat suit for the duration.

Peter filled up his air tanks and went to assess the rest of the damage. The probes were all destroyed. The ship's bridge had disintegrated without a trace, taking with it both the four pilots and the ship's computer. The Riel knew exactly where to strike—the computer held the homeworld survey, the chart of their solar system, everything. Weeks of work, more than enough to plan an attack, all gone.

Gone except for what Peter remembered. He might not know much, but Command knew even less. They weren't even sure there *was* a homeworld.

He had to get back and tell them. And that meant getting the ship online—somehow—and flying it back to the Drift.

It was two weeks of training before the team embarked for the Riel universe. Their ship, specially procured for this mission, was twice the size of a regular transport, but the extra room was filled with equipment, leaving the men tightly packed. What really bothered Peter, though, was the lack of windows; he had hoped to finally see the Drift boundary for himself.

In preparation for the crossing, the main cabin floor was cleared, and the men were strapped down flat, feet-first. The ship was tossed by violent waves of radiation, then slammed against something hard. An invisible force passed through cabin, crushing Peter on all sides as if he were being forced through a narrow pipe.

The hull screeched like it was being shoved through steel nails. The man lying next to Peter stretched and distorted, then grew as transparent as colored glass. The ship's walls sputtered and disappeared; Peter was alone, naked, the orange boundary hurling past like lava. It was terrifying and it was calming. He tried to close his eyes and realized they were already shut.

Suddenly the noise stopped and the ship was back. They were through.

Peter was too sore to move. His face and body were coated with a white crust, the salt frost of his own dried sweat. The ship's furnace kicked on, blasting hot air, and the men coughed to life.

There were no fatalities. One man had a broken leg and most had lacerations. Some suffered stranger ills—aches and stiffnesses that never went away—but, overall, they came through better than expected.

The ship fell back into routine. Nothing was noticeably different about this new universe until Peter made his first EVA. He was assigned to go outside and inspect the hull for damage, but the moment he stepped from the airlock, the thick blanket of stars overwhelmed him. After so many months in the near-empty Drift, he had forgotten what a full sky could look like. And out here, in the pure dark, it felt like the heavens themselves embraced him.

He let himself float, his duties momentarily forgotten.

Peter finished his assessment of the ruined ship by taking a walk around the hull. The Riel universe had no fewer stars now than when he had first arrived, but his interest had narrowed to one in particular, the homeworld's sun.

He stared at the painfully bright dot and then at the statistics scrolling rapidly down the side of his visor. He learned nothing.

Using his suit's tracking system, he aligned the emergency solar panel to the distant sun and felt it hum to life. The panel would provide some power—enough to recharge his suit.

The ship's power core had been hit during the attack. While the damage looked minimal, Peter had no idea how to restart it or even whether he should. Technically speaking, there wasn't much difference between a ship's power core and a missile's warhead.

He locked the solar panel in place, connected the power output to the ship, and walked to the back of the hull to inspect the engine. The engine appeared intact, but with the bridge demolished, he had no way to operate it. He queried his suit, which brought up the ship's manual.

Since the expedition was self-sufficient, the computer in each man's suit was loaded with manuals. Peter had step-by-step instructions for any situation imaginable, from mining an asteroid for conductive materials to generating electricity from his own methane emissions.

Given enough time, Peter thought, *I could re-create civilization from scratch.*

Peter found a section titled "Running the Engine's Self-Diagnostic," which pointed him to a small control panel on the bottom of the engine housing. The engine was mounted on a fin, leaving just enough room for Peter to slide under it.

Opening the panel's cover required a special ten-point screwdriver, but the ship's toolbox was nowhere to be found. Fortunately, in its unerring completeness, the manual had instructions for making new tools.

Peter needed both a duplicate of the screw and a metal rod that was thin enough to fit into the cover's recessed housing. The screw was common but the rod was not. He had never before noticed how much of the ship was made from molded plastic.

Peter's search was exasperated by an electrical short in his suit's heating coils that caused his batteries to run low every couple of hours, which meant he would have to stand at the charging station for thirty minutes at a time.

He didn't like having to stand around, not with so much to do. His idle mind obsessed over the odds of success and wondered why he was still striving to complete a mission that had so obviously failed.

In some ways it was a curse that he had survived the Riel attack. If he had died, he would have just woken up on base as he always did. Maybe he wouldn't remember any of this—Linda said he didn't always—but what would that matter?

The problem was that he had survived. And if he, the version of himself that was here right now, wanted to get back, then he had no choice but to press on.

His batteries finally charged, Peter was relieved to get back to the search. But it took him half a day and four more charge cycles before he located a metal rod inside the latch of a door.

Making the screwdriver was straightforward. Peter heated the tip of the rod with an impulsor rifle until it glowed red; then he hammered it into the screw's head, molding it to shape. He repeated the process a dozen times, until the rod slid all the way in. He bent it for leverage. It didn't look like much, but Peter was proud of himself. He had never really made anything before.

"Works like a charm," he said as he unscrewed the cover, though no one was around to hear.

The control panel was about an inch square, and its buttons were so small that he had to press them with the screwdriver. Following the manual, he typed in the code to start the self-diagnostics. The indicator light was supposed to glow green if the engine was intact, blink a code in yellow for a known problem, or turn red to indicate a problem that it couldn't identify. Peter waited two minutes; it remained dark.

With a sigh he turned to the next step in the manual.

The ship had suffered minor damage from the boundary crossing, requiring a two-hour delay while the crew effected repairs. From there they took a circuitous route, steering well clear of the three enemy bases. It was a boring, weeklong journey capped by disappointment: they detected nothing at the spot where the probe had indicated.

"Likely it's just planetary revolution," one navy pilot said. "If the homeworld has orbited to the far side of their sun, the solar radiation would block all transmissions."

The four pilots conferred, deciding to hide nearby and check back at regular intervals. Their plan didn't sit well with the marines—it might take months for the planet to come back into range—but this part of the mission belonged to the navy, leaving no room for debate. And the marines, having spent five idle weeks parked on a barren planetoid, had run out of patience.

Boredom in a crowd is far worse than boredom alone. While company helps to pass the time at first, conversation quickly grows stale and the small irritations of others are magnified to intolerability. Peter longed to get outside, to escape the cramped ship and lie under the stars, but the pilots forbade it. Everyone had to remain onboard, they said, in case the ship had to make a fast escape. It was a sound policy but, in practice, inhumane.

There was no physical interaction between the marines and the navy. The latter remained sealed in their cockpit, communicating only by video. The navy seemed unaffected by their containment, maintaining a callous cheer as the weeks crawled on.

"Two men and two women," one sergeant grumbled. "Probably feels like a party in there."

Though the comment was made in jest, the image of it stuck. Morale deteriorated rapidly. Returning from its sixth weekly expedition, with no sign of the Riel homeworld, the ship was in open mutiny. The marines demanded that they go deeper into the Riel universe to search for the planet, but the pilots refused, insisting it would be an unnecessary risk. The marines were getting ready to take a cutting torch to the cockpit door when the proximity alarm sounded.

Discipline returned instantly. The navy killed the ship's power to avoid detection, and the marines strapped in for evasive maneuvers.

A ship was passing at the very limit of their sensor range. Its profile didn't match anything in the UF's records, and its transmissions were uncoded. Peter's team had lucked onto some sort of civilian cruiser, and judging by its weak engine signature, a short-range one.

"Build electrical generators from rocket packs."

"Fuse missile to ship's hull."

Peter read aloud from the manual's list of "alternative ways to propel a disabled spacecraft." It was a depressing inventory; every option required either something they hadn't brought or something the Riel had destroyed.

"Build chemical thruster by mixing oxygen with hydrogen" had promise, until he read the details. Not only would he need several hundred times more oxygen than what was in the tanks, but, with the expected top speed, it would also take several thousand years to reach the Drift boundary.

His only real hope was to somehow produce enough electricity to fire the ship's engine. Five minutes would be enough—he could coast the rest of the way—but the emergency solar panel didn't even have enough amperage to heat the preignition chamber. Most ships, he read, were equipped with backup batteries, but this one was not. In case of power core failure, Command had determined that the men on board could simply stay in their suits while they repaired the ship.

That was it, Peter realized. *Every suit had its own batteries.*

He quickly searched the manual, compiling information about how much power the engine needed and how much each suit could provide. *I can do it*, he thought, calculating.

He needed eighty suits' worth of batteries, and there had been ninety-six marines on the mission. Most were still out there, floating in the debris. All he had to do was get them back inside.

Stumbling upon the civilian cruiser meant they wouldn't need most of the equipment that was crowded into the storage bay. They just swung into the ship's wake and it led them straight to the Riel homeworld.

Tachyon drives created a blind spot at the back of the ship, but just to be sure, the men remained on alert for the duration of the two-day journey. Marines lived in their combat suits and the navy kept a finger on the ship's main breaker, ready to cut the power at a moment's notice. The trip was uneventful until, just as a disk-shaped solar system appeared in the distance, the alarm sounded.

Peter linked to the bridge's video feed and watched a hatch open at the back of the Riel cruiser. It released a puff of gas, followed by a few dozen cube-shaped objects. The gas dissipated and the objects just floated there, doing nothing. A moment later, the computer returned its analysis: trash. Disposal was common before a ship entered the gravity of any populated system. They had arrived.

There was something else to that event, something that didn't come to the surface until several days later, during a routine spectral analysis of the video. The gas coming out of the ship was rich in oxygen.

Even though the Riel didn't breathe, their ships were still pressurized to provide a medium for sound and heat. Because the air's composition didn't matter, they generally avoided combustible gases like oxygen. So why was this one different? Further analysis determined that the air inside the cruisership was a near-match for their own.

The men voiced any number of theories but always came back to one: that whatever was on board that ship, it breathed just as humans do. And that meant they had just discovered the third race.

The technical challenge of gathering the combat suits was nothing compared to the emotional one.

The bodies hadn't strayed far, having the same momentum as the ship itself, and in the vacuum of space a feather falls as fast as a cannonball. Peter had no fuel for his rocket pack, so he tethered himself to the ship with a long rope, leaped out, grabbed a body, then pulled himself back in. Soon he was getting one on every try, but it never got easier to manhandle his dead comrades—to rip them from their peaceful orbit only to strip them for spare parts.

Peter had seen plenty of death, but nothing this depressing. Corpses piled up in the main cabin—he had to keep them on board to know which he had collected—and the ship had become a mortuary.

The quiet was too much. Peter began to regularly talk aloud. To himself at first but later to Linda.

He walked her through his work, but that grew boring. So he told her stories from his life on Genesia—stories, he realized, that she already knew. She had read his memory scan. She knew him better than anyone.

The navy held at the edge of the solar system for hours, until they were certain the Riel cruisership was out of sensor range. Then they aimed for the outermost planet in the system—a rock so small and cold that it could barely be called a planet.

The location was ideal. The Riel homeworld was only five planets away, and in near-perfect orbital alignment. The planetoid didn't rotate, so they parked the ship in the cover of the dark side and gave the pilots a turn at being bored.

The marines hauled the equipment into position by rocket pack, the low gravity making everything practically weightless. Their biggest challenge was to keep their speed down, lest they shoot off into space. The men were cheerful, happy to be free of the cramped ship.

Peter worked with several others to install a catadioptric telescope. They wouldn't be able to see much, just the main cities, but they could monitor the traffic to and from the planet, which would hint at where the spaceports were—important details when planning an attack.

Once the telescope was in place, Peter volunteered to monitor it alone, and the others were happy to leave it to him. They hauled out a week's worth of supplies and left him to set up camp. Peter patched into the telescope and spent days watching the homeworld's lazy spin.

The homeworld was backlit by the sun—so beyond a crescent of light along the right edge, it was cloaked in perpetual night. Several large landmasses floated on even larger oceans, with two sizable deserts in the middle and a white frost at the poles. There were a few dozen cities, which lit up as they rolled into the twilight and winked out as they passed deeper into the night. Somewhere just beyond Peter's sight, their sun would again rise. He tried to envision what that might look like.

The images he pictured came from his own memories: the forests and rivers of Genesia, and the pungent, fertile smell of farmland. The third race, he decided, was much like his own—warm-blooded, planet-dwelling folks. They probably weren't Riel at all, not as Peter knew them, but some other race entirely that was aligned with the Riel.

His thoughts eventually fell on Amber. Their life together was a shallow memory. While he could still describe what she looked like, he could no longer call up her image in his mind.

Was she still sending letters? He hadn't checked his mail in months. *More important*, he thought, *who was she sending them to?*

Certainly not him. He knew that now. It hadn't been him on that ride to the spaceport, and her special good-bye belonged to someone else.

It doesn't matter, he decided. *I've haven't lost anything; her love was never mine.*

It was time to let go, to put aside those borrowed feelings and make room for his own.

Peter used every fiber of muscle, his own and his suit's, to pull the cable taut. He hooked the looped end around an L-shaped door handle and released it gently, making sure it held. Then he pulled himself across the main cabin to where the cable joined with a spring that was welded to the opposite wall. Everything looked good.

He walked to the dark corner where the bodies were piled. Only a few dozen left, he assured himself, lifting the top one. "J. Barberis" was stenciled in white on its back. The suit rattled as he moved it, and he peered into the visor; the body had frozen and shattered, its remains floating inside like frosted rubies.

"You're next, brother," Peter said, thinking back to the man this had once been.

He hooked the suit's arms over the cable, aiming it at the hole in the ship's side. Then he pulled up the standard funeral service onto his visor and read:

> *God of unceasing change,*
> *We are always unfinished,*
> *And you are not through with us yet.*

Peter had cleared the ship of anything that could be unbolted to lighten the load for the journey, but he'd put off the corpses until the end. Rather than just tossing them out, he rigged up a catapult to make sure they went far from sight. They had been piled inside for three weeks now, and he never wanted to see them again.

As for the funeral service, partly it was to pass the time—charging the batteries with just the one solar panel was a slow process. But, more than that, the ceremony differentiated these men from the rest of the garbage he had to clear out.

> *We journey to the other side,*
> *To find your warm embrace,*

Peter had recovered ninety-two suits, all but three, which should have been twelve more than he needed, but he had to check the batteries for damage. Each suit contained six, distributed in the arms, legs, and torso. That balanced out the weight but, unfortunately, also increased the odds that one had been hit during the attack. So far, one in five wouldn't hold a charge and, unless that ratio improved, he would come up short. According to the manual, being even one short was too few.

But while the spirit passes,
The body remains.
And with it, the memories of family and brothers.

Peter had stripped the first few suits of anything that might be useful, but the one thing that he really needed to replace—the heating coil in his suit—was built into the ceramic casing. It would be impossible to switch suits without an airtight room; he would freeze solid before he had even undressed.

The short in his heating coils had grown worse. His batteries barely lasted an hour now, and plugging them into the charger meant delaying the rest.

And so, my brother,
I send you on to greener pastures,
And stay behind
To guard all that you loved.

He closed the service and grabbed the L-shaped door handle. He turned one side, freeing the wire loop from the other. The spring recoiled, whipping the cable forward and launching the body into space. He watched it fly away, catching glints of sunlight as it spun into the distance.

It was strange to hold funerals for men who might be alive and well back on the base, with no memory of their own death. But Peter felt it was important. He had served with these men for three months. Their bodies could be replaced, but their memories were dead forever.

Honoring their remains showed that each life had value, that their bodies weren't just empty shells to be used and replaced. And if their lives mattered, then maybe Peter's did too. All he wanted was for this struggle to mean something, that it was more than just bringing intel to Command. He wanted to believe that someone back there was waiting for him. That someone would be glad to see him.

It didn't seem like too much to ask.

Peter returned from his outpost at the telescope to find the ship buzzing with news. The men had managed to tune in to the homeworld's video transmissions, picking up their news and entertainment and giving them their first look at the third race.

Sergeant Craft met Peter at the door and led him straight to the monitor. The others had already seen it, but they gathered around to see Peter's reaction. At first Peter took it for a joke: the third race didn't just resemble humans, they *were* humans. At least they looked exactly the same.

"How could they...?" he started, not sure of what to say next.

"We first saw this three days ago," Craft said. "So we've already asked every question you could think of. It's answers we don't have."

Peter hurled the soldering iron across the empty cabin and howled in frustration. He pumped his stiff hand and stared at the mass of wires and solder that had been his sole occupation for the last nine days. It was a molten mess; Peter had no idea what he was doing.

The suit batteries were complicated. They had chips inside to regulate the power, and unless he wired everything correctly, he got nothing. The manual had instructions, but they read like pure gibberish. The suit had given Peter a course in basic electronics, teaching him to strip and solder wires, but the electrical diagrams, intricate maps of lines and symbols, were beyond him. He used the pictures as a rough guide and hoped for the best.

The lead wires, those that actually carried the power, had to be wired in sequence, while the auxiliary wires, which controlled the chips, had to be run in parallel. Some wires led directly to the engine, while others were connected to the other batteries. Peter labeled each wire with tape, but by now there were hundreds of them, crossing and re-crossing each other. The chaos was overwhelming.

He gently laced the two power leads out from the spaghetti and wired them to one of the remaining batteries. There were sixteen left, which was still five shy of what he needed to fire the engine. He knew this for sure; he counted them daily. That left one option: to use the batteries from his own suit. He didn't know exactly how that was going to work, since he also needed those batteries for his life support, but he'd figure it out when the time came.

Peter twisted the leads onto the pigtails that he had already soldered on the battery, then did the same with the six auxiliary wires. He wrapped each of the connections with black tape to keep them from shorting and stacked the battery with the others in a metal box. He started to count the batteries but gave up with a sigh.

He walked across the room and retrieved the soldering iron.

The videos of the third race sparked a heated debate among the marines. Some felt the discovery so important that they should return immediately to report it. Others insisted that they should wait until the survey was complete. The latter group won, arguing that knowing what your enemy looked like wasn't nearly as important as knowing how to kill them. The team stayed another two weeks.

A small fleet of warships was waiting at the edge of the solar system. The ships were sleek, ceramic-hulled, and unlike any Peter had seen before. Peter's ship tried to run, but the Riel blocked them with lazy ease. A single ship closed to engage. The battle was short and decisive. Peter alone survived.

This he owed to luck. When the first missile exploded, it drove a cabinet at him, pinning him to the wall. By the time Peter worked himself free, the battle was lost and everyone dead. He remained hidden for as long as he could, hoping the Riel would leave before his oxygen ran out.

Peter flipped the six batteries out of the charger, then, in three fluid movements, switched them with the batteries in his legs, arms, and chest, which he then slapped into the charger. The exchange had taken only eight seconds; after days of practice, that was as fast as he could go.

His goal was to bring both sets of batteries as close to full as possible, but his heating coils had degraded such that they would suck his batteries dry in only a few minutes.

He was gaining time with each flip-flop, but the margins were tight. When he started this an hour earlier, his empty battery took five minutes to charge. Now, nearly full, it was going to take only forty-five seconds. Soon he would find out if this entire gamble was going to pay off. *Not a gamble*, he corrected himself. *It wasn't gambling if you had nothing to lose.*

The charger's timer fell to single digits, and Peter placed his hands on the batteries. It hit zero, and he flipped the batteries out, again switching them with the ones in his suit. The charger clicked back on, counting down from thirty seconds.

Peter had planned to do this yesterday but had procrastinated, wasting time trying to pull power directly off the solar panel with the hope of keeping the batteries inside his suit. The experiment had been a disaster: something inside the panel fizzled and, for one heart-stopping moment, Peter thought he had ruined everything. Fortunately, the charger still worked. He decided to stick to the original plan.

The timer dropped to zero, and he again switched the batteries. This time it started with twenty-two seconds. Peter's heart raced. He looked toward the bow of the ship, in the general direction of the Drift.

A few hours earlier he had moved around the ship with a small bundle of batteries, manually firing stabilizers and steering at the shortest course to the Drift boundary. It was a broad target, but it was also millions of miles away. If his adjustments were off by even a hundredth of a degree, he would miss it completely.

If he did reach the Drift, then the rest was up to providence. He could end up anywhere inside, and without power he couldn't even produce a distress signal. He would be just another hunk of trash floating through a vast empty space, hoping someone would notice him.

Peter almost missed the countdown. He frantically switched the batteries.

Twelve seconds.

He kept his hands on the batteries as the seconds dropped, and he swapped them back. Again the timer read twelve seconds. This was as close as it was going to get. He counted aloud with the time, jogging in place to keep his legs loose and warm.

Three.

Two.

One.

Peter popped the batteries from the charger and slid them into a mesh bag at his waist. Then he pulled the batteries from his own suit and did the same—he was going to need all the power he could get, and his suit's insulation would keep him warm for several minutes. He raced toward the hole in the side of the ship.

It took forever. His artificial muscles, stiff from lack of power, fought him every step of the way. Worse still, his right arm wouldn't move. He had no idea when it had gotten hurt—between his artificial muscles and the painkiller from his Life Control System, he had no way to notice. He cursed the suit for hiding this from him but knew it was his own fault. He should have done a dry run.

He was sweating when he reached the engine, and the cold was seeping in. The box of batteries was strapped to the engine, with twelve sets of leads hanging over the edge. He fished a battery from the pouch, using his foot to hold it down as he awkwardly twisted the wire with his left hand. He did a quick wrap with the tape, dropped it into the box, and started on the next one.

He made it through eight batteries before his fingers were too stiff to grip the wire. He slapped his hand against his thigh, forcing the blood in, and managed to finish one more. But the tape got mangled, sticking to itself more than anything else, and he finally just tossed the whole jumble into the box. He scooped the tenth battery from the bag, but it slipped from his hand and floated away.

There was no point in chasing it or trying to wire in the last two batteries. He had to press on.

Peter had strung his homemade screwdriver around his wrist, and it took a minute to maneuver it into his hand. He pressed the back of his fingers to the engine case, tightening them to the screwdriver, then dropped onto his back and shimmied under the engine.

Using the screwdriver, he tapped the tiny preignition button, and the indicator light blinked yellow as the engine ran its self-test. The manual said this could take from fifteen seconds to two minutes.

Peter's body shook uncontrollably. He pedaled his legs in the air, trying to raise his body temperature, but he was losing heat far faster than he could hope to generate it. Space was just too cold.

The yellow light turned solid green. The engine had passed.

Peter jabbed at the ignition button, his hand trembling so badly that it took three tries. Sparks flew from the batteries, and the box danced as they exploded inside. But the ship began to vibrate, and the engine's exhaust glowed from deep within, warming up. He had done it.

As Peter relaxed against the hull, his eyes fell on a coil of rope at his feet. He jerked up—he had forgotten to tether himself to the ship. A white blade of light shot from the engine, the tip fading into the distance. The ship began to move, leaving Peter behind.

Peter dived for the rope, ducking below the engine's blazing exhaust. He drove his good arm through the coil, but the rope unspooled around it. He twirled his arm, bringing the rope between his fingers, but they wouldn't close. He clamped it between his knees, but it slipped through. The coil was running out; the ship was speeding away.

Peter kicked a leg up and spun, swinging it over the rope, then scissored it back down and twisted. The rope slid up to his crotch and wrapped around his legs like they were a mooring cleat. The knot tightened, snapping his legs together. Peter was flipped head over heels and jerked forward. He slammed into the hull, bounced off, and swung toward the ship's center—straight at the searing white tachyon exhaust. If he touched it, it would shred the suit from his body.

He kicked at the hull to straighten himself, but his reflexes were tuned to his artificial muscles; lacking their strength, he only face-planted. His visor scraped across the hull, then struck something with a deafening crunch. Peter blacked out.

He woke up a moment later. He couldn't see much because a thick rod—one of the ship's sensors—had punctured his visor right between his eyes. The sensor curved up, either into his skull or over the top. Peter didn't feel any pain, but he wouldn't expect to.

His visor wasn't leaking air and, between the rod and the rope, he was held firmly to the ship. He tried to look ahead, but all he could see was hull.

Peter wasn't cold anymore, only tired. It had all been so much work, but he was done. He could relax, maybe even take a nap. Felt like he hadn't slept in days.

Wake me up when I'm home, he thought. He couldn't wait to get back, to open his eyes and find Linda looking down at him. He missed her. He never wanted to be away from her for this long again. Or this far.

It was a long trip back. He hoped to sleep the whole way.

[14.08.2.78::3948.1938.834.2D]

"Ah, there you are," the voice said. A friendly voice. A man's voice.

Peter opened his eyes, blinking against the white light. The man who looked down at him sagged with weight and was bald except for a laurel of white hair. He gave Peter a fat smile, his teeth as small as a baby's.

"What's the last thing you remember?" he asked.

"I..." Peter cleared his throat; it was burned raw. "The engine fired. Am I home?" Peter tried to sit up, but his right arm didn't move; it was gone, his shoulder nothing but a nub.

"Easy, son," the man said, laying a firm hand on Peter's chest, then looking back over his shoulder. "How about that?" he said. "The boy wants to know if he's home."

Peter craned his neck and saw two other people: Linda and her supervisor. Neither looked happy.

"Hello," he said to Linda, his voice wavering. She crossed her arms and glared at him with something deeper than anger. It was hate.

Colonel Chiang San burst into the room in full parade dress. He motioned everyone to attention as General Garvey followed him in.

Seeing himself in the Great General's uniform wasn't as shocking the second time around; Peter was more conscious of their differences than their similarities. The General was in his early fifties, both thinner and shorter than Peter. He had a cleft scar cutting his face from brow to cheek, passing right over his left eye. He inspected Peter, then turned to the balding man.

"Good work, technician," he said.

"Thank you, sir," the man replied. "It's a similar procedure to what we do here every day. I simply adjusted the—"

"Yes," the General cut in; then he turned to Peter. "Sixteen months ago I sent thirty-seven teams into the Riel universe, each with the same mission. You are the only man to return. My question is, did you find the Riel homeworld and can you tell me where it is?"

Peter swallowed and, clearing his throat, managed, "Yes."

The General glared.

"Yes, sir," Peter corrected, the effort searing his throat. He would have said more, but the General raised a hand.

"The colonel will take your full report," he said. Then, to the technician: "How long until he's on his feet?"

"Two hours, sir. Maybe three. First time we've ever done this."

"Bring him to me when he's ready," the General said. He turned to Linda's supervisor. "As of now, this is model 375," he said. There was a gravity to the words that Peter didn't understand. Linda choked up, her eyes red and wet.

"I'm sorry," the General said to her gravely. He turned on his heel and strode out.

"You heard him," the supervisor barked at Linda. "Reset the—" But Linda fled the room, hands over her face.

The General grunted noncommittally, closing Peter's report and laying it on his large oak desk. "How accurate are these coordinates?" he asked.

"Very accurate, sir," Peter said. "I remember them clearly."

The General nodded, motioning to the seat opposite. Peter practically collapsed into it. The General had kept him at attention for a half hour as he studied the transcript of Peter's debriefing. It was an officer's privilege to keep his men on their feet, but given Peter's condition, it felt like a message: we might look alike, but only one of us is the General.

Peter was just glad to sit. It had only been two hours since he was revived.

"You're a colonel now, if you hadn't noticed." The General pointed to the silver eagle on Peter's empty right sleeve, which was folded up and pinned. Peter hadn't noticed; he had been rushed in here as soon as he could stand.

"No, sir. Thank you, sir."

"Don't thank me," the General said. "I didn't promote you."

"Yes, sir."

"So you have no memory of Officer Training?"

"No, sir."

"No memory of anything you did on base over the last thirteen months?"

"No, sir. Should I?"

"Apparently not," the General said. "No one can agree on how your memory works, other than that you have to die. You didn't. Your ship was found and you were resuscitated, thus your missing arm. We don't actually heal anybody out here; we rebuild them from scratch. Is something amusing?"

"I was just thinking, sir, about all the times I supposedly froze in space. Now I actually have."

The General scrutinized Peter. "Yes," he agreed dryly. "Speaking of which, I apologize for having you shot. It's against regulation for men in the lower ranks to meet their own clones. At the time I had no idea that you would remember anyway."

"Apology accepted, sir," Peter said.

"Everything I'm about to tell you is classified way above your rank, but you already know a great deal more than you're supposed to. You've kept your mouth shut so far. Continue.

"The UF charter allows us to clone any resident of the Livable Territories, provided that they volunteer. We sample their DNA and scan their memories, then we create a soldier. One soldier. The charter is specific on that point, and as far as the civilian population is concerned, one is all we make. But as you can plainly see, that's not the case.

"We were losing the war, badly, and we had far more resources than blueprints to build. So the government signed a secret order to give us more flexibility. There are still limitations, specifically that we can't duplicate lines once we advance them—the memory of each clone must start as that of the original.

"I don't see the point, myself, but I'm not woman-born. I trust the homeworlders have their reasons.

"This rule, however, has created a situation. Three months after you left on your mission, your team was declared missing-presumed-dead, then reinstated from their last recorded scan. Since that time, you—Peter 375—have had an impressive record, not the least of which was your promotion to colonel and the receipt of top honors in Officer Training. Your other version has been very successful, and it's a shame to lose him. But I guess it can't be helped."

"Sir?"

"I need the information in your head. It is invaluable. So I'm reinstating you as Peter 375."

"Thank you, sir," Peter said.

The General raised his eyebrows. "I'm simply making a strategic decision. Your report here is a good start, but I'll have more questions. I'm planning the largest offensive in UF history, and every detail is important. Frankly, if it wasn't for that..." The General trailed off, frowning.

It was a long minute before he spoke again.

"The privileges of a colonel—the rank your counterpart officially earned just last month—include private quarters. Private quarters he may share with a woman."

Peter's stomach sank. "Linda."

"Yes. Linda."

"I—"

"I ordered all records of the other version destroyed," the General cut in. "You are 375 now. There is no going back."

"And Linda?" Peter asked.

"Are you questioning me?" the General asked, rising to his feet.

Peter snapped to attention. "No, sir," he said.

"Entire worlds are at stake here. Billions of lives. I don't have time for trivialities."

"No, sir."

"Good," the General said, again calm. He sat down and turned to his terminal, ignoring Peter as he spoke.

"You're demoted back to sergeant—you haven't got the knowledge to be a colonel—but I'm electing you for Officer Training.

"This promotion has nothing to do with the other 375. He earned his rank through hard experience, by winning unwinnable battles and gaining the respect of his men. Your promotion is political. You are under-qualified, but you have demonstrated unprecedented determination in bringing back valuable information, and in that you've succeeded where all others failed. Rewarding you sets a good example for the men."

"Thank you, sir."

"Dismissed."

"Sir." Peter walked to the door.

"One more thing, sergeant."

"Yes, sir?" Peter turned back.

"Per her request, I've granted Linda 75 reassignment, but only after the battle. You're in poor health, and medically speaking she knows you better than anyone. So for now the two of you will have to put your feelings aside. That won't be a problem, will it, sergeant?"

"No, sir," Peter said.

"Good. Now get some rest. We've got a lot of work ahead."

Peter walked to his bunk on autopilot—nothing had changed in the year and a half he had been gone—but when he got there, it was already occupied.

"Sir?" a sergeant asked, standing and saluting. Peter didn't recognize him, but the sergeant obviously knew who he was.

"Nothing," Peter said, stepping back and letting the door close.

Peter made his way to the officer's quarter and was only half-surprised when the door opened for him. Halfway down the hall was a door with his name on it. He hesitated, but the door slid open automatically. He stepped inside.

Linda had left in a hurry. Drawers hung open and hangers were scattered on the floor. His own clothes filled exactly half the closet.

He sat on the wide bed. It had been carelessly made, and there were dents in both pillows.

[14.08.2.79::3948.1938.834.2D]

"We have a rare opportunity in front of us—a chance to turn the tide of the war. It won't be easy. In fact, it will be the toughest battle in the history of mankind. But also the most important."

General Garvey was addressing a crowd of some ten thousand men. Peter sat with Chiang San in his office, watching on the monitor. He remembered viewing these briefings in the barracks with his platoon when he was a private. Back then he hung on every word, hunting for clues about the mission. But this time he already knew the plan, so he wondered about the other men in the room. He had never attended a briefing personally, and it occurred to him that he didn't know anyone who had.

"It's all canned," Chiang San said, as if reading Peter's mind. The colonel was leaning back in his chair, feet on the desk. "If there's a room like that anywhere on this base, I've never seen it. Figure the audience is pre-recorded or computer-generated. I don't even know whether the General delivers the speech himself or just lets the computer handle that too. I asked him one time, but he just laughed. Told me I'd find out when I got promoted."

"How many of me are there?" Peter asked. It was an obvious question, but he had never thought to ask.

"Just the one, now."

"But what about…?" Peter pointed at the monitor.

"Oh, he's not you. Not exactly. But that's complicated. Let's talk about you.

"Each line typically starts with ninety-six copies. Some advance and others are eliminated. Not only because they fail, mind you, but also because others succeed. Sergeants have a lot more access than privates, so there are fewer of them running around. After the first dozen privates get promoted, the rest are retired. That's why the base is divided into twelve even parts."

"And I've never seen the other parts?" Peter asked.

"Of course not," Chiang San replied. "That's the whole point. As a sergeant, you get the run of your section, and everyone in it knows only that one version of you. Not that you could tell the difference: each section is exactly the same. The whole base is divided out from the center, like slices of a giant pie. It's only us colonels who can move between sections. Of course, that means once a sergeant gets his commission, all of his dupes are iced.

"Most lines don't produce a colonel, though. We're a rare breed, you and I."

"We're not just fighting over another piece of empty space," the General continued on the monitor. "Even as I speak, the base is advancing toward the Drift's far boundary, bringing us within striking distance of a Riel homeworld. This time, we're taking the battle to the enemy's doorstep."

Applause erupted in the room, seemingly spontaneous.

"Towing the battle to the enemy's doorstep," Chiang San corrected from his chair. "The base hasn't got engines. There was even talk of taking it straight through the boundary, but we decided against that. Took months to repair the damage from bringing it in here in the first place, and no matter where we'd cross, it wouldn't take long for the Riel to find something this big. Better to go in shooting."

"What will the casualties be like just getting the men across?" Peter asked.

Chiang San winced. "Not so bad. We've ironed out a lot of the kinks since your trip. Hardened the equipment and the men."

"*I'll clear up the rumors right now,*" the General said. "*We have discovered the third race. Our objective is their homeworld. They may look like us, but make no mistake: they are our enemy just like the rest.*

"*This is an unprecedented opportunity—a chance to win the war in a single stroke. To ensure, once and for all, the safety of our loved ones.*"

"Another homeworlds-approved message," Chiang San grumbled.

Peter smiled, taking it as a joke.

"You don't believe me?"

"How could it be?" Peter asked. "The Livable Territories are light-years away. They couldn't even know about the attack yet."

"You study physics?" the colonel asked. Peter shrugged. "Then don't make like you're smart. They got it figured, trust me. They keep a hand in every little thing we do out here and don't you ever forget it."

Applause erupted as the General left the stage. A projection appeared where he was—a combat suit, but not a marine's. It was white and shiny, and while its proportions looked normal from the front, they were elongated when seen from the side. The suit looked familiar, but Peter couldn't place it.

"*Meet the new enemy,*" a colonel said, walking up from the audience. He was a stout man, with dark hair and olive skin. "*It may not look as fierce as the others,*" he continued, "*but it's just as deadly. Probably more so.*" The colonel reached the stage and turned around—it was Chiang San.

"Just like an onion, ain't it, kid?" said the Chiang San who sat across the desk from Peter. "You peel back a layer and there's always another."

Peter divided his attention between the colonel on the screen and the colonel in the room. He tried to gauge the nearby Chiang San's reaction, to see if he already knew what his on-screen self was going to say. But Peter's companion watched without expression, offering no comment about his performance onstage.

On-screen, the colonel gave a summary of the new race, which he called the Threes. He talked about where they lived, what they breathed, and what it took to kill them. He knew a lot more than Peter's expedition had dug up, and he wondered how much of it was embellished.

The colonel said moving the base into position would take two weeks, during which the marines would train on new weapons—ones that fired both impulsor and projectile ammo.

Peter tuned him out; he wasn't going to be fighting. He would spend the next two weeks with Chiang San, getting a crash course on the Battle Map, the complicated system the generals used to control the entire battle. General Garvey wanted Peter on the commandship in case he thought of anything relevant, and so he needed to be able to follow the action.

During Peter's first session, Chiang San had told him: "The Battle Map may look like a more complex version of the Sim Test, but it's far more than that. The Sim Test is meant only to identify men capable of strategic thinking, not to simulate actual battle. There are no false positives, no enemy decoys, and the outcome of every engagement is predictable. In the Sim Test, three platoons of marines will always defeat a squad of four Gyrines. That's not how it works in real life.

"There's a lot more guesswork and chance in a real battle. The Battle Map collates information from all over the board—information that is changing constantly, not just for the Riel but also for our own side. A general's job is to weigh what he sees and make decisions—up to hundreds of them a minute, depending on the size of the conflict. It takes training—two years of it—but it also takes talent, which is something you have to be born with.

"So to speak," Chiang San added, giving Peter a wink.

"Not bad," Chiang San said as his on-screen self finished his lecture, "if I do say so myself."

"Was that—?" Peter asked.

"Wait for your promotion," the colonel cut in, "like the rest of us did. Right now, there are more important things to worry about. As in, you've got a meeting with the General."

"We do?"

"*You* do. Right now. He wants you to review his initial battle plan."

Chiang San was already on his feet. Peter followed him out.

Command was a long hallway lined with colonels' offices. It bulged at the end to accommodate five doors, one for each general. Chiang San knocked on the one in the center.

"Don't let him rile you," Chiang San whispered with sudden urgency. "He doesn't like you much."

"Why not?" Peter asked. He had only had two brief conversations with the General.

"Nothing you did," the colonel said. "Just who you are."

Before Peter could respond, the door swung open. A man in a black uniform motioned him in—the very man who had shot him.

A short passage connected the General's office to an interior replica of a commandship. The Battle Map dominated the dimly lit room, a three-dimensional projection of the Riel universe rising from its massive steel table. Five generals stood beside it. Peter had met two of them before. There were no introductions.

"Ah, 375," General Garvey said, motioning him to the projection. "I wanted your input on this."

"Yes, sir," Peter said.

"We drop the formalities in this room, sergeant." The General's tone was uncharacteristically warm. "Look here."

The General scrolled the Battle Map past the three Riel bases, zooming in on the homeworld's solar system. "This is how the system will look when we attack. And this"—the General twisted his hand above the table, revolving the planets backward around the sun—"is how it was when you surveyed it. You reported heavy radio use on this planet here, and this one as well. Both planets are uninhabitable, so they are either outposts or mines. Did your team investigate?"

"We did, but I didn't see the report."

The General nodded. "When you completed your survey two weeks later," he said, twirling the system forward, "you were still seeing activity on this planet, but this one was silent. Is that correct?"

"That's what I heard. I didn't witness it myself."

"Relax, sergeant. This isn't a trial. My suspicion is that this planet has a small, isolated base, somewhere in here." The General drew a circle onto the projected planet, his finger leaving a green mark. "And when we advance the clock to zero hour, these are the only two planets in the fourth-quadrant approach. More important, this one has created a blind spot on the other." The General scrolled the planets around to demonstrate.

"My plan is to send the main invasion force through here, led by two naval destroyers. We'll skip the less active planet—leave it for clean up—and send the destroyers straight for this one. What do you think?"

Peter inspected the map, nodding his head as if he understood. "That sounds very smart, sir." he said.

The General glared at him. "I'm glad you approve," he said. The other men laughed. "But I think we'll do without your tactical advice. The question is, do you remember anything useful?"

"Yes, sir," Peter said. He studied his boots, his face burning. "Of course, sir." He caught the eye of another general, who frowned back.

"Well," General Garvey prodded.

"I..." Peter's mind raced. He looked from one planet to the other, unable to remember any of what the General had just told him. "I don't think so, sir."

The General gave Peter a hard look, then walked over, close.

"Colonel San has access to this," he said gently. "Go over it again with him tonight." Peter flinched as the General placed a hand on his shoulder. "And take your time, son. It's important."

Peter nodded and the General dismissed him. Peter took a walk to see what else he could remember about the Riel solar system. He knew every detail was important but that only made them harder to remember.

As hard as Peter had found the Sim Test, the battle computer was a level beyond. Everything moved twice as fast and there was a lot more to keep track of. Each blue dot was labeled with a string of numbers that were meant to tell him, at a glance, the platoon's armament, mobility, and condition. But even after two weeks of practice, Peter still had to stop to work out the code. And with dozens of platoons on the table, there just wasn't time.

Even more frustrating were the Riel markers, which were shaded in hues from translucent pink to solid red, depending the strength of the intel. Peter learned that any marker that was not bright red—indicating the enemy was being observed at that very moment—was extremely unreliable. The Riel moved quickly, especially on their home turf. And they were nearly impossible to track. More than once, Peter had sent his men to fight a single squad, only to find four more waiting.

Peter blundered through several hours of simulated battles every day, feeling worse for the practice. And so far he had managed only twenty platoons—a couple hundred men. A general managed a couple million.

On the eve of the battle, Chiang San led Peter to the conference room for their final briefing. Every colonel on the base was crowded into the room, along with the generals and their staffs. The naval officers, as usual, attended by video. Peter wondered if they were even allowed to leave their ships.

General Garvey entered to muted applause. The Riel universe appeared on the projector, and Garvey opened with an overview of the battle plan that Peter had watched develop over the previous weeks. The first objective was to get past the Riel bases, which they would soften up with atomics. The bases themselves would be unaffected—their deflectors were too strong—but any patrolling fighterships would be incinerated and the rest would be grounded. They'd nuke the bases for ten minutes, which was long enough, the general believed, to sneak the fleet past.

The General had ruled out trying to capture the bases but planned to leave behind a decent-size force to convince the Riel that they were his principal target. "The bases will give us a rough time," he said, "but at least we know what to expect there. What lies beyond is entirely new territory."

The projection scrolled to the Riel homeworld.

"We've never locked horns with the third race before, and we have precious little information about them. Perhaps they are weak—bonded or enslaved by the others—but I don't think so. I believe the Threes are the master race, reigning over the others.

"When I consider the size of the enemy bases that protect this planet, and the ships that attacked our scouting mission, I see a homeworld of utmost importance. I see the center of the entire Riel kingdom.

"I said we could win the entire war tomorrow and I meant it, but it won't be easy. We'll be facing a massive force, and as with any dominant race, the Threes will have reserved the best technology for themselves. Our one advantage is surprise. We must knock the Riel off balance, scatter their defenses, and keep them scattered until we plant our flag in the rubble of their capital.

"Our assault will come in two waves. The first will use every marine we have—a full ninety-six divisions built and ready to go. The second wave is a duplicate of the first, printed and waiting in cold storage, to be resuscitated the moment the first wave is off base. The organization of both waves will be the same—platoons, regiments, and divisions all under the same chain of command unless I specifically order otherwise. This includes everyone in this room; so all second-wave officers will refrain from open-channel communication until the death of their first-wave counterpart. Myself and other noncombat officers will be replaced as necessary, per standard battle procedure."

Next the General outlined the force deployments. The first wave would concentrate on the outlaying defenses with only two divisions targeting the homeworld—and those just to probe their defenses. If all went well, the entire second wave would head directly for the homeworld.

The briefing lasted two hours. Afterward the men filed into the Officer Resuscitation Center, which was far more refined than what the troops used. The hallways had frosted glass and nurses were stationed at every door. Now that they had their orders, their brains would be scanned. Each man could expect to be killed several times during the course of the battle, and with the exception of Peter, this moment would be the last they remembered when they awoke.

Colonel Chiang San guided Peter to a doorway and clapped him on the back. "See you in the morning," he said with a wink.

The nurse waited for him inside. It was Linda, but she wore a mask over her face and a scrub hat pulled low on her head. Peter started to speak, but she looked away, motioning him to the bed. He lay down and she raised a long needle.

[20.74.9.72::1938.7493.738.8D]

Peter stood at the large bay window at the front of the commandship, watching the disk-shaped base slide underneath. He had forgotten how large it was, like a flattened steel moon.

He tried to distinguish the pie-shaped sections that Chiang San had described, but he saw no seams on the hull's corrugated surface. Each section must be laid out sequentially, he decided, with the printing machines in the center, the resuscitation area next, and then the barracks and the docks.

But how do you get from one section to another? Peter wondered.

The ship angled up and accelerated, passing through the shield's triangular gateway. The entire fleet waited outside, a dark mass like a black sun against the shimmering orange Drift boundary.

Peter remained at the window while the crew scurried about. He had no task or duty, and there was little chance he'd remember anything useful. Even the General seemed to realize this, relieving Chiang San from babysitting duty and giving him a proper command.

Woven throughout the commandship's cold efficiency was an air of suspense, perhaps even dread. They had towed the base to the very border of the Riel universe, which was necessary to rapidly deploy the second wave, but that put the entire United Forces at risk. A loss today meant losing the entire war. If General Garvey were telling the truth, the coming battle would be the most important in human history. But Peter couldn't stop thinking about Linda.

She had barely spoken to him during the scan, and when he tried to apologize, she walked away. Not that it had been much of an apology—more of a boneheaded attempt at conversation. The man she loved had been killed, utterly destroyed, so that Peter could take his place. How could he apologize for that?

She must hate the sight of me, he thought.

"Strap in for the crossing, sergeant," the captain said, appearing on a nearby monitor. Peter shook his thoughts away and joined the men on the floor, lying down and pulling straps over his body. He peered up at the window as thick steel shutters began to close. The asteroids rolled by outside like malformed dice, tossed by the boundary's violent radiation. The shutters locked with a deep thrum, sealing out the light, and then the crossing began.

A wave of pain rolled over Peter, washing away all other thoughts.

Peter was alone on the floor when he woke. The generals were across the room, huddling over the Battle Map, and their staffs orbited around them. He tried to sit up but lacked the strength.

A man in a black uniform strode over and helped him to his feet. Peter was embarrassed, but it was the third time he'd crossed the Drift in this body.

"I let you sleep," the man said in a hushed voice. "Still a few hours before the hammer drops."

Peter nodded. He needed distraction, so he went to inspect the map.

There wasn't much to see yet. The fleet was marked in faint blue—an estimated position, not their actual. The rest of the map was nearly blank. There were no charts of the Riel universe, and for stealth the commandship's sensors were throttled to a few thousand miles—just enough to avoid a collision. The only other features were the three orange Riel bases and, off in the far corner, the blue homeworld.

The man who had helped Peter to his feet took up station behind him, his hands clasped behind his back like an aide. Or maybe his job was to make sure

Peter didn't bother anyone important. Peter himself wasn't important. He was here only because General Garvey had once decided he might be useful. This had since been proved otherwise, but the General wasn't going to admit that he was wrong.

All Peter wanted was for someone to hand him a gun and send him out to fight.

The battle started without a countdown, without a word. The General simply ran his hand over the map and it began. The room stood motionless, all eyes following the blue tracers racing across the map. The dots blinked when the atomics reached their target, then disappeared as they detonated.

That was the signal to drop radio silence. The battle computer connected to the other ships, receiving their actual positions, and the map flashed as every blue marker brightened at once. The fleet shifted into a narrow line, slipping past the besieged bases.

On the map the commandship was moving at high speed, keeping pace with the fleet, but there was no engine noise and no sense of motion. The inside of the ship was as staid as an underground bunker.

Red dots appeared. Just a few at first, but as the General scattered sensor pods, they popped up across the map, tightening around the UF fleet in a horseshoe formation. All the generals leaned in, their hands darting around and sending men to meet the enemy.

Peter stood on his toes, peering over shoulders, but the men were too fast—he couldn't follow their actions, only see the results. Soldiers died by the thousands. The only sound was the electronic hum of the Battle Map.

After a minute of deafening silence, a brigadier said, "First-wave placement, ninety-five percent." He was the youngest of the generals, and his forehead was beaded with sweat. General Garvey acknowledged him without looking up.

"Eden is in sight, sir," the brigadier reported, using the code name for the Riel homeworld.

"Location?" the General asked.

"Exactly where we expected her."

The General smiled—a twisted, disturbing smile—and looked straight at Peter. "Good job, sergeant," he said.

Peter surprised himself by blushing. "Thank you, sir," he replied, but the General had already turned back to the map.

"Give me an ETA on the second wave," the General said, but his words were lost under a piercing alarm. Something exploded against the roof and ripped it open.

The escaping air sucked Peter up, slamming him into the ceiling. He struggled to breathe, but the suction was too strong. The alarm faded and became tinny as the air thinned.

Below him General Garvey dangled from the Battle Map,

holding on with one hand while the other moved calmly over its surface, issuing his last orders before the air ran out.

Linda's face emerged from the white light. She was leaning over him, ripping the steel needles from his head and flinging them into a tray. Her mask was off, her lower lip clamped in her teeth. A loose clump of hair swung in front of her face.

"Sorry," she said when Peter winced. "They need you as soon as possible."

She jabbed a needle in his arm, plunging it so fast that her knuckles whitened. She tapped a button and gray ceramic panels rose on all sides of the bed, encasing Peter. "I'm going to cook you," she said, hidden from view. "Try to hold still."

There was a loud buzz and Peter's senses lit up. He felt like he was being tickled over every inch of his body, inside and out. The process lasted several minutes; then the noise stopped and the panels slid back down. Linda leaned in and laid a cold towel on his forehead. He smelled burned hair.

"What was...?" Peter tried to ask, barely able to speak.

"Microwaves," Linda said. "They accelerate the resuscitation process. It's a very complicated procedure, VIP only."

"I should be flattered," Peter mumbled. Linda smiled, producing another needle.

"This, too. A strong mix of painkiller and stimulant. Highly addictive. Sometimes we have to toss a body after just a single dose." She gave him the shot and raised the bed to a sitting position.

"No questions?" Peter asked.

"No time," Linda replied, taking his hands and yanking him up. Peter came forward too fast, falling over her. She locked him in a bear hug to hold him up.

"I've done that better," Peter said. Linda laughed, then caught herself and looked away. Peter started to speak, but she cut him off.

"I don't want to talk about it," she said.

"I know," Peter said. He found his balance and she released him. Neither moved. They just stood there, close, he gazing at her and she at the floor. Then the door opened and Peter's aide, or whoever he was, came in.

"Ready, marine?" he snapped.

"Yes, sir," Peter replied. The aide turned on his heel and led Peter into the hall.

Peter followed the aide down the hallway, the stimulant surging through his body like raw power. He pulled on his jacket and was momentarily surprised to notice that he had a right arm again.

They joined up with a cluster of two-dozen men, all racing giddily for the docks. A heavy-set general in the back read out the battle's highlights from a portable screen, right up to the point where the commandship was destroyed. General Garvey was in the front, where two aides supported a monitor between them—a scaled-down version of the battle computer. A third aide had his hands on the General's shoulders, guiding him from behind. The General worked furiously, ignoring everyone else.

The thin brigadier dropped back alongside Peter. "You remember?" he whispered. There was awe in his voice, like he was witnessing a miracle. Peter nodded. "What happened?" the brigadier asked.

"Maybe a missile," Peter replied, shaking his head. "It was over fast."

A naval captain appeared on the device in the brigadier's hand—a different one from the last time. "Engines warm and ready, sir," she said.

"Very good," the brigadier replied. He shortened his step, dropping behind Peter, and quizzed the captain about Riel proximity.

The officers passed through the airlock into the glass-lined docks. It was the same route as before, but now, with the docks empty, they had a panoramic view of the raging Drift boundary. Peter stared, fixated, then noticed that the green plasma shield was turned off.

"Riel scouts are prowling about," his aide offered, catching Peter's look. "The shields give off an energy signature like a homing beacon. We'll turn them back on if we need them."

At the end of the long hallway was another command-ship, one of several stashed around the base, the only reserve in this all-out battle.

Green light filled the hall as the base's shield hummed to life. The group stopped unevenly, the men in back knocking into those in front. They all looked outside, searching for the cause of alarm.

A swirling hole appeared in the orange boundary, sucked from the inside like the birth of a black hole. An enormous steel wedge slid out of the middle, the tip of something very big.

What came out of the Drift boundary was a monstrous battlecruiser so large that Peter couldn't even guess its scale. It resembled a giant spear, starting with the wedge-shaped bridge and tapering to a long, narrow body. There was no end to it—the ship emerged with unhurried ease, growing longer and longer.

The base opened fire with massive tachyon cannons and swarms of rockets, pounding the incoming ship mercilessly to no noticeable effect. The enemy ship drew overhead, casting its shadow on the men in the hallway, who stared wide-eyed. And still the ship grew, sliding out from the dark hole.

Round doors opened along the ship's hull, pumping out streams of fighterships. They swooped under the base, disappearing from sight.

Two missiles fired from the back of the battleship's bridge, making a lazy arc and slamming into the base's plasma shield. Sparks flew as the missiles pushed forward, bending the shield as if it were made of rubber. Then the shield gave way and the missiles popped through. They shot below view and the whole base shook from their impact. The green shield flickered and died.

There was a loud clatter as the two aides dropped the portable Battle Map. They picked up the General, one under each arm, and rushed him to the commandship. No one else moved. Peter looked up and down the hall, ready to run but unsure where.

Square hangers opened along the battlecruiser's body, and a string of dots dropped out. As the dots grew closer, Peter saw their spidery legs and red flesh: Typhons, dozens of them, dropping to the base like commandos. They attacked the hull with Delta-class impulsors, cutting loose whole sections and shoving them into space.

Decision made, Peter thought, running for the commandship. But then a squad of fighterships swung around the base, heading toward him. Glass shattered as bullets ripped through the docks. A rocket exploded, tearing the hallway in half. A long section of hall spun away, the burning commandship attached to the end.

The other men still hadn't moved. Another wave of fighterships swooped down on the hallway, spraying bullets, slaughtering them. Peter's aide stood placid, almost distracted, as the bullets sliced him into three pieces. Only the brigadier reacted, dodging back and running toward the base.

Peter leaped over the edge of the four-sided walkway. As he dropped, the gravitational field of the perpendicular walkway pulled at his side, slamming him against what was now the floor. Bullets sparked against the grating. He shoved to his feet and raced for the base.

Air streamed from the open airlock, sucked through the broken windows behind him. It was a powerful wind; Peter leaned forward as he ran.

There was a loud bang as the airlock's emergency charges fired, slamming the doors shut. The brigadier was caught in the middle, his chest crushed.

The walkway collapsed. Peter jumped.

He nearly reached the airlock, but the wind threw him back. He scrambled for a hold on the smooth glass walls, finding none.

The windows shattered as the docks broke away from the base. A seam appeared at Peter's feet, and he threw himself forward, grabbing an empty window frame as the rest of the hall tore loose and spiraled into space.

Peter held the very edge of what was still attached to the base, a section of the hallway some thirty feet long. Above him the airlock doors were wedged open by the brigadier's body. Air rushed from the base, flapping Peter like a flag.

He clung dearly to the window frame, hanging in space with nothing to protect him but the thin fabric of his dress uniform. The cold ached in his bones and clamped at his chest. But for the escaping wind, he would have frozen in seconds.

Peter's hands grew weak. He looked up at the airlock, squinting against the stinging wind, which cooled below freezing in the short distance between him and the base. But it was better than nothing, which was what he'd have if the airlock weren't propped open.

Peter tried to pull forward, but the wind was too strong. He swung his legs back and forth, building up momentum, then kicked up. The heel of his boot caught the inside of a fractured window. He doubled one hand over the other and pulled, throwing an arm over the frame. A shard of glass pierced his bicep. Peter jerked back, but he was skewered, stuck.

Blood welled from the cut, spraying his face. He blinked to clear his eyes, but his vision grew dim. Darkness crept in at the edges. Exhausted and freezing, Peter slumped back, suspended by arm and leg. His eyelids drooped.

Something clapped Peter on the head. His eyes popped open and he glimpsed a boot flying past. He looked up at the brigadier's corpse in the doorway. His shredded clothes streamed in the escaping wind. One foot was bare.

I owe you one, Peter told the dead man, adjusting his grip on the frame. His arm was numb, the bleeding stemmed by a red crust of ice. He pulled forward, throwing his other foot over the window frame, then freed his arm from the shard of glass and reached for the next frame. Most of the windows were shattered, leaving empty framework. Peter climbed toward the airlock.

He made rapid progress, rising to within a body length of the base. But the remaining windows were intact and the walls were too smooth to climb.

Peter leaned into the hallway, breathing the rich air inside and trying to figure out how to reach the doors. They were too far away to jump and the windows were too tough to break. His sole option was to climb, and there was only one thing to hold on to.

He slipped his legs through the window frame and locked his feet to the edge, reaching for the brigadier's body, which dangled in the middle of the hallway like the clapper of a bell.

The wind pressed against Peter and his stomach trembled. He was losing strength. He grabbed at the general's leg, clamping on to the man's calf. It was as hard as a block of ice.

Peter tugged, wondering if it would hold his weight. It seemed solid, and there were no other options. He locked the calf in both hands, slipped his legs loose, and swung out to the middle of the hallway.

The brigadier's leg stretched under Peter's weight and the knee cracked, bombarding Peter with iced flesh. The calf broke loose and Peter fell.

He dropped three feet and lurched to a stop. A thin strand of tendon stretched between the calf and knee. Peter twirled in the wind, gripped by vertigo unlike any since Basic.

He curled into a ball, clamping his feet around the brigadier's ankle, then pushed with his legs, reaching up and digging his fingers into the tattered pants. He eased his other hand up to the man's belt, then drew his legs up and clamped them to the brigadier's thigh. He pushed up again, his head rising to the doors.

The wind was strong here, and Peter kept his face down to as he felt around. He found the thick rubber seal that ran between the doors, grabbed tight, and let go of the brigadier.

The door bowed and the brigadier's body slipped free. It slammed into Peter, rebounded, and shattered against the wall, its crystal fragments scattering into space.

Something clamped around Peter's hand. The airlock had shut. The flow of air was cut and the vacuum of space sucked at Peter's lungs. Ice formed on his skin and his eyes froze, fracturing his vision. He didn't have long.

He kicked at the door, wedging his foot in the seal, then pried and pulled. The doors wouldn't budge. Peter kicked one foot with the other, driving it farther in. The rubber fluttered as a thin line of air rushed out.

Peter pressed his lips to the seal and let the warm air fill his lungs. He leaned away and the air was sucked back out. He breathed like this three times, clearing his head, then straightened his back and pulled with all he had. The doors spread fractionally. He shoved his foot farther in and locked his arch on the lower door's edge. He pulled harder; the doors yielded slowly.

Air poured over him, warm and moist. Peter slipped his shoulder in, then tucked his head and leaped inside.

The wind threw him back, but the doors slammed shut, catching him.

The roar of the wind echoed in Peter's ears and his skin burned in the warm air. The gravity generators were out, so he floated in midair, catching his breath.

His arm throbbed where the glass had pierced it. He pulled off his jacket and tossed it away. When he rolled back his shirtsleeve, he saw that the cut was jagged and bruised, but the blood had clotted. He checked himself further, finding no other damage. He kicked off from the airlock doors and sailed down the hallway, heading toward the center of the base.

The gravity started to return some fifty yards in. Peter sank like an old balloon and paddled over the floor with his hands. He dropped farther, crawling, then finally stood and ran.

He passed through Command and into the resuscitation hall. An alarm blared, but everyone was gone. All of the doors were open, all of the stations abandoned.

He cut over to the larger hallway, the one used to transport freshly printed bodies. The alarm was even louder here and sharp white lights strobed on the ceiling. Peter saw movement in the distance and sprinted toward it.

The crowd was a mix of small nurses and smaller technicians, with a few towering, black-uniformed guards. They all shoved against one another, panicking, each trying to get to the front. Peter overtook them easily.

She was near the back. He touched her shoulder and she turned.

"Linda," he shouted over the alarm. "I know you're angry with me, but you have to listen..." Peter saw the confusion on her face. He looked down: her badge read Linda 19.

He looked up and saw several faces staring at him, all of them Lindas. It was too much for Peter; he shoved Linda 19 away. She knocked into the others, who all turned and scrambled away, merging with the crowd.

Peter watched the confused mass push down the hall. A thousand bodies, but only a few dozen clones. He didn't know where to go, but it wasn't with them.

The noise of the crowd faded beneath the shrieking alarm. He looked to a speaker in the ceiling and walked to a wall console. "Alarm override," he said.

"Authorization required," the console replied.

"Sergeant..." Peter started, then had a better idea: "General Peter Garvey."

The alarm stopped, its noise fading down the hall. In the silence, Peter heard the sounds of war: pounding explosions, the moaning hull, and distant gunfire—Riel were inside the base.

His first thought was to find a weapon. He was in the Purple Area, which put the armory in the wreckage behind him. On either side of him, dark machinery slept behind glass walls. A half-printed body defrosted on a metal bed, its blood draining to the floor.

Am I alone? he wondered. *The last marine on the base?*

Even if the others came back, what good would it do? That colossal Riel battlecruiser would shred the entire UF fleet long before it reached the base. No, the battle was lost. The war was over. Peter's only hope was escape.

The base shuddered, from impact or explosion, and Peter was thrown to the floor. Fractures laced up the glass walls.

Not without Linda.

⇥ ⇥ ⇥

Peter pushed to his feet and raced up the hallway, chasing after the crowd. They were bunched up at a doorway, all of them shoving to get through.

"Linda," he yelled over the panicked din. A number of Lindas turned to him. "Seventy-five?" he asked. They all shook their heads, then waited. But he had nothing to tell them, so he pushed past though the doorway.

"Linda Seventy-Five!" he shouted.

The crowd spilled out into a large, circular room. A dozen doors were spaced evenly around the walls, like spokes on a wheel. This was the center of the base, the hub that connected all twelve sections.

People poured in from all directions and, having arrived at their destination, milled around as if at the end of a fire drill. Peter pressed through the crowd, shouting for Linda, his voice straining. He drew a deep breath and bellowed with all his might, "Seventy-five!"

Right in the middle of the chaos, a head turned. Their eyes locked and she said his name—or maybe she just mouthed it—and then she smiled.

Peter started toward her, but a horrible shriek filled the room. The ceiling broke loose and enormous red fingers wrenched it back, bending it up like the lid of a can. Hideous golden eyes peered down from the darkness above. A Typhon.

The cacophony of the crowd united in the single scream of a thousand throats.

Every instinct told Peter to run, but Linda was trapped. He plunged into the room, shouldering through the crowd.

The Typhon's giant hand swept through the room, plucking up a technician and lifting him to its shadowed face. The man screamed and screamed as he was flipped and turned, inspected from every angle. The room grew still, watching and waiting.

The Typhon bent his thumb under the man's chin and popped his head off. The head plopped to the floor, spraying blood and gore. The crowd shrieked, retreating. A monstrous smile glinted high overhead.

The crowd panicked, shoving violently in all directions. Several more Typhons appeared at the wall. Their large arms swung into the confusion, grabbing people at random and tearing them apart. The monsters seemed curious, inspecting the dead bodies the way a child might look inside a doll. A guard opened fire but only drew attention to himself.

Peter bent his elbow to a point and tried to drive forward, but the flow of the crowd changed every time someone was pulled from it. Linda dropped from sight and then whipped past a moment later. Peter reached out too late; his fingers brushed her shirt.

Frustrated, Peter balled his fists and began to swing, clearing a path by knocking people down and stepping over them. He reached Linda, grabbed her arm, and towed her toward the nearest exit.

His breakout caught the attention of a Typhon. It dropped the nurse in its hand and lashed out at Peter. The hand swung low, its shovel-thick fingernails raking gouges in the steel floor.

Peter dodged to his right, but the hand shifted, staying on him. He moved to his left, but it was no good—the thing was just too fast.

He stumbled into a guard, a man about his own size. He tossed Linda aside and grappled the man's neck, twirling him in a forced dance. They spun around and Peter let go, flinging the disoriented guard right into the approaching hand. The red fingers closed around the offering, passing so close that they brushed Peter's jacket.

Peter hefted Linda over his shoulder, bulled through the crowd, and escaped from the room.

They were in a hallway, but Peter wasn't sure which one. Chiang San had said that each of the twelve sections was identical, so it probably didn't matter.

The hall was empty. No one else had thought to flee or even to follow him as he did. The glass door closed behind him, muffling the noise.

Peter ran through the Purple Area as fast as he could, stopping short at a door marked Armory. Only then did he notice Linda pounding on his back. He set her down and reached out to calm her. Tears streaked up her forehead.

"What are they?" she asked.

"Typhons," Peter said, surprised. He assumed that everyone knew about the Riel. "They're too large to follow us here," he assured her. Linda nodded, unconvinced.

"So what now?" she asked.

"We get out of here," Peter said. "Off the base." He turned to the armory door and identified himself as the General. The door slid open, revealing a large, long room. Racks of combat suits lined one wall, crates of weapons the other. Peter pulled Linda inside, shut the door, and searched through the suits.

"Where can we go?" Linda asked. "If they destroy the base…"

Peter found a suit his size. Open and empty, it looked like a tailor-made casket. He stepped into it backward, closing the hinged plates around his shins and thighs. Next he pulled a yoke-shaped piece through his legs, raising it over his torso. He swung the chest plate down and locked the two pieces together.

A dull thump shook the room, rattling the equipment. Peter stopped and listened, waiting for the next impact. None came.

"We retreat," he said to Linda. "Head for the Livable Territories." He slipped his arm down the suit's rigid sleeve, wiggled his fingers into the glove at the end, and snapped it to his shoulder. He repeated with the other arm.

"That's ridiculous," Linda said. "We'd have to cross the entire Drift. And then how would we find it? The universe is a big place."

"The commandship will have charts," Peter said. *But will it? Was there even a commandship left?* He slipped his helmet on, cutting off the conversation. The control link clicked to the interface port on his neck, and the suit hummed to life. The pain in his arm numbed and his body swelled with the strength of artificial muscles. He soaked it in for a moment, fueling his confidence, then took the helmet back off.

"We get off the base and then figure out the rest," he said firmly. "Let's get you into a suit."

None of the combat suits were even close to Linda's size. Peter put her in the smallest one that he could find, but it was still so large that she barely peeked out from the neck. Her joints didn't match the suit's, which meant that if Peter tried to drive it remotely, it would break her bones.

At least she'll be armored, he decided, clamping on her helmet and opening the communicator link between them.

"You okay?" he asked.

"No," Linda replied. "Please take this thing off of me."

"You're safer this way," Peter said. He closed the link, cutting off her reply, and propped her in the corner. He turned to the weapons and dug in.

Peter strapped a rocket pack to his back, slid eight explosive charges into his belt, and clipped a pistol to each leg. He dragged an X-910, a bazooka-shaped impulsor with a fat rectangular lens at the tip, off the heavy weaponry rack. It was so heavy he could barely hold it. He didn't know if it was strong enough to kill a Typhon, and he was hoping not to find out.

Peter wrapped a four-shot powerbelt around his waist and tied some webbing to the gun's stock so he could lug it from the top. His artificial muscles strained as he lifted the gun in one hand and Linda in the other. He started for the docks.

Peter moved as quickly as he could, which, with all the weight he was carrying, wasn't very fast. His heart skipped at every groan or shudder; he expected the roof to rip away at any moment. He tried to push himself faster, but he was exhausted. He stumbled.

Peter let the gun drop as he fell, spinning so that Linda landed on top of him. He saw through her visor that she was speaking. He opened the comm.

"...running around like a crazy person when I should have..."

"Sorry," Peter said. "I tripped."

"Oh, you're listening again? Wanna take this helmet off? My hair is caught on something."

Peter sprung her collar and set her helmet on the floor. Linda shook her hair out, trying to squeeze her hands up through the hard collar.

"Yours, too," she said, nodding at his helmet.

"I don't think that's a—"

"Peter!" Linda barked. He obeyed.

"Good," she continued. "Now, let's get some things straight. First off, I'm not in love with you."

"I never thought—"

"The man I love is dead, and... shut up and let me speak."

Peter closed his mouth, nodding for her to continue.

"I don't blame you or anyone," Linda said. "I've always known better than to get involved with a marine, that he would either get killed or discontinued or—the worst—stuck in one version for months, forgetting everything I told him. But you—*he* was different. He could remember. And he grew into a wonderful man. But now he's gone, and we're back to... you.

"I made a deal with the General. Get you through this battle and be done with it. Put you and him behind me and start fresh. Well, the battle is over.

"Thank you for trying to save me. It was very gallant and, in any other circumstance, I'd count myself lucky. But as it stands, I'd rather just go ahead and die."

"You can't mean—" Peter started.

"Don't," Linda interrupted. "I know that look, Peter. You don't believe me, but it's true. I want to die. I don't even care if it hurts, because *I won't remember.*"

They fell silent. Even the distant fighting had grown still.

"Then why did you come with me?" Peter asked.

"I was just scared, Peter," she said, then turned away. "Oh, you wouldn't understand."

"I understand," Peter said, though it didn't make sense. "Things are different now. We've lost the war. No one is coming back."

"They'll figure it out. They always do."

"Not this time. There's no one left."

"Just let me out of here," Linda said, shaking the suit in frustration. Peter began to reach forward but stopped. Something tickled the back of his neck, something that wasn't there. Instinct.

He threw himself on top of Linda as the wall exploded. A half-dozen Gyrines raced up the hallway, directed from behind by two men in elongated white space suits. *Threes.*

Peter shoved Linda into an alcove. He grabbed the large gun by the strap, pointed it down the hall, and fired. The shot went wide. It ripped a twenty-foot section out of the wall, punching through several rooms and continuing out of sight.

The Riel scrambled for cover.

Peter kicked both helmets to Linda, then leaped into the alcove as bullets tore up the walls around him.

He sat Linda up and locked her helmet in place; then he put on his own and dialed up the gun's status—it needed twenty seconds to charge.

The rest of his visor was unnervingly blank. There was no map, no battle computer, and no suggested tactics. He opened a new battle scenario, as Chiang San had shown him, and a diagram of the base appeared. There were red dots pretty much everywhere and only two blue—Linda and himself.

He zoomed in on the eight red dots down the hall. Videos slid in from the side, fed from nearby security cameras, showing him the Riel from the front and back. They were advancing, the Gyrines in front of the Threes.

The suit offered Peter a firing solution and he took it. He spread the gun's focus wide and hefted it up. He eased to the corner of the hall as it finished charging.

The gun was too heavy to hold around the corner, so Peter braced it against his waist and stepped out. Gunfire erupted, but the bullets never reached him. He aimed down the center of the hallway and squeezed the trigger.

The gun surged with power, raising the hair over Peter's entire body. A wide impulsor wave rolled out of the barrel, shredding walls and shattering fixtures as it passed. The bullets melted in midair and the Gyrines dissolved into green paste. The blast wave knocked into the Threes, sending them flying from sight. Peter stepped back into the alcove, giddy.

His suit counted off the kills. One, four, all six of the Gyrines. But there were still two red dots in the hallway—far away but coming fast. The security cameras were destroyed, but Peter knew it was the Threes. He compared the gun's charging time against their speed. It was going to be close.

Peter checked on Linda. She nodded. He peeked around the corner and was met by the strobe of machine guns. He pulled back and replayed the video caught by his helmet's camera.

The hallway was dark, but the Threes were visible under light-amplification. Their white suits had massive rocket packs with large, round stabilizers mounted on rods that angled up from each shoulder. Guns were built right into their forearms—short-barreled, wide-caliber, and piston-driven. They were fast and powerful, evidenced by the minced walls behind him.

The Threes seemed unharmed by the impulsor blast, and a quick spectrogram showed why. Their suits were polyceramic and had plates of crystal shield fused to the surface—a nearly impregnable combination.

"What is it?" Linda asked.

"It's bad."

Peter peeked out again. This time the Threes didn't fire; they had slowed to a walk and seemed to be having a discussion. His suit drew a trajectory based on their new speed, and Peter tightened the beam on the large gun, deciding to hit one of them with everything he had.

The gun finished charging. He hefted it up to his shoulder, caught his balance, and stepped out. The Threes stood about fifty feet away, exactly where they had been before, facing each other. They cast a glance at Peter and he hesitated, unsure of what they were doing. But they weren't doing anything. They just stood there, waiting. Peter fired, the thin impulsor wave searing the air as it sliced down the hall.

A translucent yellow bubble formed around the Three he had targeted, some sort of personal shield. The focused energy of the most powerful weapon Peter had ever held in his life slammed against the bubble and fizzled away in a few green sparks.

Shit.

Peter leaped back into the alcove as bullets ripped the hallway to confetti. He stumbled into Linda, knocking her into the corner. She yelped in surprise but bit it off.

Peter counted his assets. The X-910 had one shot left. He had two pistols, but those would be as useful thrown as fired. He had eight explosive disks, but those had to be stuck directly to the target. In short, he had nothing.

"Time to punt," he said.

"What does that mean?" Linda asked, alarmed.

The large gun still needed 30 seconds to charge—the last one always took the longest. "We're going to split up," he said, unstrapping the powerbelt.

"No," Linda said. "This isn't right."

"Hold that thought," Peter said. He peeled the adhesive from two explosives and palmed one in each hand. He dove into the hallway, pressed them to the far wall and twisted to set the adhesive. Then he leaped to the ceiling, setting two more charges on an exposed beam. He landed flat on the floor and rolled back into the alcove. The Threes didn't fire. They strolled casually up the hall, not ten yards away.

Too close, Peter thought. He emptied a pistol blindly around the corner. It wouldn't do much, but maybe they didn't know that. He tossed two more explosives at the floor and reached his arm into the hallway to twist one to the nearest wall. Eight more seconds to charge the gun. He peeked around the corner, knocking helmets with one of the Threes.

The white helmet was long and narrow, the darkened visor split in two like the eyes of an insect. The man inside was surprisingly small, maybe half Peter's height. The suit extended his arms and legs, bringing him up to size.

The Three was as surprised as Peter. It stepped back involuntarily, as if to let Peter pass. His gun was pointed right at Peter's face, but he didn't fire. The other Three appeared behind the first, peering curiously over his shoulder.

Peter turned away and came back with a wide roundhouse. His fist drove into the Three's chin, bowling him over.

The Three's gun fired wildly, spraying the wall and ceiling.

A bullet caught Peter's arm, shoving it back.

"Here we go," Peter said, scooping up the giant X-910. He aimed it at the floor as the last second ticked off the charger. The light went green and he fired.

The force of the blast drove Peter into the air. The impulsor wave ripped through three floors and finally out the hull itself.

A perfect escape route, he thought, lifting Linda over his head. *For one.* It would work only if he stayed behind to cover her exit.

"Peter, don't," Linda said. But it was already done. He cast her into the hole and the vortex of escaping air sucked her into space.

She'll be safe for now, hidden in the debris, Peter assured himself.

Bullets tore apart the hallway. The Threes fired as if making a show of destruction.

Pissed someone off, Peter thought.

He set the explosives' timer to three seconds and dove into the hallway. He landed flat on his stomach and fired his rocket pack.

Two seconds.

His rocket pack was designed for space; in gravity it lacked the power to get him airborne. He scraped along the floor.

He shoved his elbows down to raise his head but careened sideways, clipping the wall. His legs flipped over his head, and he rolled into a ball. As he bounced down the hallway like a loose tire, the rocket pack was spinning him faster and faster.

One second.

Bile splashed up his throat and blood filled his head. He let himself roll until he was about to pass out, then killed the rocket and threw his arms out, slapping against the floor. His body stopped, but his brain kept spinning. He staggered to his feet, wavering, disoriented. Bullets plinked against his armor, knocking him around. Then came the explosion.

The shock wave curled the walls on four sides, rolling them toward him. Peter was shoved forward by a blast of air. A wall of fire—hot gas mixed with molten metal—bore down on him. He ran.

He sprinted with all he had, but the fireball rolled over him. The flame engulfed him, triggering every warning light in his suit. Then the floor shattered and he fell through.

Peter fell. Ten, twenty, forty feet.

The flame burned out, and he plunged through the dark. He slammed against something solid. It shattered and he continued down.

He turned on his sensors and saw he was inside a wide steel duct. Thick steam filled the air and Peter didn't see the floor until he crashed into it.

He bounced from the impact, then settled onto the grate flooring. Dark vapor streamed around him, swirling, dancing with shadows. Peter stood up and eased forward blindly, arms out, feeling for the wall. His foot landed on nothing—he had reached the edge. He jerked back, then leaned forward, peering out from the curtain of steam.

The room was massive. Peter couldn't even see the walls. Titanic equipment loomed overhead and enormous metal pipes twisted and mingled as they dropped into the depths. Everything was too far to reach. Peter was stuck.

A familiar screech echoed through the room: Ricl fightships. Peter killed his sensors, but too late. Two fighterships whipped around a large pipe, heading straight at him. They popped off four rockets and then curved back and away. Peter bent his legs, ready to leap into the abyss, but the rockets angled up. They weren't meant for him.

He watched them fade overhead and saw the flash of their explosion. There was a moment of silence, then a deep groan. It grew louder, trembling the grate under his feet. Peter waved his arms, trying to keep his balance.

Fragments of pipe and hunks of malformed plastic rained from above. A metal gear sheared a support cable, its frayed end whipping toward Peter. He ducked. It whistled by, but the grate beneath him flipped, tossing him over the edge.

Peter fired his rocket, directing his fall toward a doughnut-shaped coupler that bulged out from a colossal pipe. White lines appeared on its casing; then a massive turbine tore through, ripping it apart. He was falling straight toward it.

Peter fired his rocket again, but it only sputtered—out of fuel. He dropped through a crack in the casing to the coupler's cavernous interior and splashed into some frothy white liquid at the bottom.

The turbine crashed down, its blade a gleaming steel tidal wave two stories tall. Peter tried to scramble back, but his feet slipped on the smooth surface. He raised his arms uselessly as the blade closed in.

A hunk of pipe tumbled from the sky, shearing the turbine at the neck and sending the ungainly blade forward. It rolled overhead, rupturing the walls around him. The coupler fell and so did Peter.

Peter shoved away from the coupler just as it smashed against another pipe. The pipes merged and grew thinner as he fell. Floodlights shone up from below and lit the framework of a transportship.

The ship was only half-finished. Robotic arms hung over it, lifeless. There were blocky extruders attached to their tips, with hoses connected back to a large crucible. It looked like a giant printing machine—one that could build entire ships. Peter passed through its frame and continued down.

The corrugated steel of the base's hull appeared in the distance. Peter could see the stars through a gaping hole. He was about to fall out the bottom of the base.

He used his stabilizers to angle at the side of the hole. If he missed, he'd plunge through space indefinitely.

His stabilizers didn't offer much propulsion, and it didn't look like he was going to make it. But Peter wasn't falling as quickly as he had first thought. In fact, he was slowing. The gravity had shifted. He had dropped below the gravity generators, and they were now pulling him back up.

He slowed to a halt, the hull just beyond his reach, then fell back up.

He rose toward the half-finished transport, catching its skeletal frame in his hands and pulling himself onto one of the wide I-beams. He tried his boot magnets, but the ship was made from high-density plastic. He peered down and saw debris from the wrecked pipeworks floating in a thick blanket. *That must be the midpoint of the base's gravity,* he thought. He scanned around, but there was only debris. He'd have to find a different way—up or down—if he didn't want to end up trapped in the middle.

Peter searched the cavernous room. Under the floodlights he could see the dividing lines between the twelve sections of the base. But not twelve, he realized. Thirteen. He looked at the ship beneath his feet. *A thirteenth section*, he thought. *For the navy.*

Something caught Peter's eye: a pair of rockets punched through the layer of floating debris. But they were too big to be rockets.

The Threes were coming for him.

Peter had no weapons, no rocket fuel, nothing. *The only bright side*, Peter thought, *is that they're chasing me instead of Linda.*

The Threes opened fire. Bullets riddled the transportship's frame. He ran down the beam, but there was nowhere to go. Then, just as a bullet clipped his heel, they swerved away—one of the Threes had knocked the other's elbow, saving Peter's life. But only, it seemed, because he was trying to kill him himself.

The second opened fire, but the first one retaliated, playfully slapping his friend's arm. They rocketed past, horsing around, ignoring Peter. They flew through the break in the hull and disappeared outside.

Peter walked to the end of beam, leaped to one of the robotic extruders, and slid down the hose to the crucible. Molten plastic bubbled inside, fed from a pipe that ran out the bottom—back toward the center of the room. He couldn't see where it led, but having only one option made for an easy choice. He shimmied down.

Peter had gone just twenty feet when he heard the screaming of the fighterships. Two of them swung around a wide pipe, and the one in front fired a single rocket. It came right for him.

Peter clasped the pipe in both hands and drew his legs to a crouch. He timed the rocket's approach, springing forward right before it hit. The rocket passed beneath him so close that he could feel the heat of its exhaust.

He fell toward the layer of floating wreckage. The rocket arced around, releasing a plume of flame as it accelerated toward him. Peter looked from the rocket to the debris, trying to gauge which one would reach him first. It would be close.

Peter plowed into the debris. A large hunk of steel pipe cracked against his helmet, sending a jolt through his spine. He fell out on the other side, the wreckage sealing behind him.

The rocket should have exploded against the wreckage, but somehow it pushed through. It flew up alongside Peter. It was nearly as tall as he was and slender. It was seemingly unaware of him, but then something clicked and it turned sharply. Peter seized it with both hands, holding it back.

The two spiraled through the air. The rocket kept pivoting to aim at Peter, but since he was latched on to it, the rocket just spun him faster and faster. Peter's hands were slipping, so he kicked his legs in and locked them around the rocket, hugging it with his whole body. He raised his face over the tip of the cone. The rocket, sensing Peter in front of it, flew straight.

He leaned his head to the side and the rocket turned to follow. He considered steering it down, through the break in the hull, but the Threes might still be out there. Instead he took it straight up, back to where he started.

Peter and the rocket soared up the vaulting room, passing through a halo of fire—the damage of the earlier rockets. Pipes and machinery were torn and mangled. Something important had been destroyed, but Peter had no idea what.

They flew higher, into the dark. Peter turned on his headlamp, but it was another minute before the ceiling came into view, glinting like steel. He certainly hoped it was.

He tightened his hands on the rocket's cone, and just before it struck the ceiling, he flipped his legs up. His timing was off, too early, and he almost fumbled his hold. But the roof was indeed made of steel; his boots locked in place.

The rocket swung wildly and Peter nearly lost his grip. He jerked the rocket back, keeping the nose from the ceiling, and tucked it under his arm. He knew that if he let it go, it would circle back for him, so he punched the rocket's stabilizer, an oval bulge at the rear of the housing, pounding it inward.

The stabilizer sparked, releasing a puff of smoke. Peter aimed the rocket away and let go.

The rocket spiraled into the dark and, unable to control itself, exploded against a distant pipe.

Peter found a ladder welded to the side of a nearby pipe. He grabbed a high rung, released his boot magnets, and flipped right-side up. He climbed to a hatch in the ceiling.

Peter emerged into the glow of the Drift boundary. The hull had been torn away, and he saw the gridwork of rooms outlined by stubby remnants of their walls. Strings of metal twisted into the sky to where four dark shapes—fighterships—hovered overhead. Peter clicked off his helmet light and froze.

The ships gave no indication that they had seen him. Their trapezoidal windows all faced the middle, as if huddled in conference. Peter waited several minutes and then decided to try for cover.

He was at the bottom of a crater—the product of some massive explosion. Ahead, high on a wall, an intact hallway led into the base. Peter carefully lowered himself flat and rolled into the channel of a half-destroyed pipe. He shimmied forward.

Halfway there he had an overpowering urge to look back. Something glinted above the fighterships. A combat suit, Peter thought, his heart sinking. But it was only debris. Linda was still out there. He pressed on, faster.

The melted ruins curved upward until Peter was climbing. He made slow, decisive movements, easing up the coarse surface. A mangled door blocked the lower half of the hallway. He grabbed the top and flipped over, then peered back. The fighterships hadn't moved.

He crawled down the hall until the ships were blocked from view; then he stood and ran.

The hallway was pitch-black; even his low-light sensors registered nothing. He didn't dare use his headlamp—it would make him a target long before it revealed any—so he turned on his intermittent radar, the lowest-power sensor in his array. The hallway appeared in intervals, bright green pings that slowly melted to black. He was back in the Purple Area, heading toward the center of the base.

He had hoped to resupply at the armory, but that was behind him in the center of the crater. Once again the Riel had known exactly what to target. It seemed certain they would've also destroyed the remaining commandships, but he had to keep looking. He needed a way off the base.

He continued up the hall and found a general infantry rifle on the floor. The battery had a full charge, and he had two spares on his belt. It wasn't much, but he was happy to have it.

The artificial gravity dropped for a moment but kicked back on. The entire base drummed as everything inside it floated, then dropped. The gravity fluctuated steadily, jerking Peter's guts and making it difficult to walk. He tried to time his steps, to lock his boots to the floor when the gravity dropped, but he had mixed success, like dancing to a tune he didn't know.

The gravity stabilized again a few minutes later, just as Peter reached a door at the end of the hall. It was glass, but to his radar it was as opaque as any wall. He ran through his passive sensors, registering nothing. He touched his helmet to the door and listened. Silence.

He wedged his fingers into the doorjamb and pried it open, the dead motor inside whining in protest. When the door was about a foot open, someone jumped out and tackled him.

Peter swung the butt of his rifle. It connected with a dull thud and his attacker fell away, landing on the floor. Peter raised the gun like a bat, retreating a step and waiting.

His radar pinged; a small man lay facedown on the floor. Peter waited several more pings, but the man didn't move. He flipped him over with his foot. The man's chest was hollowed out. Peter recoiled, startled.

His radar pinged and he looked to the open doorway. The room was filled to chest level. His radar pinged and he saw an arm sticking out from the pile. Then a foot. This was the central hub. Twenty minutes ago the room had been full of screaming people. Now it was dead calm.

➤← ➤← ➤←

Peter steeled himself and stepped to the doorway. A long second passed before his radar pinged. The room was a slaughterhouse, heaped with mangled corpses. Most were decapitated.

He looked up at the opening in the ceiling. There was no sign of the Typhons. His instinct told him to wait, but he knew that was more fear than strategy. The death in the room unnerved him, but he had to keep moving.

He forced the door and bodies spilled around his legs. He stepped onto them, balancing on the wobbling flesh, and started into the room.

Now that he knew what to look for, the thirteenth section was obvious: a longer section of wall between two doorways. He crept around the room, holding the wall for balance. He kept his eyes up, not to watch for Riel but to avoid what was underfoot.

Halfway around the room, he heard a muffled cry.

He froze. The sound was gone, but he was sure he had heard it. He worked backward, probing the corpses with his foot. The noise came again. Peter felt a chill of recognition. He dug through the bodies, tossing them aside. She was at the bottom.

The radar painted Linda's face in green and black, her movements separated into one-second intervals. She looked in his direction—at the noise of something that she couldn't see—terrified. Then she was trying to pull free of the corpses, to escape. A crescent-shaped wound spanned her chest, the shape of a Typhon's fingernail. Peter slipped his helmet off and whispered, "It's okay."

"Peter?" Linda asked the dark, hope leaking into her voice. "Is that you?"

"It's me," he said, forgetting for a moment that he wasn't. He pointed his helmet at the floor and turned on the spot, creating a puddle of light. He slipped his glove off and stroked the familiar cheek. Her skin was cold. His fingers left long dents, like she was made of wax.

"Oh, Peter," she said. "It was awful. Just awful..."

"Shhhh," he said. "It's over now. You're safe." He looked down, but her badge was smeared with blood. *Does it matter?* he wondered.

"Hold me," Linda said. Peter pulled her to him, gently pressing her body to his stiff suit. She rested her head on his bare neck, her breath rasping in his ear. Peter knew she was in pain, knew there was no way to save her. He laid the rifle softly on the floor and slid his hand down to his boot, drawing a long knife.

"It's okay, Linda," Peter whispered, running his fingers through her hair while his gloved hand raised the knife to the back of her neck, where the spinal cord meets the brain. *A clean cut and she'll never feel it,* he assured himself. *The nerves will be severed instantly.* His heart pounded, the knife trembled.

Peter pulled Linda to him, kissing her, losing himself. She responded, weak but sincere.

He wanted to lift her up, to take her with him, but she wasn't the one. All the Lindas might look the same, but they weren't.

He pulled away and smiled warmly at the Linda in his arms. Then he gripped her head and drove the knife in. The blade sliced through her neck, its point clinking against his collar.

Linda threw her head back and gasped. She tried to speak, but her larynx was severed. Then the shock passed and she was calm. She looked into Peter's eyes, nodded, and laid her head back on his neck. Her breath slowly tapered off.

Once he was sure Linda was dead, he lowered her gently to the floor and stood up. He put on his helmet and glove, leaving the knife. He stumbled through the room, shoving bodies out of his way as he walked to the long section of wall. He couldn't see a door, but he knew where it was. He kicked the wall repeatedly, angry, mindless of the noise. The door's outline appeared as it bent inward. He kicked until it collapsed. The hallway on the other side was small; he had to duck to fit.

The first hall ended at another, with curving glass walls that glowed a dim orange. He cupped his hands and looked out, expecting to see the Drift, but it was something else.

The hallway spiraled upward like a giant spring. In the center was a power core, a massive, pill-shaped object suspended in space by thick wires. It was the same power core as on any ship, but a thousand times bigger. Its shell was cracked, the tail of a missile sticking out of the billowing fire.

He didn't know whether the core would explode, but he didn't want to be around if it did. He sprinted past a large sign, not catching a word of it, and the hall straightened out.

A portable terminal lay on the floor, discarded. He picked it up and scrolled through; it was unintelligible. A deep rumble shook the floor. Peter dropped the terminal and continued.

The hallway grew dimmer and a low mist covered the floor, swirling around his feet. He slowed his pace, feeling with each step, but the back of his neck itched. He looked back, searching the dark fog, but saw nothing. He turned and ran.

He moved faster than his radar could see, chased by the echoes of his own footsteps. He rounded a corner and saw a blue light. He dropped to a crouch and raised the rifle. Nothing moved. He killed the radar, allowed his eyes to adjust, and saw the frosted window in a door.

Peter knew he should keep moving, but something was working on this otherwise dead base. He had to find out what.

Peter was so conditioned to automatic doors that it took him a moment to realize this one had a handle. He shifted the rifle to one hand, stretching his fingers around the stock to the trigger, then eased the handle down and pressed his shoulder to the door. It sprung open and he leaped inside.

Eyes glared at Peter from his left and right, high and low. Tall racks covered both walls, their shelves lined with disembodied heads. A thousand steel needles perforated each head, leaving only the face exposed, and each needle was wired to a flat metal box at the base of their necks. Peter waved the gun around, but they didn't flinch. They were all dead, their faces bloodless, frozen in some final moment of horror.

The only movement was on the far side of the room, where bubbles trickled up the edges of a glowing blue tank. Another head floated inside the tank, eyes closed, gently bobbing in the water. The needles stopped halfway across the skull, as if unfinished.

Peter crept forward, his gun pointed at the tank but his eyes shifting to each face he passed. Some of them were familiar.

Three feet from the tank, the head opened its eyes and began to scream.

Peter jumped back and leveled the rifle. The noise grew more frantic—not screams, but some coarse, unintelligible language. And the sound wasn't actually coming from the head—its face was frozen, its mouth gaping lifelessly—but from a speaker at the base of the tank.

"Hold it there, marine," the tank ordered, suddenly intelligible. "Secure that weapon."

Peter lowered the gun to his waist, keeping his aim.

It was an older man's head, with thin, white hair and a meticulously cropped beard. Its skin was pale and smooth, like plastic. Only the eyes moved, following the gun's barrel.

"My apologies," the tank continued. "I expected you to speak Sakazuarian." The eyes squinted at Peter. "Is that you, General Garvey?"

"Yes," Peter said, but then corrected himself. "No, Sergeant Garvey."

"Oh," the tank said with sudden disdain. "The other Garvey."

"Yes."

"Yes, *sir*," the tank said. "I'm Captain Nicholai Andić. Now stand down."

"Yes, sir," Peter said, letting the rifle droop.

"You've never seen a navy man in the flesh before, have you?"

"You're...?"

"The navy, yes. What's left of it," Andić glanced at the inanimate heads. "Now give me a status report, sergeant."

"Sir?"

"What is happening out there? With the battle?"

The question was absurd. "There is no battle, sir," Peter said finally. "It's over."

"Ah," the captain replied. He was still for a moment. "And the technicians?"

"Dead."

"No," Andić said. "That's not possible."

"I saw them myself. Back in the hub."

"Not them," the tank said, relieved. "Those are *your* technicians. Mine are human—Originals, as you call them."

"Originals? Out here?" Peter asked. It seemed incredible, but so did everything about this room.

"They've probably left by now."

"They have ships?"

"Genius," the captain muttered, then fell motionless.

Peter waited for any sign of life. "Hello?" he said, tapping the tank.

The head glared at Peter's hand. "I'm not a fish, sergeant," he barked.

"Sorry, sir." Peter had meant tapping the tank, but the captain took it the wrong way.

"Sorry?" the tank boomed. "At least I know what I am."

"Sir?" Peter asked, wondering why he was still talking to this thing, much less kowtowing to it.

"Forget it. What's your interest in ships?" the captain asked.

"I just—" Peter started.

"Don't lie."

"We have to get out of here."

"By which, you're not including me."

"No, sir," Peter said. "Linda."

"Ah," Andić said. "Of course."

"It's not like—"

"I'm not jealous," the captain said. "These wires are far more complex than that interface port on your neck. I've got complete sensory input, you know. And full access to the libraries. Any memory I want. Any."

Enough, Peter thought, starting to the door.

"Where would you go, anyway?" Andić called after him.

Peter kept walking.

"Because there is a ship..."

Peter stopped, turned. Andić's blank face seemed to smile.

"Maybe we can come to an arrangement," he said.

"You want to come," Peter said.

"No. That would be impossible. Besides, you don't need me. Human ships are designed to be piloted by humans."

"Then what?"

"The batteries on this tank are fully charged. They'll last a week, maybe longer." The captain's eyes dropped to a red switch at the base of the tank.

"Oh," Peter said.

"Please," Andić said. "You'll only be expediting the inevitable."

"And you'll tell me where to find the ship?"

"To find it, and how to fly it. This section has its own docks, for humans only."

Peter nodded, walking back to the tank.

Peter jogged along the low-ceilinged hall, keeping his head down and his legs bent. He took the third hallway on his left, then the next one on his right. He chanted Captain Andić's directions under his breath so he wouldn't forget.

"There will be an autopilot," the captain had said. "But it will be in Sakazuarian." He taught Peter the symbols for the Livable Territories, verbally guiding Peter's finger as he drew them out in the air. Peter wasn't sure he got the symbols right and quickly forgot most of them anyway, but Andić's final advice stuck in his mind—that if he did find Linda, he should just shoot her, then turn the gun on himself.

"It's not worth the struggle," he said. "Just sleep it out like the rest of us."

Peter rounded a corner and saw a single dock jutting out into space. It was the same octagonal glass hallway that the marines used, but smaller and with only one walkway. Portals lined either side to couple with ships, but as far as Peter could see, there were none.

He pried the doors open and stepped inside.

The giant Riel battlecruiser floated serenely overhead, backlit against the orange Drift boundary. It was fully visible now, twice as long as the base was wide.

Gleaming steel fighterships patrolled through the detritus, which were mostly fragments of the base. The fighterships moved at a lazy pace; the battle was long over.

Peter waited at the door as a squadron flew past; then he started down the hallway deliberately, as if he belonged there. He even put a wobble in his gait, aping that of the short-legged Gyrine. *It could work*, he thought. *From a distance.*

He looked up at the battlecruiser. It was large beyond imagination. How had the United Forces ever hoped to defeat such a thing? He could see now that the war had been doomed from the start.

Peter saw the ship parked outside, coupled to a door at the very end of the hall. It was as sharp as a missile and flat white like the armor worn by the Threes. For a second he feared it was a Riel ship, but then he saw the winged UF logo on the side.

A squadron of fighterships curved around the base, heading toward him. Peter tried to remain calm, but every step was an eternity. He wanted to dash to the ship, to fly away.

The fighters closed in, near enough to see through his farce. He was certain that they had—they were aimed right at him—but he had to play it out. Certainly the Riel knew about this ship and certainly they were keeping an eye on it. Were they expecting him? Was it a trap?

The ships arced upward, passing over the hallway, so close their exhaust buffeted the glass. And then they were gone, shrinking into the distance. Peter reached the ship; its door was wide open. He allowed himself a smile, but it didn't last.

There was a flicker of movement, something fluttering behind the ship. A large piece of metal swung up and over the hull, pressing against the roof. Another came around the front. Giant, red-skinned fingers gripped the cockpit and the ship rolled back on its mooring as it took the weight. A monstrous golden eye rose up in front of Peter; the lustrous cornea rippled as the iris tightened to an angry dot.

Peter staggered backward as the Typhon rose on its spidery metal legs. It had a devil's face, with pointed teeth and shark-smooth red skin that turned black at the top, resembling hair. Thick horns curved out from its forehead, one of which was half broken. The creature towered into space, looking down at Peter through the dock's glass ceiling. It spread its heavy arms, either for balance or to attack.

The very sight of a Typhon usually made Peter freeze with fear, but he now saw it with clarity; it wasn't some terrible, nightmarish demon. It was a manufactured soldier, just like Peter. It was dangerous and horrifying, but it could be killed.

It'll have to be, he thought.

The Typhon gazed down at him with the same curiosity that Peter had witnessed in the central hub. It was curious what he was. Curious why he was here. It stretched a leg out and tapped the glass overhead. The noise was deafening, the point chiseling the glass. Peter forced himself to remain still. The creature tilted its head, perplexed by his inaction.

There was no point in dashing for the ship; the Typhon could tear it apart. Peter backed up calmly, smiling casually at the Typhon. He got about twenty paces before the Typhon's face twisted with anger, its mouth opening as if to roar. Peter turned and ran.

The Typhon leaped onto the hall, which bowed under its weight. Then it jumped again, landing right over Peter and driving its spiked feet at him on both sides. Glass shards flew through the room and a sharp-pointed foot grazed Peter's back. He ran faster and the Typhon chased behind.

Metal legs jabbed through the glass around him. Peter ducked under one leg, then hurtled over another. A third caught his calf, slicing through both suit and flesh. Peter staggered and fell as another knocked the back of his helmet. He rolled with the fall, coming up on his feet, but another leg blocked the way. The Typhon, watching through the glass, withdrew the leg to let him pass.

Why doesn't it just kill me? he wondered. It had enough weaponry to wipe out a regiment. Peter thought back to the base's hub, to how the Typhons had toyed with their victims before killing them. Toyed with people. Fury welled inside Peter, but he held it back. Anger wouldn't help. He needed to be cunning.

He strode toward the base, taking measured steps, an easy target. The Typhon curled up to pounce, shaking with excitement, eyes riveted on Peter.

Peter tightened the focus on his rifle and aimed at the airlock. He held down the trigger and used the beam to draw a circle around the doorframe. The Typhon shifted its legs, eyes wide.

The doorframe was glowing orange when the first clip ran dry. Peter swapped in the second without taking his finger from the trigger. The Typhon pounced.

Peter hopped forward as the metal legs sliced through the walls. He sprinted at full tilt and the Typhon bounded after him, batting at him like an oversize kitten.

The second clip ran dry twenty feet from the airlock. The doorframe glowed like a bright red lasso. But the floor was no longer shaking. Peter looked back.

The docks were ruined, a twisted metal frame that spiraled into the distance. The Typhon was perched on top, looking first at Peter and then at the airlock. The weapons at its midsection—machine guns and rocket launchers—ratcheted forward.

Does it know? Peter wondered.

He slapped the last battery into his rifle, switched to rapid pulse, and fired right into the Typhon's eye. The gun wouldn't do any real damage, but he hoped to piss it off.

He did.

The Typhon leaped at Peter, landing on the glass overhead. It ripped the hallway in half and shoved the back part away—along with the escape ship—to squeeze inside. It shot forward, legs closing around Peter like a giant claw.

Peter dropped the gun and body-slammed the airlock. The door fell away, glowing metal strands stretching like taffy from the molten frame. The Typhon's legs pierced the walls, shredding it as they clamped together, coming at Peter on all sides. The spiked points zeroed in on his head and chest, then suddenly stopped.

The Typhon's space-cold legs had frozen the molten doorframe on contact, trapping the legs in a metal ring. Its joints twitched harmlessly against Peter's suit.

The Typhon twisted and bucked, shaking the entire room. In moments it would tear the whole wall out, but Peter was already on the move.

He rolled, turning upside down and using his boot magnets to run up the underside of one of the Typhon's legs. He dove for the disk that separated the metal from the meat, grabbing the edge and flipping smoothly to the top.

The Typhon's machine guns strobed and its rockets flared, but too late. Peter jumped inside the circle of weaponry. He didn't doubt that the monster would turn its weapons on itself, but it didn't seem able to.

Peter swung his feet onto the Typhon's rugged stomach. It was as hard as rock and, he was happy to discover, iron-rich. His boot magnets locked to the red flesh and he sprinted up its torso. He ducked a swipe by one massive arm and dodged left to avoid the other.

He sprung off the chest, caught the chin in both hands, and leap-frogged over the snapping teeth. He landed on the bridge of the nose; the giant eyes crossed to look at him. A large hand swatted at him, but it was too far away.

Peter pulled the last explosive from his belt, ripped off the cover, and slammed it down with both hands, dead center on the Typhon's forehead. He twisted it in place and then pulled, flinging himself forward.

The moment his hands were clear, he triggered the charge and flipped around to watch the explosion. The monstrous head blew apart, disappearing in a cloud of black blood.

The Typhon's body struggled for another minute before realizing that it was dead. Peter sailed off into space, his own laughter echoing painfully inside his helmet.

[20.74.9.72::1938.7493.738.8D]

Peter twirled slowly off into space. He locked the motors in his suit to blend in with the other debris and watched the base shrink into the distance. No one investigated the dead Typhon for two hours. After that Peter was too far away to see.

A flurry of shuttles ran between the Riel battlecruiser and the remains of the base. *Were they studying it? Stealing food?* Whatever they were doing, Peter hoped they would finish soon.

He was desperate to link to Linda, to find out if she was okay, but to transmit when the Riel were nearby would be fatal to them both. Instead he studied the shuttles and tried to fathom what the Riel were after.

A flat chunk of the base's hull floated past. Peter got a hand on it and pulled it in front of him.

By the tenth hour Peter was a wreck. His air was half gone and he had floated deep into space; the base was the size of a coin. Shuttle activity had continued nonstop, and he worried that the Riel were moving in.

He worried about Linda too. Had he sealed her suit properly? Minor leaks were common and easy to fix, but Linda had no control over her suit. By now even the smallest leak would have bled her air tank dry.

He tried not to imagine Linda suffocating, but he couldn't escape it. There were few distractions, and the need to contact her itched under his skin.

After two more grueling hours, there was a swarm of light as the fighterships and shuttles returned to the battle-cruiser. The cruiser, a distant needle under full magnification, rotated to face the Drift boundary.

A translucent blue cone grew from its bow, drilling a hole in the orange haze. The massive engines fired, as bright as any sun, and the ship plunged in, heading back to its own universe.

The hole closed behind it and all was still.

He managed to wait another fifteen minutes before opening the comm.

"Peter?" Linda's response was both urgent and thick with disbelief.

"It's me," he said.

"I..." she stammered, "I can't believe you made it."

"We both made it. How do you feel?"

"Cold," she said, "it's very cold out here."

"We'll get you warm soon. It's all over."

"Yes," Linda said, "I saw them leave. You made it."

"*We* made it," Peter said, embarrassed by how eager he sounded. He had a lot to say, a lot to explain, but he wanted to wait until they were together.

"I'll get us a ship," he said. "You keep watch. If you see anything, anything at all, just say 'incoming' and then go radio silent. You got that?"

"Got it."

Peter tried to think of more to say but couldn't. He turned back to the wrecked base.

Peter raised the piece of hull over his head, used his stabilizers to aim directly away from the base, and heaved with all his might.

Tossing the debris in one direction sent him in the opposite. He turned to watch the base approach, but his speed was so slight and the distance so great that he had to use his suit's tracking system to see that he was moving.

A half hour later his boot magnets clicked to the base's hull. He stayed on the edge, jogging to the Section 13 docks. The airlock door had been cut away and the dead Typhon removed. *Do they know we're still alive?* he wondered. He looked out at the white ship. It floated nearby, the broken hallway still attached. *Was it a trap?*

Peter decided to leap. It would have been safer to get a fresh rocket pack, but he didn't know where to find one and he'd rather not go back inside to look.

He sprang from the hull and soared through space, catching the framework and scurrying to the ship's open door. The interior was like a standard shuttle—a single room behind the cockpit with three rows of seats and room for cargo. But the scale was minuscule; the ship was designed for someone half his size.

Sakazuarians, Peter thought. *Or whatever they're called.* He crawled to the cockpit. He was too large to fit, so he leaned in, squeezing his shoulders through the doorway.

The controls looked simple enough. There was a stick for direction and a throttle to control the speed. He poked around the console, pressing the most likely buttons, and the engine hummed to life. He then released the dock and flew the ship in a slow figure eight, getting the feel of it.

"Linda?"

"Still here."

"I need you to talk, so I can triangulate on your signal."

"Talk about what?"

"It doesn't matter. Just keep transmitting." Then, as an afterthought, "Tell me a story."

"I can see the promenade deck from here," she said.

"The room with all of the windows?"

"Yes, that one. I was married there."

"What?" Peter blurted. He cut the comm, suddenly short of breath. *They were married.* It was several minutes before he could reopen the link.

"—ter, are you there?" Linda asked, spooked.

"I'm right here," Peter said. "Everything is fine. Tell me about it."

"I don't know if—"

"Please."

"Okay," Linda said. It was a few moments before she spoke. "Nobody had ever been married on the base before, so we made up our own ceremony. You had proposed to me right after officer training, but it took weeks to arrange everything. We kept it a secret as best we could, afraid of what the General would do. But even that was fun, sneaking around and talking in code. We called it the Event.

"The morning of, the other nurses surprised me with a dress. They had sewn together some old uniforms and made a train out of bedsheets. It was horrible, but it was wonderful. You should have seen it."

Peter's fists were tight, mangling the throttle. He forced his hands open, raised them to the air, and tried not to punch anything.

"Peter... I mean, *my* Peter, ordered the promenade deck shut for repairs. Chiang San officiated and all of your sergeants were there. We even had a honeymoon of sorts, locked in the cargo bay of a naval destroyer. The ship spent three days pretending to chase an enemy scout while we... It was amazing, Peter. It was a gift."

Peter cut the comm.

He found Linda among the wreckage below the base. He parked at a distance, not trusting his piloting skills, then tethered himself and leaped. He kept the comm shut as he pulled her to the ship and stowed her in the back. He left her in the suit. *The ship's not safe until I check the airlock*, he told himself. But he knew better.

He circled around to the cargo bay and landed with extreme care, using quick taps of the thruster. He unloaded Linda, leaned her against the ship, and opened the comm.

Neither spoke at first. When they eventually did, it was awkward. Peter wanted to discuss supplies and living arrangements, but Linda wasn't interested. The base's life support had completely failed, so Peter left her in her suit and got to work.

First he inspected the ship, checking the solar panels, water reclamation, and oxygen generators. Then he loaded it up.

Being in the cargo bay meant that finding supplies was as simple as opening crates. Peter stuffed the ship with a year's worth of food, a couple extra suits, a crate of batteries, and two of every type of weapon he could find. Experience had taught him to be prepared.

He tore out the backseats and laid in a full-size mattress—no doubt intended for some officer's quarters. It was going to be a long trip, so they might as well be comfortable.

Peter worked quickly, worried about what the Riel had left behind, then loaded Linda and flew the ship back outside. When they were safely distant from the base, he released her from the suit. She crawled into the bed, stretching her muscles and inspecting her bruises without comment.

Peter had been fiddling with the Nav computer for close to an hour when Linda squeezed under him and into the cockpit. She was just small enough to fit inside, and it turned out she knew a bit of Sakazuarian.

"You're sure about this?" she asked.

"It's our only choice," Peter replied.

Linda brought up the autopilot, keyed in a quick sequence, and the ship began to move. Peter watched the base shrink in the rear monitor. First it blended with the other stars; then it disappeared completely.

Once they were at speed, Linda peeled off Peter's suit and attended to his wounds with the ship's medical kit. The painkiller she injected made his skin tingle and made him all the more conscious of her touch. Her hands felt soft, even as she stitched the bullet hole in his arm and the long, deep cut in his calf.

"If you really think this is your last body," she said, "you might want to take better care of it."

It took five weeks to cross the Drift, most of which Peter spent lying in bed, drugged and healing. He wanted to climb back into his suit to numb the pain, but Linda wouldn't allow it.

"Your suit's drugs are too strong. They don't heal you, they only keep you operational."

So Peter accepted the pain and held out as long as he could before asking for another injection.

He had nothing to occupy his mind—the room didn't even have windows—so he spent his time fretting about Riel patrols. Linda avoided him, shutting herself in the cockpit except to tend his wounds or feed him.

The food came in cartons of raw powder; lacking the equipment to reconstitute it, she simply mixed it with water. The result was a chalky paste. There were a few flavors, but they all tasted like ground flour.

A couple of weeks into the journey, the sterile smell of antiseptic gave way to the acrid smell of their bodies. The ship lacked a shower, which Peter found odd, given the length of the journey, and they had to clean themselves with wet towels.

Peter's own smell embarrassed him, but he was attracted to the sweet coarseness of Linda, which added to his feelings of awkwardness.

The muted tension of the trip was broken by the reappearance of the Drift boundary—they had reached the border to their own universe. Peter, fully healed, squeezed his head into the cockpit and chatted with Linda about what lay beyond the shimmering curtain.

Next Peter went though the familiar routine, strapping both of them flat to the mattress.

"Don't worry," he said, "I've done this before."

Linda nodded, dubious, and then the hull began to shriek.

Peter was surprised at how easily his new body handled the crossing; he felt no more than a sinking feeling, like he was nodding off to sleep. Linda didn't fare as well.

She lay still at first, eyes closed, then let out a low moan. Her body started to shake, as if the ship were passing through heavy turbulence. Bruises appeared on her neck and arms, seemingly caused by nothing. Peter called to her, but she didn't seem to hear. When they finally reached the other side, he ripped off the straps and sat her up. She doubled over, gasping for breath.

She sat there for over an hour, panting heavily, then lay back and fell into a troubled sleep. Peter sat beside her, watching her chest rise and fall, and listening to the rattle of her breath. He spread out the medical kit and tried to guess what might help.

Linda woke up feeling better, but her skin was pale and she could barely talk. She guided Peter as he injected her with painkiller, but she wouldn't allow anything else. When he pressed her, she only looked away.

Peter wanted to leave, to give her a moment alone, but there was nowhere to go. He turned away and kept quiet.

Another hour passed and he grew restless. He got up and mixed some food; the scraping sound of the spoon filled the room.

"Thank you," she said, taking a bowl from him and setting it, untouched, at her side.

Three days after they entered their own universe, Peter put on his combat suit and went outside. He told Linda he was going to inspect the hull, but the truth was that he just had to get away. Linda was very sick. He could smell the decay on her breath, the sickness inside, but she refused to talk about it. It was dismal. It was driving him crazy.

Stepping outside of a moving ship was jarring. The stars streaked past, racing from the glowing white mass in front of the ship, arcing overhead, then melting away behind. Peter clung dearly to the hull as he climbed to the roof.

The ship was encased in the shimmering bubble of a warp envelope. Green dots flashed in the air—microscope particles incinerated by the force of the ship's passing. They reminded Peter of the fireflies that swarmed the fields of Genesia on warm summer evenings.

Home, Peter thought, settling on the roof. They would be there soon, and he was nervous. He'd been so young when he left, and the war had barely started. Would he even recognize it?

"Are you excited to see your homeworld again?" Peter asked over breakfast. They had been in their own universe for three weeks now, and while Linda's condition hadn't improved, last night they had detected a large energy source that had to be the Great Barrier, the giant shield that protected the entire Livable Territories.

"It isn't really my homeworld," Linda said.

"You know what I mean."

"I do," Linda said, nodding. "But to be honest, I'd rather not go."

"Really?"

"My memories of that place...her memories. They aren't mine, but they're just as real. Just as inescapable. I was relieved to learn I am a clone."

"I'm sorry," Peter said, thinking back to the drawings in her desk, the dark images in heavy pen.

"Don't be. That was a long time ago. And as for my original, I'm sure she's long dead."

"Why?" Peter asked.

"Do you have any idea how old I am?"

Peter shook his head.

"I'm ninety-two, Peter. Not counting the age of my original."

"You don't look it."

"Clones don't really show their age, but we do wear out. We last about a century."

"And you're still on your first body?"

"My only body. Technician-grade clones don't have a neural web. There's no way to get my memories out."

"So then what? You just die?"

Linda stared at him, sober, then coughed into a blood-stained napkin.

Peter looked away, stirring the yellowish paste on his plate. Several minutes passed before he said, "He married you anyway. Even though you only have a few years left."

"Yes," Linda said. "Even though he would have to watch me die. Even though I would forget everything. Do you know how much that means?"

Peter shook his head. "No," he admitted.

Linda gave him a hard look, probing, and smiled. "You might just, someday."

"Someday? How old am I?"

"You have thirty months of active service. Add that to the age of your original and you're about twenty."

"Not that. The real total."

"Active service is all that matters."

"For others. Not for me."

Linda shook her head, but Peter only waited. She gave in: "I was seventy-four the year they rolled out your line."

"Eighteen years?" Peter asked. "We've known each other that long?"

"I've known you that long. You've only known me as long as you remember. And you've forgotten a lot."

Peter nodded.

"And the war?" he asked.

"I arrived at the base when I was twenty-two," Linda said, "and even back then nobody could say when it had started."

Peter spent as much time as he could outside. It was painful to watch Linda waste away, painful that he couldn't help. That she wouldn't let him.

Her attitude was frustrating. She was a nurse. She knew about medicine, but she refused to take any. And she wouldn't even discuss finding help when they reached the Livable Territories.

"I don't want to die in a hospital," she said. "Besides, I don't know what you think will happen when we get there. It's not like an unidentified ship coming out of the Drift is going to be met with a hero's parade. There's a war on."

Peter had been napping on the ship's roof when he woke to a warm glow. He squinted at the shimmering green wall in front of him, a plasma shield so broad that it sliced apart space itself. He scrambled inside.

He found Linda in the cockpit, examining the shield with the optical enhancer. The shield was an epic polygon, flat triangles interconnected by satellite. And there were millions of satellites, their protective green bubbles studding the massive sphere. It was the Great Barrier.

"Any sign of the Riel?" Peter asked.

"No other ships in range," Linda replied. "Maybe they're not coming."

"I wouldn't count on that, but at least we beat them here. Where are we headed?"

Linda pointed at a large rectangular frame. "Looks like a gateway," she said. "It's sending us a transmission, either asking for identification or an access code."

"Is there one in the computer?"

"I checked," Linda replied with a shrug. She was wrapped in a blanket that had worn to the shape of her body. Her skin was chalk white and her lips were stained brown.

"You'd better cut the autopilot," Peter said. "I doubt they'll just let us in."

"You've got some clever idea?"

"Extremely."

A few hours passed before a ship appeared on their long-distance scanner. It was a large one, judging from its energy signature, and it was coming toward the gateway.

Peter worried it was the Riel battlecruiser, but the computer identified it as a cargoship, the same model that supplied the base. *Maybe even returning from it*, Peter thought.

Peter's plan required that they make themselves hard to detect, which meant getting back into their suits and turning off the ship's life support. Peter encased Linda and strapped her in the back, then wedged himself in the doorway to the cockpit, freeing both hands to fly. He backed the ship up beside the gateway and killed the engines.

Six hours later the running lights of the cargoship twinkled in the distance. Another hour and its hull glittered in the shield's green light.

The cargoship was headed straight toward them with no sign of slowing down. Peter's hand hovered over the throttle. He didn't want to risk detection, but the alternative was worse: they would shatter across the larger ship's bow.

The proximity gauge switched from miles to yards. The ship filled the cockpit window and grew larger still. The vacuum of space was dead silent, but the large ship's engines thundered in Peter's mind. The distance dropped to double digits, then single. The *U* on the cargoship's hull looked to be thirty stories tall.

Peter yanked the throttle back, but just then the cargoship stopped.

He reset the throttle before the engines could fire; then he watched the cargo ship pivot toward the gateway.

Peter was hit by a blast of light as the cargoship's twenty-story impulsor stack swung into view. He threw the throttle forward, flying in its wake. His ship was engulfed in white tachyon exhaust.

The small ship was getting tossed around, so Peter jerked the stick to compensate. He stayed in the middle of the turbulent exhaust, where his own engine would be undetectable.

Once their speed matched the cargoship's, Peter dove, breaking free of the light storm and into the quiet shadow below. He cut the engine and the ship seemed motionless as it flew alongside the other. They were close enough, he hoped, that the gateway's sensors would register the two ships as one.

The shield approached slowly, growing razor-thin as they passed through. Peter craned his neck and looked back. From the inside looking out, the shield was translucent; the stars shone like reflections on a shimmering green sea.

Once inside the Great Barrier, the cargoship turned, steering toward its final destination. Peter let his own ship glide until he was certain they were out of scanner range of both the cargoship and the shield; then he reversed the throttle just enough to stop.

"We're in," he said over the comm.

"Congratulations," Linda replied. "You want to get me out of this suit now?"

"I want to wait a few minutes, to be sure we weren't noticed."

"Why am I not surprised?"

Peter spent a quarter of an hour tracking all the ships nearby until he was certain that none were headed his way. At the same time, he sifted through the incoming radio transmissions, gathering the names and coordinates of the occupied planets: Anteries. Sakazu. Carallaries. And, finally, Genesia. He had never realized how close they were to each other.

No other ships approached, so he removed Linda from her suit. Dark bile had collected on her chin; she wiped it away as soon as her arms were free.

"Just to be clear," she said firmly, "I'm never doing that again."

"I promise," he said, sliding her from the suit to the mattress.

"So what does it look like out there?"

"Like space," Peter said, "but crowded."

"I want to see," she said.

Peter found her blanket and helped her to the cockpit. Her arms were thin, her skin tight to the bone.

Outside the window the lights of a thousand ships moved through the system. "Oh, Peter," she gasped.

"This is only the very edge," he said.

"So many ships."

"And planets," Peter added. "Hundreds of them."

Linda furrowed her brow. "That's a lot more than I remember," she said.

"Yeah," Peter replied. "Me too."

[01.14.6.3::9234.1427.937.5L]

The Nav Computer had nothing to offer about the interior of the Livable Territories, so they studied the flight patterns of the other ships. The only thing out there was civilian craft—if the United Forces were preparing to repel a Riel invasion, they were doing it somewhere else.

Linda flew the ship in a small circle while Peter triangulated on Genesia's radio transmissions; it seemed like the safest bet. It took an hour to fix the planet's coordinates, after which Linda felt weak and had to lie down, leaving Peter at the controls.

At the core of the Livable Territories, a dozen suns were tightly clustered. Each was surrounded with planets that revolved on several axes or, in one case, were strung along the same orbit like a pearl necklace. It was as if humanity had designed the heavenly bodies for its own convenience.

Peter expected to continue on to a more remote location, but it turned out that Genesia was inside one of the busiest systems. He trailed some larger ships as they passed the planet, then he circled back, approaching in the shadow of a smooth white moon the way transportships approached Riel-controlled planets. He couldn't hope to avoid detection but saw no reason to be obvious.

He circled the planet to find a landing site as Linda sifted through the terrestrial radio signals. She was looking for Peter's hometown, but the closest she found was Bentings Naval Base, from where he had left Genesia all those years ago.

Peter remembered Bentings surrounded by farmland, but as they approached he saw it was buried in the middle of a city. In fact, the whole planet was just one endless metropolis.

They decided to land near the base, in what appeared to be a large city park with a small forest inside. Peter would have preferred somewhere more remote, but there weren't many choices.

The ship wasn't streamlined for planetary entry and the Nav System rejected any course to the surface. Peter knew nothing about landing a ship except that there was a strong danger of burning up if you descended too fast. So he aimed the ship away from the planet and backed into the atmosphere with a heavy burn of the tachyon drive. It wasn't subtle—the engines scorched the air, creating a thick column of smoke—but no ships came to investigate.

At a thousand feet he cut the engines for fear of burning down the forest. With only the stabilizers to slow their decent, they plunged through the trees and smashed to the ground. The rear hull crumpled, cushioning the impact. The ship teetered for a moment, then flopped down to its landing gear.

The computer screamed at Peter in a language he didn't understand, but nothing was on fire. He switched it off and went to check on Linda.

The two of them stood in the doorway, gazing out at the trees. Peter was in a black thermal bodysuit—the underlayer of his combat suit—and Linda wore an oversize camouflage coat like a dress. The air here was crisp and wet, alive. After so many years of filtered air, it was intoxicating. Peter drew deeply though his nose, taking in the smell.

"You first," he said, waving her outside.

"Help me," Linda replied. Peter stepped out and lifted her down. She tested the ground with her feet, checking that it was really there. "It's marvelous," she said, threading her arm through his for support.

They walked through the woods, treading over soft pine needles. They came across a gravel path and followed it to a field of manicured grass. Next they trudged up an embankment that overlooked a blue lake. Finally, Linda dropped onto a bench, panting. Peter joined her, surprised to find himself also out of breath.

The late-afternoon sun was warm and the park's colors were bright and rich. It was a little overwhelming—back on the base, everything that wasn't steel was colored to match.

Peter threw his arm over Linda and she curled into him. They looked up at the moon high overhead, half faded against the pale sky. But it wasn't the moon. It was too big, and patched in blue and gray. It was a planet. And there was another one nearby, smaller or more distant. Peter knew this wasn't right, but he didn't care. He was happier now than he'd been his whole life. Or, at least, what he could claim as his own.

Linda suddenly turned away, coughing sharply into her towel.

"So what's next?" she asked, mopping her chin.

"One of us should scout around," Peter said.

"And that should be you," Linda said. "I'm happy right here." She stretched out her arms, embracing the sun.

Peter smiled, her joy feeding his own. He didn't want to leave her, but she was in no condition to travel. He had to find help.

"I'll show you around later," he said, getting to his feet.

"I'd like that," she said. Peter waited awkwardly, wanting to say more, then turned down the path. "Peter," she called after him. He looked back.

Linda sat framed by the green grass and the blue lake, the sun highlighting her hair. "This is really lovely," she said. "Thank you for bringing me."

Peter nodded, not trusting himself to speak, and continued on. The sound of her cough faded behind him.

Once he was out of Linda's sight, he started jogging, then running. At the end of the path was a high brick wall over which the city rose like endless smokestacks in a gray haze. Peter slowed to a walk and passed through a gate.

Everything outside the park was paved. The trees that lined the sidewalks were plastic, planted in green cement. The air was burned, and the relentless din of cars' horns and engines filled his ears. Peter searched for anything familiar.

Two small women shoved past him. They looked like miniature humans, no taller than Peter's waist. The older lectured the younger in a thick accent that he didn't recognize. The younger looked back, ogling Peter. She tapped her companion's shoulder and pointed. Peter escaped into the street, dodging traffic.

The street was ten lanes in each direction. Peter worked through the slow-moving traffic. A tiny car screeched to a halt in front of him, and the driver gaped at him in horror. Peter ran faster.

More cars stopped and more little people got out to look at him. At the far side of the street he ducked into an alley where impossibly tall buildings blocked out the sun. Small shops lined both sides of the alley, but he saw nothing that could help Linda. He looked into a window; the man inside was startled by the sight of him and ducked behind a counter.

Then a small woman came out of a doorway. She had dark hair and a low-cut, strapless dress that was black against her smooth, tan skin. She walked right up to Peter, chasing him back a step.

"You look like you could use a stiff one, friend," she said, raising a clear bottle. Slivers of ice slid down the side.

"I need to find a hospital," Peter said. "Or a doctor."

The woman stared for a moment, blankly, then said, "Come on in. We'll get you sorted." She winked at him and sauntered back inside.

Peter checked both ways—the alleyway was empty—then followed, ducking though the small door.

The room was just tall enough for Peter to stand. A short bar was set against one wall and a few dozen tables were scattered about. Everything was lit, but there was no source of light. It was as if the air itself glowed. The woman was nowhere to be seen.

"What are you drinking, friend?" a man asked from behind the bar. He was middle-aged and wore a paisley felt vest over a white plastic shirt. He craned his neck up at Peter, giving him a welcome smile.

"I need to find a hospital," Peter said.

"A what?"

"A hospital," Peter repeated. "The woman outside said you might be able to help me."

The bartender frowned.

"Or a doctor," Peter said. "A medic?"

The man remained still as a picture for several seconds and then brightened. "Perhaps you'll start with some food?" he asked, gesturing at a machine in the corner. It was a miniature of those in the Purple Area of the base. "We print a fine selection of meats here, with vegetables as good as fresh."

"That's not what the man wants, George."

Peter turned. Three small men stood behind him, dressed in gaudy felts and plastics. The one talking had plastic glasses so large they covered his face.

"He asked for a medic," said the second man, who wore a wig of solid rubber.

"How's the war, soldier?" said the third, taking a drag from a toothpick-thin cigarette. "Kill the nasty Riel today?"

"What kind of amusement is this anyway, George?" the man in the glasses asked the bartender.

"No idea, friend," the bartender replied.

"Stupid projection," the smoker said, flicking his cigarette at the bartender. It flew through him and struck the wall. The bartender didn't seem to notice.

Peter saw for the first time the shimmering translucency of the man's skin. *He was a projection.*

"Like talking to a wall," the wigged man said, waving a hand at Peter. It connected, slapping against Peter's leg. The man jerked back, shocked.

"Hang on," he said. "It's real."

"Real like what?" asked the smoker. "A robot?"

The man in glasses reached out tentatively, pinching the skin on Peter's arm. "Flesh and blood."

"Hey," Peter said, raising his fist. The man in the wig backed away.

"Scared?" chided the man with glasses, shoving his friend at Peter.

"So you're what?" the smoker asked, lighting another cigarette from a glowing plug.

"I'm a sergeant," Peter said. The small men only looked confused. "A marine," he added.

"A reproduction?" he asked, incredulous. "For real?"

"I heard they were big, but..."

"A drink for the sergeant, George," the man in glasses told the holographic bartender.

"Do you drink?" the smoker asked Peter.

"I can't," Peter said. "I've got to find a—"

"A medic," the man in glasses cut in. "We heard it. So why are you here?"

"I have to go," Peter said, starting for the door. Then he stopped. "I need to tell you something important," he said.

"Go on, then," said the man in the wig.

"The base was destroyed," Peter said. "Wiped out."

The men stared blankly.

"There's nothing left to stop the Riel from invading the Livable Territories," Peter continued.

The men only stared. Peter took their reaction for fear, but then they burst out laughing.

"Don't you get it?" Peter shouted. "We lost the war. The Riel are coming!"

"You sure he's real?" asked the smoker. He reached out, but Peter slapped his hand away. There was a crunch. The smoker collapsed, clutching his wrist and screaming.

"What the hell?" said the man in glasses, retreating. "Cops, George."

"I already called them, friend," replied the bartender.

Peter went for the door, but the two men blocked him.

"You'll wait here," said the man in glasses.

"I don't want to hurt anyone," Peter said.

"Too late."

"By far."

The men puffed up their small chests, seemingly ready to fight. But they jumped out of Peter's way as he bulled past, knocking the door from its hinges and out into the alleyway.

Sirens blared, growing louder. Peter was greeted by the shriek of a crowd gathering at one end of the alley. He ran in the opposite direction, away from the park.

Peter shoved through awnings hung at chest level, tearing the fabric and snapping the metal underneath. He scattered tables and chairs and reached the far street just as two police cars squealed to a halt in front of him.

The police leaped from their cars, drawing projectile guns and taking cover. Peter raised his hands to surrender and one of the cops fired. The bullet caught him square in the chest.

Peter staggered back, hands clutching his chest. The wound hurt, but not much. He lifted his hands; there was a hole in his shirt and a blemish on his skin, but no blood.

The cops, terrified, opened fire. Their bullets stung like hornets.

"Stop," Peter yelled, kicking one of the cars. The bumper caved, crumpling the hood, and the car hopped backward, landing on a cop. The other three retreated, still firing. When their ammo ran out, they turned and fled.

Peter lifted the car off of the cop and tossed it aside. The small man was mangled, but alive. He moaned in agony.

Peter stared, horrified.

More sirens approached and Peter ran, from himself as much as the police.

People scattered as Peter raced down the sidewalk, shoving each other and diving into traffic. The path cleared except for one man, as large as Peter, wearing a charcoal-black suit. He stepped from a shop and stood right in Peter's way, facing the other direction. Peter aimed to the left, but the man swung into his way and turned around. It was another Peter.

The clone reached into his jacket as Peter scrambled to stop. The clone broke into a wide grin. "Just admit it," he said. "You look better in a Blanshim suit." He winked at Peter and dissolved. It was only a projection.

Four police cars raced around the corner. An officer leaned from a window, leveling an automatic rifle. Peter hopped to his feet and ran as the cop opened fire. Bullets drummed against Peter's back.

He quickly outpaced the police cars and took a left down a long, wide avenue, heading deeper into the city. The sky was a thin ribbon of yellow smog.

Halfway down the block, narrow stairs led below the sidewalk. Peter hopped down them four at a time and kicked through the metal door at the bottom. He ducked inside.

He followed the steps down past giant metal girders that looked sturdy enough to support the entire city. Machines clanked and hammered, hidden in the dark. Greasy dust coated the handrails, and the acrid stink of chemicals was overpowering. Far below, the room opened up to a wide expanse where trains crisscrossed one another, riding on cushions of sparkling blue electricity.

The stairs ended at a narrow catwalk. Peter followed it, moving carefully in the dim light. He passed several massive supports, each with a staircase leading down, and then the catwalk split into three directions. He didn't want to get lost, so he sat on the steps to get his bearings. He was breathing hard, and the room was spinning.

He tried to think, to make sense of what was happening, but his head was thick, fuzzy. All he knew was that he had to find help for Linda. He needed a plan, but the rhythmic mechanical sounds were a lullaby.

His eyelids grew heavy and sleep washed over him.

Peter woke to the sound of footsteps. He bolted upright and saw two dark figures walking toward him. They stopped when they saw him, mumbled excitedly, and retreated.

He rubbed his head, aching with the dullness of a hangover, and wondered how long he had slept. His legs and chest were sore and his stomach was tight with hunger. *That can wait,* he decided, getting to his feet. *I've already wasted too much time.*

He climbed unsteadily to the streets.

There were few indications that it was night. The strip of sunlight overhead was gone, and there were more gaps in the lighted grid work of offices in the surrounding buildings. The sidewalk was empty but for a small huddle of people on the corner. Peter walked in the other direction back toward the park.

He stopped at a holographic projection of a man and woman that was behind a plateglass window. The man's nose was enormous, nearly a foot long, and his skin was as smooth as car paint. The woman's eyes and lips were unnaturally large, and her hair exploded from her head like mortar fire. Their mouths moved, and when Peter looked at them directly, their voices were projected into his ears.

"…the big news tonight is a reproduction on the loose in downtown Bentings," the woman said. "This was scanned earlier today—"

Suddenly it was daylight. A car was overhead, falling in slow motion. It knocked Peter down; he felt the weight of the car and heard bones breaking. Then the car rose again and Peter saw his own face staring down at him, wearing a queer expression.

"UF officials have teamed up with police to track it down," the woman continued from behind the desk.

"This is a nightmare scenario," a policewoman said. "A military-grade weapon running around on our streets. They told us this could never happen."

Peter turned away from the projection as several motorcycles raced toward him. They whizzed past, engines echoing through the tall buildings.

They're after me, Peter thought. He needed to hide, but he still hadn't found help for Linda. He'd go check on her, he decided, but as he stepped to the curb, a yellow car squealed up beside him. The door slid open, but the car was empty—no driver and no room for one, just two bench seats facing each other. A red laser pricked his eye, followed by a voice from the car.

"Hello, P. Garvey, ident 765697897," it said. "May I offer you a ride home?"

Peter took a step back. The car eased sideways, staying close. "Maximum travel time is seventeen minutes guaranteed," it insisted.

"Yes," Peter decided, suddenly certain. "Take me home."

"Please enter the vehicle and fasten your seatbelt," it said, a tinge of impatience in its electronic voice.

The car was tiny. Peter squeezed inside by tucking his feet back and propping his knees on the opposite seat. His head was bent nearly to his lap. The car pulled away the moment he was inside.

The sudden momentum rolled Peter's stomach. He wiped the cold sweat from his face. It wasn't nerves. His throat was raw; he was getting sick.

They traveled through the city, passing clusters of nightlife—restaurants and bars spilling over with well-dressed people. They giggled and laughed, as if the war didn't exist. *Do they even know they've lost?* Peter wondered. *Do they even care?* He turned away, staring down the road.

The car stopped in front of a narrow cement building and bid him goodnight, whisking away without asking for payment.

Probably goes right to my account, Peter thought. He leaned back and looked up; the building faded into the heights. He corrected himself: *His account.*

The door opened heavily as Peter approached, giving way to a lobby of shining white plastic. Three elevators stood opposite the door; one was open. There were no buttons. The doors closed behind him and the elevator rose.

Numbers scrolled rapidly on a brass-colored plate, coming to rest at 2174. There was a slight rise as the elevator stopped and the doors opened on a dim hallway. A sign on the far wall offered directions by apartment number. Peter tried to the left.

The carpet and wallpaper were matching green-on-green paisley. Brass-colored chandeliers clicked on, leading Peter forward and dimming as he passed.

Halfway down the hall, a door clicked.

>I<   >I<   >I<

"Hello," Peter whispered, leaning through the doorway. It was dark inside. "Hello," he repeated, louder. No response. He stepped in.

It was a spacious apartment. A short hallway led to a living room that was dominated by a U-shaped leather sofa. Sheer curtains hung over bay windows on the far wall. Peter walked over and looked out.

He was miles in the air; he couldn't even see the street below. The city lights were a panorama, stretching out in all directions, twinkling like stars in dark space.

He let the curtain fall and spotted a glass-framed photo—a man and a woman. He tilted it to catch the light, but then heard a metallic clink behind him.

"Don't move," said a trembling voice. Peter turned slowly.

A small man, wrinkled and aged, stood across the room with a projectile gun in his hand. His eyes grew wide when he saw Peter's face.

"My God," the man said.

"I'm not going to hurt you," Peter said, raising his hands.

"I said don't move." The old man crept sideways, toward a phone on the table. Peter examined him, trying to peel back the cloak of age and find himself inside.

He was half Peter's height and thin with hunched shoulders. His ears were overlarge and his nose hung down at the tip, as if it had grown too long and then drooped. A few threads of white hair were strung over his mottled skull, and his eyes—magnified behind thick spectacles—were either green or yellow. Peter's were blue.

"Why am I here?" Peter asked.

"What?"

"A cab brought me here. It said this was my home. Why?"

"How should I know?" The man said, feeling for the phone.

"Am I you?" Peter asked. "Are you my original?"

"Don't be ridiculous," the man said, raising the phone. "This is Donald in—" he started, but Peter was on him, ripping the phone away and crushing it in one hand.

"Stay back," Donald hissed, jabbing the gun into Peter's ribs. Peter didn't move.

"My name is Peter Garvey," he said.

"I know who you are," the man snapped.

"You know Peter?"

"There is no Peter."

"You're lying."

"I want you to leave," he said, raising the gun to Peter's face.

"That thing is useless," Peter said, staring him down.

"I know," he said. He slumped into a chair with a hand over his face. "What do you want?"

"I need help."

"Help?" Donald was incredulous. "With what?"

"My...friend. She's sick."

"So go to a hospital."

"Where?" Peter asked. "How?"

"She's like you?"

"She's a nurse. Technician-grade."

"But she's—?"

"A clone, yes."

"We call them reproductions," Donald said. "You're...you're Petra's."

Peter was confused.

"My wife," Donald explained. "You were made from her code."

"But I'm..."

"All marines are male. They make you that way. But everything else about you is her. The hair. The face. The eyes." Peter shifted uncomfortably under Donald's gaze. "She was very proud of you," Donald continued. "You're a general?"

"No. The General is dead."

"No matter. The general dies, the soldiers die. Millions every day, billions every year. It's all just a game, isn't it?"

"They were people, fighting to—"

"Reproductions, you mean," Donald said impatiently. "And what are we even fighting over?"

Peter didn't answer. He didn't have an answer.

"The great Drift Wars," Donald sneered. "This is what? Our third?"

"I don't know," Peter said weakly.

"Petra liked it, though. She'd watch the Battle Channel most nights. If she could see you here, talking to me…" Donald smiled wistfully.

"What happened to her?"

"She died. We all do." Donald looked down at the gun in his lap. "Some days there's nothing to do but wait for it."

A minute passed. Neither man spoke.

"You can't take your friend to a hospital," Donald said finally. "They'll destroy her."

Peter nodded.

"I'm sorry," Donald said.

Peter looked around the dim room, his eyes stopping at the picture by the window—the photograph of Donald and Petra. He took a step toward it, then stopped.

"I should go," he said.

"Yes." Donald pushed to his feet, set the gun on the table, and led Peter to the door. "Good luck," he said. "I mean it."

"Thank you," Peter said. Then, struck by a thought: "May I ask you something?"

"Please."

"Do you know a woman named Amber? Amber Taylor?"

Donald thought for a moment, then shook his head. "No," he said, "I can't say as I've ever heard of her."

Peter stumbled down the sidewalk, light-headed, sweating profusely. He was breathing hard and the air burned his lungs like smoke. His stomach turned sour; he turned in to an alley and vomited. He leaned against the wall, retching out thin strings of fluid.

After a few minutes he straightened up. Light shined on him from all directions, surrounding him. He had stumbled into some kind of arcade set in a small courtyard. It was closed for the night, but projections for the various entertainments glowed above him. Peter was drawn to one in particular.

The billboard was shaped like the wings of the service. It showed two marines, a man and a woman, firing guns at a comically distorted Typhon. Glowing letters announced: "UF Marine IX: Retribution."

"Immerse yourself in the war experience," it read. "Fight as the United Force's most dangerous weapon: a Grade 6 Military Reproduction."

A game, Peter thought. Just like Donald had said.

Peter made slow progress. The sky was a light gray when the park appeared in the distance. The sight encouraged him. He pushed forward on rubbery legs.

A radio chirped behind him. He turned and saw a police officer following him from a few blocks away. The cop turned and fled, yelling into his handset.

Peter picked up his pace, jogging at first and then running. Every muscle ached and he choked on the air. He had halved the distance to the park when an engine roared overhead. A small ship raced into view and stopped high overhead, hovering. Another craft took up position down the road.

Peter took a left, away from the park. *I don't want to lead them to her*, he thought. But a wide, flat tank pulled into the road, blocking the way. The dark eye of its main cannon rose toward Peter's head, but it didn't fire. Peter backed up and continued down the street. The tank followed.

Each time he tried to change direction, he met another tank. Soon a small division crowded the road behind him. His last hope was to lead them beyond the park, but there were more tanks waiting at the entrance, forming a barricade that led to the arched gate. It was all machinery; there wasn't a human in sight.

They already know, Peter thought. The tanks crowded up behind him and he stumbled forward into the park. A single tank moved to the gate, blocking his return. Neither it nor the airships followed him inside.

The sun peered over the forest, and he squinted as he walked up the path. Linda wasn't at the bench by the lake. He hadn't expected her to be, but it still made him anxious.

He took a minute to rest, bracing his arms on the back of the bench, not trusting himself to sit. His body hurt all over and his eyes wouldn't focus. He hadn't felt this bad since catching the flu as a child.

"As a child," Peter laughed caustically. He pushed to his feet and started into the trees.

He found the ship lying calmly among the trees, its white hull catching the early light. Its door was open. He called out Linda's name, but there was no response.

Peter rushed to the ship, heart pounding. She was inside, sleeping peacefully. He steadied himself on the door, watching, holding his sleeve to his mouth to muffle his breath. But something was wrong. He stepped softly inside, reaching for her forehead.

"I wouldn't do that," said a familiar voice behind him. "You won't want to remember her that way."

Peter turned. The dark outline of a man stood against the morning sun. Red light caught his shoulders and reflected off four brass stars.

[01.14.6.2::9234.1427.937.5L]

"You killed her," Peter said, too shocked for anger.

"She was dying," the General replied.

"You bastard!" Peter lunged, grappling for the General's neck. But the General slipped to the side, batting him to the ground with casual ease.

"Crossing the Drift boundary killed Linda," the General said. "Bringing her here killed her. I simply offered her mercy."

"Mercy?" Peter spat. He tried to stand but toppled back, coughing, clutching his chest.

"You get a different offer," the General said, holding out a clear plastic mask. "Put this on. The air here is poisonous."

Peter hesitated, suspicious.

"I am going to kill you," the General said, "after we talk."

Peter took the mask and breathed deeply. He felt his head clear. "How can the air be poisonous?" he asked. "This is our home."

"Actually we're of Sakazuarian manufacture. We're only modeled after Genesians. Our memories—our entire lives—were created from scratch. But you already know that, don't you?"

Peter nodded.

"You and I were born in the Drift," the General continued, "and we're meant to stay there. The air on Genesia is poisonous to us because we're nitrogen intolerant. It builds up in our blood and makes us sick. It's a kill switch designed into our bodies to keep us out of the Livable Territories. Both you and Linda would be have been dead in another twenty-four hours."

"So you murdered her?"

"We don't have time for this, sergeant. I offered her pills and she took them. From the look of her, she would have taken them weeks ago. If anyone had asked."

"And how are you even alive?" Peter asked. "The whole base was destroyed. I saw it."

"Do you really think we take such risks?"

"There's another base?"

"There are hundreds, maybe thousands, for all I know. Don't give me that look. You've kept your share of secrets. You were told why no one below the rank of colonel knows he is a clone?"

"Because people fight harder when they believe their lives are at stake."

"And?"

"And because battles are decided by how motivated we are to fight."

"Not just battles, kid. Wars. Clones are expensive. Suits and weapons are expensive. We can't have our boys throwing their lives away like it was some video game. They need to have a stake.

"The same principle applies to a base. If you think the fate of the entire war hangs on its survival, then you'll fight like hell to defend it."

"All of those lies," Peter said, "just to make us fight?"

"Oh, it's more than that. We aren't as advanced as you might think. Sure we're big and tough, but we're still human. Our improvements are merely the result of genetic trial and error. We're nothing compared to the Riel.

"Gyrines and Typhons were designed from the ground up, not only as fearsome killing machines but also as perfect soldiers. Order them to guard a rock and they will—for a week or for a decade—and never even ask why.

"You and I, on the other hand, inherit the frail emotions of our originals. We require purpose. We must be inspired, given a reason, simply to do what we were created for."

"So they give us memories?" Peter asked. "Make us think we're human?"

"It's a subtle trick. Take this planet, for example." The General looked around, grimacing. "Disappointing, isn't it? Where are those small towns? The earnest people? And let's not forget, the pretty women."

The General pulled a locket from his coat pocket and tossed it in Peter's lap.

"Amber," Peter said.

"Someone you'd die to protect. Every marine is given a cause. Ours was her."

"It's cruel," Peter said.

"Maybe," the General said. "But it works. Look how far you've come to save the woman you love."

Peter looked at the ship's dark doorway, where Linda lay dead.

Forever.

"So here's your choice," the General said. "Either I'm going to kill you, or I'm going to scan your memory and then kill you."

"That's a choice?"

"Either you go back, or we restore the colonel—the version of you who married Linda. The version who has never seen this planet, the Threes, or the inside of the Riel universe."

"You said he was destroyed," Peter said, "wiped from the memory banks."

The General gave Peter a disdainful look and glanced at his watch. He drew a needle from his pocket and filled it from a small bottle.

"Why did you bother coming here?" Peter asked. "Why not just let me die?"

"Because you're me," the General said, distracted.

"What?"

"You are me. Same genes, same memories. My own line, restarted from scratch."

"Why not just clone you?"

"Oh, they have. Hundreds of times. There's a General Garvey running nearly every base in the UF. And that makes the originals nervous. They're afraid that the Riel will catch on to my tactics, that one day I'll start losing like the robots lost the first Drift War. It's not a flattering comparison, but you get used to it, answering to optimates.

"The trouble is, none of the other lines have shown much potential. And that's where you come in: you're a variation on a proven line. New and improved, or so I'm told. Now hold still."

The General knelt down, pressing his gun to Peter's temple while he jabbed the needle into his neck.

Peter's head went light. The General eased him to the ground.

"All generals are told the truth," Garvey said. "We know who we're really fighting for. This isn't how you're supposed to find out, but since you have, I'm here to see if you will."

"Will what?"

"Fight."

"Fight?" Peter mumbled. "To defend these...?"

"Self-important worms?" the General suggested. "Pathetic mice?"

"Yes," Peter agreed. "Why do you fight for them?"

The General shrugged, stirring pine needles with his boot.

"What else is there?" he said. "We are made to fight."

"We're pawns," Peter said.

"We're warriors," the General said, "fighting the greatest battle in history.

"We're not human. We're gods. We die a thousand deaths but live forever. Every day brings a new thrill, a new battle, and another chance to prove ourselves in the face of death. The ancients dreamed of a life like ours. They called the place Valhalla. To them it was heaven—a myth. But we live there.

"You're not a boy anymore, Peter. You don't need any made-up, romantic nonsense." The General motioned to ship. "You killed a Typhon for her. Would you dare to just live your life for her?"

Peter concentrated on the General's words, but they were fuzzy. He turned to the ship, to Linda.

"You're running out of time," the General said. "Choose."

Peter didn't have an answer. She was gone. Everyone was gone. The sky faded and, in the last twinkle of light, he mouthed his choice.

Then everything went black.

[16.45.19.8::4783.9183.722.8D]

White.

White so thick that Peter couldn't see his hands. His gloves appeared as he dropped below the clouds, but everything else remained white—an overcast sky and a snow-covered planet met seamlessly at the horizon.

Marines plunged from the clouds, speckling the sky. Two hundred thousand men—a full division—all under Peter's command. Colonel Garvey's command.

Peter was leading from the front. An unnecessary risk, but today he just felt like it. And this mission was only a decoy, a feint to draw the enemy's attention from the real invasion, which was at the other end of the solar system. He wasn't going to win, so he might as well have some fun.

Being out front also gave him a chance to watch his new men in action—the freshly christened Asigma

Garvey division. Recruits all, with no memories past Basic. These men believed that Peter had personally supervised their entire training. In reality, this was the first time he'd laid eyes on them. So far he wasn't impressed.

They were a nervous, uncoordinated bunch. They jerked around in the air, their virtual training out of tune with their newly minted bodies. It always took a couple versions to settle in. And they hadn't found their balls yet, either. They had been as silent as corpses on the way here, no doubt fearing for their very lives.

And with good reason, Peter thought, turning to study the empty field below. He was expecting a volley of bullets to greet them, but it hadn't come. Something was wrong. Not ten hours ago, the satellites had spotted a Riel garrison in the area.

"They're catching on to us," he muttered. He logged the enemy's absence into the battle computer and fired his rocket—a thermal-ionic booster pack with enough fuel to fly around for hours. One of the privileges of rank.

He hovered as the other men, clumsy and howling, fell past; then he oriented himself with a distant mountain range. Three miles to the south was a Riel outpost, their official target. He decided to rough out some sort of assault, just in case. He dialed up the mission intel.

This time of year, he read, the outpost was buried under a hundred yards of snow. The only access points were the front door, the back door, and a half-dozen ventilation shafts. They were all heavily fortified, so there was no chance he'd actually get inside. "But if you are prudent with your men," General Garvey had advised, "you should be able to stretch the assault out for a couple of hours."

And it'll be good experience, Peter decided, *for any who survive.*

His thoughts were interrupted by an explosion, which was followed by several more. Puffs of black smoke rose from the white landscape. *Shit*, Peter thought, almost laughing. *Land mines.*

Explosions cracked in the morning air and a blanket of dark smoke covered the plain. Clusters of blue dots disappeared from Peter's map and the comm was flooded with screaming sergeants and moaning men. *So much for that*, Peter thought. *A whole fifteen seconds' worth of distraction.* He killed the comm and focused on his own landing.

There was no map of the land mines yet—satellite coverage wasn't scheduled until they were groundside, and their suits' sensors weren't strong enough to penetrate the snow. For now, the only way to find them was to set them off.

He drew his pistol and fired in a spiral pattern at the ground. A mine exploded, splattering snow on his visor. He landed gently, the webbing on his boots spreading his weight and allowing him to stand on the fresh powder.

Peter was the last to touch down. The battle computer reported that three-quarters of his division had been killed on impact. He set a meeting point for the remaining men and slapped a fresh battery into his gun. As he started forward, bullets ripped up the snow at his feet.

Finally, he thought, *something to kill.*

His suit calculated the bullets' reverse trajectory, highlighting his target. Peter checked which of his forces were nearby and, racing ahead, opened the comm. "Sergeant Graff," Peter said.

"What?" Saul replied.

"Live target in your sector. Sending coordinates."

"I'm standing right on it," Saul said. Peter saw a group of men ahead, where the target was supposed to be. There was nothing else. Then the snow swelled, bursting in a red flash as a Typhon leapt from a trench. It landed in front of Peter, its column-thick legs sinking in the deep snow.

Peter's hand went for his belt, but he wasn't carrying explosives.

Oh well, he thought, as a monstrous hand swung down at him. *I wouldn't get to pull that trick twice anyway.*

The Typhon grinned, scooping him into the air. It lobbed off a couple of rockets, opening its hand as they struck him on both sides.

Black.

White.

Peter blinked. There was a rustle of sheets and a young woman's face appeared, smiling down at him. She was beautiful, the most beautiful woman he had ever seen.

"What's the last thing you remember?" she asked.

"Being in love with you."

"It better be," Linda said, flopping heavily onto his chest. Peter traced his hand down the cleft of her back, feeling the silken skin of her new body. He reached for the light beside the bed.

Black.

CPSIA information can be obtained at www.ICGtesting.com
Printed in the USA
BVOW05*2041230914

368029BV00004B/16/P

Nixa Jr High Library